REVELATIONS OF A
LADY DETECTIVE

REVELATIONS OF A LADY DETECTIVE

WILLIAM STEPHENS HAYWARD

———

With an Introduction by Mike Ashley

THE BRITISH LIBRARY

This edition published in 2013 by

The British Library
96 Euston Road
London NW1 2DB

Originally published in London in 1864 by George Vickers, Strand

Cataloguing in Publication Data
A catalogue record for this book is available from The British Library

ISBN 978 0 7123 5896 5

Designed by Geoff Green Book Design, Cambridge
Typeset by IDSUK (DataConnection) Ltd
Printed and bound in Hong Kong by Great Wall Printing Co. Ltd

Contents

INTRODUCTION

MIKE ASHLEY

In the same way that you can wait for a bus for hours and then two turn up at once, so the growing body of devotees of that new genre of detective fiction must have felt in 1864 when, within a few months of the publication of Andrew Forrester's *The Female Detective*, rival publisher, George Vickers released the anonymous *Revelations of a Lady Detective*.

Both books are rare. The British Library reprinted *The Female Detective* in 2012 and now provides the opportunity to enjoy *Revelations of a Lady Detective*. Both books are of historical significance. They were the first books to feature a professional female detective as their heroine, and they remained the only such books in Britain for over twenty years until the publication of *Mr Bazalgette's Agent* by Leonard Merrick in 1888[1]. But, as we shall see, they are historically significant for two different reasons.

In *The Female Detective* we encountered a rather mysterious, reserved woman who tells us virtually nothing about herself and likes to blend into the world about her as she observes, analyses and investigates. She is a genuine detective, working both as an agent for the police and in a private

---

[1] In the United States, Harlan P. Halsey created Kate Goelet in "The Lady Detective" as one of his Old Sleuth series of dime-novel detective stories set in New York. I have been unable to find the original publication date of this in the *Fireside Companion* story paper though I have seen the date 1880 cited.

capacity. We don't know her name although she calls herself, on occasions, Miss Gladden.

Likewise, Mrs Paschal, the heroine of *Revelations of a Lady Detective*, is regularly consulted by the police and serves as an undercover agent as well as investigating her own cases. But, even though she is "verging on forty", she throws herself into her cases with verve and gusto and has no hesitation in infiltrating a deadly secret society or casting off her crinoline in order to plummet into a sewer on the trail of a criminal. For those who recall the television series *The Avengers*, we can see her as the Emma Peel of the detective service.

Action woman though she is, Mrs Paschal rarely acts before she thinks. She evidently has a vast amount of experience behind her. She reveals in the first story, "The Mysterious Countess", that she "had not long been employed as a female detective" but her subsequent actions tell us that she is well versed in the ways of the world and in a later story she states that "...owing to frequent acquaintance with peril, I had become unusually hardened for a woman."

She also makes a statement that may be the first rendition of a phrase better known in the version stated by Sherlock Holmes: once you have eliminated the probable, whatever remains, no matter how improbable, must be the truth. Mrs Paschal's version is "I had seen a few things in my life which appeared scarcely susceptible of explanation at first, but which, when eliminated by the calm light of reason and dissected by the keen knife of judgment, were in a short time as plain as the sun at noonday." A bit more long-winded perhaps, but nevertheless the same expression of a ratiocinative mind. Evidently Mrs Paschal is the forerunner not only of Emma Peel but of Sherlock Holmes.

Mrs Paschal is entirely different to Miss Gladden and in fact comes from a different line of evolution. To understand why, we need to know who created Mrs Paschal, and in what circumstances.

The authorship of *Revelations of a Lady Detective* has always been uncertain. It had been published by George Vickers in Angel Court, one of a number of narrow, dim alleyways, just off the Strand. The original George Vickers who established the company had become prosperous by pandering to the public's interest in crime and the darker side of life. He had a phenomenal success serialising, in weekly penny parts, *The Mysteries of London*, compiled, at the start, by George W. M. Reynolds. It was reputedly selling over 40,000 copies a week, and when released as a series of bound volumes from 1846 onwards, sold over a million copies. Reynolds responded not only to the public's fascination for crime and mystery but, most importantly, their interest in what went on behind the closed doors of the rich and famous.

At the start of the serial one of the principal characters is the resourceful and resilient heroine, Eliza Sydney. The idea that a woman appeared so significantly in this series and proved capable of looking after herself in a wild and wicked world was a feature of these sensational novels. It was a literary descendant of the gothic novel, notably Ann Radcliffe's *The Mysteries of Udolpho* (1794) which follows the misfortunes and eventual triumph of Emily St. Aubert. It continued through such "penny dreadfuls" as *Ada the Betrayed* (1843) by James Malcolm Rymer, and it was one of the factors that made *The Woman in White* (1860) by Wilkie Collins and *Lady Audley's Secret* (1862) by Mary E. Braddon so successful.

Vickers died in 1846 and Reynolds fell out with his widow, Mary Ann, and his sons George and Henry who now ran the company. They continued to publish a range of "penny dreadfuls" and their slightly more superior hardcover equivalent known as "yellowbacks" because of their brightly designed binding, and by the 1860s had further success with a new package of books repeating the plot of the gothic heroine, but with a rather more intimate subject. This was the infamous Anonyma series which began with *Anonyma, or Fair but Frail* (1864), labelled "A Romance of West End Life, Manners and 'Captivating' People".

This, and its immediate sequels *Skittles, a Biography of a Fascinating Woman* (1864) and *Skittles in Paris* (1864) were fictionalized biographies of one of London's most noted courtesans, Catherine Walters (1839-1920). Her nickname was Skittles but she had earlier been dubbed Anonyma by an unnamed correspondent to *The Times* in July 1862, who signed himself simply 'H'. He described how the "charming creature" had become the talk of society in 1861 and her manners and dress had instantly become fashionable so that within a year she had many imitators. Her parlour was believed to be visited by many of high standing in society, including royalty, politicians and the aristocracy.

Vickers issued a flurry of similar titles such as *Kate Hamilton, Cora Pearl, Formosa, Incognita* – all anonymous but credited as "by the author of 'Anonyma', 'Skittles' ... " and so on. The significance of all of this to the book you hold in your hands is that when it was reprinted in the same year (1864), it was also credited as "by the author of 'Anonyma.'"

There were so many books attributed in this way – Michael Sadleir lists over twenty in the space of one year in his *XIX Century Fiction* (1951) – that it is hard to believe they were the work of only one author. In fact two authors soon became associated with the books, Samuel Bracebridge Hemyng and William Stephens Hayward. Both were still in their twenties and both had started writing only a few years earlier, Hemyng with *The Curate of Inveresk* (1860) and Hayward with his immensely popular *Hunted to Death* (1862).

Hemyng had been born in London (not India as is sometimes stated) in 1841, the son of a Registrar of the Supreme Court of Calcutta, had been educated at Eton, and had studied for the law, being called to the Bar in 1862. Hayward[2], born in 1835, whilst coming from a landed family – a local magistrate who lived at Wittenham House in Berkshire – had led a profligate youth. He was arrested in 1857 charged with rape but was discharged when the wronged woman failed to appear in court. Soon after, Hayward was arrested as a debtor, having squandered his money betting on the horses, and was thrown into a debtors' cell. It seems that the love of a young woman rescued him. He married in September 1859 and settled down to turning his experiences into money through writing.

It's likely Hayward had travelled extensively in his early years. *Hunted to Death* and its sequel *The Black Angel* (1863) are set firstly on a voyage to the United States and then across North America. It's possible that another book from this period, *Love Frolics of a Young Scamp* (1864), tells something of Hayward's wayward youth. That book is significant because a later reprint credits it as being by the

---

2   I am indebted to the researches of Steve Holland for providing many of the details about W. S. Hayward's life.

author of *Anonyma* and *The Lady Detective* (under which title *Revelations of a Lady Detective* was reprinted). Another of Hayward's books, *The Beautiful Demon* (1864), which has a preface initialled W.S.H. and is credited to the author of *Hunted to Death*, was also reprinted as by the author of *Skittles*. Although these later attributions, by a different publisher, are not absolute proof, they are one reason why Hayward, rather than Hemyng, is credited as having written *Revelations of a Lady Detective*.

Here we have two authors whose experiences gave them knowledge of both sides of the law: Hayward as a young reprobate, debtor and possible rapist, who had "done time" but who was from a well-to-do family and had travelled to some degree; Hemyng, a more affluent individual who was well versed in the law and who served (though not entirely successfully) as a barrister. Hemyng would have mixed in the kind of society that might have eluded Hayward, and could well have known the real Anonyma and her clients (was he the 'H' of the letter to *The Times*?) and through his own clients would have known the underbelly of London. The fact that Hemyng contributed the section "London Prostitution" to Henry Mayhew's *London Labour and the London Poor* (1861) shows his knowledge of lower-class London even while he was studying for the Bar. Hemyng, though, denied writing the Anonyma books after an article in *The Bookseller* in 1868 identified him as the author. Whether his indignant response was an honest disclaimer or an annoyance at being unmasked one cannot be entirely sure.

There can be no doubt that the two authors would have known each other. Not only would they have met at Vickers's offices, but it is likely that Hemyng completed one of Hayward's novels, *Lord Scatterbrain* (1869), when Hayward became ill. We can only speculate, but there's a possibility that the authors shared experiences, each complementing the other's work.

Hayward seems to have had a weak constitution and it's probable that his spell in prison aggravated it. He went to live in Brighton in the hope that the sea air might help him recuperate but it was too late. He died there in August 1870, aged only thirty-five. The final stories he wrote were included in an enlarged edition of *Hunted to Death*, still his best remembered work, issued in 1873. Reprints of his books continued to appear for decades and his name remained a byword for sensationalist stories, often coupled with Mary E. Braddon.

Bracebridge Hemyng, on the other hand, went from strength to strength. Soon after Hayward died, Hemyng began a new serial, "Jack Harkaway's Schooldays" (1871), the first of what would be many novels about this adventurous ultra-fit though at times vindictive youth and his adventures around the world. The first book almost certainly reflected some of Hemyng's days at Eton, but you can't help wondering whether any of Hayward's early adventures inspired later episodes. Jack Harkaway made Hemyng's fortune, though he continued to write other books, including *In the Force; or, Revelations by a Private Policeman* (1884). He lived in a grand style over his final years and died in 1901.

Seen in context it is not surprising that the character of a lady detective appeared when she did, as one of a body of books which featured dogged and resourceful heroines fighting the odds. Whereas Forrester's *Female Detective* arose out of his interest in true crime, *Revelations of a Lady Detective* expanded the tradition of the gothic novel and penny dreadful in showing that women have every bit as much true grit as their male counterparts.

REVELATIONS OF A
LADY DETECTIVE

THE MYSTERIOUS COUNTESS

THE CHIEF OF THE DETECTIVE POLICE

I TURNED a familiar corner, and was soon threading the well-known avenues of Whitehall. It was in a small street, the houses in which cover the site of the once splendid palace of the Stuarts, where one king was born and another lost his head, that the head-quarters of the London Detective Police were situated. I stopped at a door of modest pretensions, and knocked three times. I was instantly admitted. The porter bowed when he saw who I was, and at once conducted me into a room of limited dimensions. I had not to wait long. Coming from an inner room, a man of spare build, but with keen searching eyes, like those of a ferret, shook me, in a cold, business-like way, by the hand, and desired me to be seated. His forehead bulged out a little, indicating the talent of which he was the undoubted possessor. All who knew him personally, or by reputation, admired him; he performed the difficult duties of an arduous position with untiring industry and the most praiseworthy skill and perseverance. He left nothing to others, except, of course, the bare execution. This man with the stern demeanour and the penetrating glance was Colonel Warner - at the time of which I am writing, head of the Detective Department of the Metropolitan Police.

It was through his instigation that women were first of all employed as detectives. It must be confessed that the idea was not original, but it showed him to be a clever adapter, and not above imitating those whose talent led them to take the initiative in works of progress. Fouché, the great Frenchman, was constantly in the habit of employing women to assist him in discovering the various political intrigues which disturbed the peace of the first empire. His petticoated police were as successful as the most sanguine innovator could wish; and Colonel Warner, having this fact before his eyes, determined to imitate the example of a man who united the courage of a lion with the cunning of a fox, culminating his acquisitions with the sagacity of a dog.

"Sit down, Mrs. Paschal," exclaimed the colonel, handing me a chair.

I did so immediately, with that prompt and passive obedience which always pleased him. I was particularly desirous at all times of conciliating Colonel Warner, because I had not long been employed as a female detective, and now having given up my time and attention to what I may call a new profession, I was anxious to acquit myself as well and favourably as I could, and gain the goodwill and approbation of my superior. It is hardly necessary to refer to the circumstances which led me to embark on a career at once strange, exciting, and mysterious, but I may say that my husband died suddenly, leaving me badly off. An offer was made me through a peculiar channel. I accepted it without hesitation, and became one of the much-dreaded, but little-known people called Female Detectives. At the time I was verging upon forty. My brain was vigorous and subtle, and I concentrated all my energies upon the proper fulfilment and execution of those duties which devolved upon me. I met the glance of Colonel Warner and returned it unflinchingly; he liked people to stare back again at him, because it betokened confidence in themselves, and evidenced that they would not shrink in the hour of peril, when danger encompassed them and lurked in front and rear. I was well born and well educated, so that, like an accomplished actress, I could play my part in any drama in which I was instructed to take a part. My dramas, however, were dramas of real life, not the mimetic representations which obtain on the stage. For the parts I had to play, it was necessary to have nerve and strength, cunning and confidence, resources unlimited, confidence and numerous other qualities of which actors are totally ignorant. They strut, and talk, and give expression to the thoughts of others, but it is such as I who really create the incidents upon which their dialogue is based and grounded.

"I have sent for you," exclaimed the colonel, "to entrust a serious case to your care and judgment. I do not know a woman more fitted for the task than yourself. Your services, if successful, will be handsomely rewarded, and you shall have no reason to complain of my parsimony in the matter of your daily expenses. Let me caution you about hasting - take time - elaborate and mature your plans; for although the hare is swift, the slow and sure tortoise more often wins the race than its fleet opponent. I need hardly talk to you in this way, but advice is never prejudicial to anyone's interests."

"I am very glad, I am sure," I replied, "to hear any suggestions you are good enough to throw out for my guidance."

"Quite so," he said; "I am aware that you possess an unusual amount of common sense, and consequently are not at all likely to take umbrage at what is kindly meant."

"Of what nature is the business?" I asked.

"Of a very delicate one," answered Colonel Warner; "you have heard of the Countess of Vervaine?"

"Frequently; you mean the lady who is dazzling all London at the present moment by the splendour of her equipage and her diamonds, and the magnificent way in which she spends what must be a colossal fortune."

"That's her," said the colonel. "But I have taken great pains to ascertain what her fortune actually consists of. Now, I have been unable to identify any property as belonging to her, nor can I discern that she has a large balance in the hands of any banker. From what source, then, is her income derived?"

I acknowledged that I was at a loss to conjecture.

"Very well," cried Colonel Warner, "the task I propose for you is to discover where, and in what way, Lady Vervaine obtains the funds which enable her to carry on a career, the splendour and the profuseness of which exceed that of a prince of the blood royal during the Augustan age of France, when Louis XIV set an example of extravagance which was pursued to ruination by the dissolute nobility, who surrounded the avenues of his palaces, and thronged the drawing-rooms of his country seats. Will it be an occupation to your mind, do you think? If not, pray decline it at once. It is always bad to undertake a commission when it involves a duty which is repugnant to you."

"Not at all," I replied; "I should like above all things to unravel the secrets of the mysterious countess, and I not only undertake to do so, but promise to bring you the tidings and information you wish for within six weeks."

"Take your own time," said the colonel; "anyone one will tell you her ladyship's residence; let me see or hear from you occasionally, for I shall be anxious to know how you are getting on. Once more, do not be precipitate. Take this cheque for your expenses. If you should require more, send to me. And now, good morning, Mrs. Paschal. I hope sincerely that your endeavours may be crowned with the success they are sure to merit."

I took the draft, wished Colonel Warner goodbye, and returned to my own lodgings to ruminate over the task which had just been confided to me.

CHAPTER II

THE BLACK MASK

I IMAGINED that the best and surest way of penetrating the veil of secresy which surrounded the Countess of Vervaine would be to obtain a footing in her household, either as a domestic servant, or in some capacity such as would enable me to play the spy upon her actions, and watch all her movements with the greatest care and closeness. I felt confident that Colonel Warner had some excellent motive for having the countess unmasked; but he was a man who always made you find your own tools, and do your work with as little assistance as possible from him. He told you what he wanted done, and nothing remained but for you to go and do it. The Countess of Vervaine was the young and lovely widow of the old earl of that name. She was on the stage when the notorious and imbecile nobleman made her his wife. His extravagance and unsuccessful speculations in railway shares, in the days when Hudson was king, ruined him, and it was well known that, when he died broken-hearted, his income was very much reduced - so much so, that when his relict began to lead the gay and luxurious life she did, more than one head was gravely shaken, and people wondered how she did it. She thought nothing of giving a thousand pounds for a pair of carriage horses, and all enterprising tradesmen were only too rejoiced when anything rare came in their way, for the Countess of Vervaine was sure to buy it. A rare picture, or a precious stone of great and peculiar value, were things that she would buy without a murmur, and pay the price demanded for them without endeavouring to abate the proprietor's price the value of a penny piece. Personally, she was a rare combination of loveliness and accomplishments. Even the women admitted that she was beautiful, and the men raved about her. She went into the best society, and those of the highest rank and the most exalted social position in London were very glad to be asked to her magnificent and exclusive parties. Fanny, Countess of Vervaine, knew very well that if you wish to become celebrated in the gay and giddy world of fashion, you must be very careful who you admit into your house. It may be convenient, and even necessary, to ask your attorney to dine with you occasionally; but forbear to ask a ducal friend on the same day, because his grace would never forgive you for making so great a blunder. The attorney would go about amongst his friends and tell them all in what company he had been. Your house would acquire the reputation of being an "easy" one, and your acquaintances who were really worth knowing would not any more visit at a house where "anybody" was received with the same cordiality that they had themselves met with. The Countess of Vervaine lived in a large mansion in one of the new, but aristocratic squares in Belgravia. A huge towering erection it was to look at - a corner house with many windows and balconies and verandahs and conservatories. It had belonged to the earl, and he bequeathed it to her with all its wealth of furniture, rare pictures, and valuable books. It was pretty well all he had to leave her, for his lands were all sold, and the amount of ready money standing to his credit at his banker's was lamentably small - so small, indeed, as to be almost insignificant. The earl had been dead a year and a half now. She had mourned six months for him, and at the expiration of that time she cast off her widow's weeds - disdaining the example of royalty to wear them for an indefinite period - and launched into all the gaiety and dissipation that the Babylon of the moderns could supply her with. Very clever and versatile was her ladyship, as well able to talk upon abstruse subjects with a member of a scientific society as to converse with one of her patrician friends upon the merits of the latest fashions which the Parisians had with their usual taste designed.

I dressed myself one morning, after having gained the information I have just detailed, and put on the simplest things I could find in my wardrobe, which was as extensive and as full of disguises as that of a costumier's shop. I wished to appear like a servant out of place. My idea was to represent myself as a lady's-maid or under housekeeper. I did not care what situation I took as long as I obtained a footing in the household. When I approached Lady Vervaine's house, I was very much struck by its majestic and imposing appearance. I liked to see the porcelain boxes in the windows filled with the choicest flowers, which a market gardener and floriculturist undertook by contract to change twice a week, so that they should never appear shabby or out of season. I took a delight in gazing at the trailing creepers running in a wild, luxuriant, tropical manner, all over the spacious balconies, and I derived especial pleasure from the contemplation of the orange trees growing in large wooden tubs, loaded with their yellow fruit, the sheen and glimmer of which I could faintly see through the well-cleaned windows of the conservatory, which stood over the porch protecting the entrance to the front door.

I envied this successful actress all the beautiful things she appeared to have in her possession, and wondered why she should be so much more fortunate than myself; but a moment afterwards, I congratulated myself that I was not, like her, an object of suspicion and mistrust to the police, and that a female detective, like Nemesis, was not already upon my track. I vowed that all her splendour should be short-lived, and that in those gilded saloons and lofty halls, where now all was mirth and song and gladness, there should soon be nothing but weeping and gnashing of teeth. I descended the area steps, and even here there was a trace of refinement and good taste, for a small box of mignonette was placed on the sill of each window, and a large Virginia creeper reared its slender limbs against the stuccoed wall.

A request to see the housekeeper brought me into the presence of that worthy. I stated my business to her, and asked her favourable consideration of my case. She shook her head, and said she was afraid that there was no vacancy just at present, but if I would call again, she might perhaps be able to give me a more encouraging reply. I knew perfectly well how to treat a lady of her calibre. Servants in gentlemen's families are generally engaged in making a purse, upon the proceeds of which they are enabled to retire when the domestic harness begins to gall their necks, and they sigh for rest after years of hard work and toil. They either patronize savings banks, where they get their two and a half per cent, on the principle that every little helps, although they could at the same time obtain six per cent in foreign guaranteed government stock; but those who work hard, know how to take care of their money, because they understand its value, and they distrust speculative undertakings, as it is the duty of all prudent people to do; or if they distrust the parochial banks, they have a stocking which they keep carefully concealed, the contents of which are to help their possessors to furnish a lodging-house, or take a tavern, when the time arrives at which they think fit to assert their independence and retire from the servitude which they have all along tolerated for a purpose. Armed with a thorough knowledge of the class, I produced a five-pound note, and said that it was part of my savings from my last place, and that I should be happy to make her a present of it, if she would use the influence I was sure she possessed to procure me the situation I was so desirous of obtaining.

This offer produced a relaxation of the housekeeper's sternness. She asked for a reference, which I gave her; we always knew how to arrange those little matters, which were managed without any difficulty; and the result of our interview was, that I was engaged as third lady's-maid at a salary of fifteen pounds a year, and to find myself in tea and sugar. I entered my new place in less than a week, and soon had an opportunity of observing the demeanour of the Countess of Vervaine; at times it was restless and excited. Her manner was frequently pre-occupied, and she was then what is called absent. You might speak to her three or four times before you obtained an answer. She did not appear to hear you. Some weighty matter was occupying her attention, and she was so engrossed by its contemplation that she could not bestow a single thought on external objects. She was very young - scarcely five-and-twenty, and not giving evidence of being so old as that. She was not one of those proud, stern, and haughty aristocrats whom you see in the Park, leaning back in their open carriages as if they were casting their mantle of despisal and scorn to those who are walking. She was not pale, and fagged, and bilious-looking; on the contrary, she was fat and chubby, with just the smallest tinge of rose-colour on her cheek - natural colour, I mean, not the artificial hue which pernicious compounds impart to a pallid cheek.

Now and then there was an air of positive joyousness about her, as if she was enamoured of life and derived the most intense pleasure from existence in this world below, where most of us experience more blows and buffets than we do occurrences of a more gratifying nature. Although pretending not to do so, I studied her with great care, and the result of my observations was, that I could have sworn before any court of justice in the world that, to the best of my belief, she had a secret - a secret which weighed her down and crushed her young, elastic spirit, sitting on her chest like a nightmare, and spoiling her rest by hideous visions. In society she showed nothing of this. It was in the company of others that she shone; at home, in her bed-room, with her attendant satellites about her, whom she regarded as nobodies, she gave way to her fits of melancholy, and showed that every shining mirror has its dull side and its leaden reverse. There are some people who are constituted in such a manner by nature, that though they may be standing upon the crater of a volcano given to chronic eruptions, and though they are perfectly cognizant of the perilous position in which they are, will not trouble themselves much about it. It was my private opinion that the ground under the feet of the Countess of Vervaine was mined, and that she knew it, but that she had adopted that fallacious motto which has for its burden "a short life and a merry one." There was something very mysterious about her, and I made the strongest resolution that I ever made in my life that I would discover the nature of the mystery before many days had passed over my head. The countess had not the remotest idea that I was in any way inimical to her. She regarded me as something for which she paid, and which was useful to her on certain occasions. I believe she looked upon me very much as a lady in the Southern States of America looks upon a slave - a thing to minister to her vanity and obey her commands. Lady Vervaine was one of those fascinating little women who charm you by their simple, winning ways, and you do not dream for a moment that they are not terrestrial angels; did you know them intimately, however, you would discover that they have a will and a temper of their own, such as would render the life of a husband miserable and unhappy if he did not succumb to her slightest wish, and put up with her most frivolous caprice. She was frequently tyrannical with her servants, and would have her most trivial command obeyed to the letter, under pain of her sovereign displeasure. One day she struck me on the knuckles with a hair-brush, because I ran a hair-pin into her head by the merest accident in the world. I said nothing, but I cherished an idea of retaliation nevertheless. We had dressed her on a particular evening for the Opera. She looked very charming; but so graceful was her manner, so pleasant was her bearing, and so unexceptionable her taste, that she could never look anything else.

"Paschal," she said to me.

"Yes, my lady," I replied.

"I shall come home a little before twelve; wait up for me."

"Yes, my lady," I replied again, in the monotonous, parrot-like tone that servants are supposed to make use of when talking to those who have authority over them.

It was a long, dreary evening; there was not much to do, so I took up a book and tried to read; but although I tried to bring my attention upon the printed page, I was unable to succeed in doing so. I was animated with a conviction that I should make some important discovery that night. It is a singular thing, but in my mind coming events always cast their shadows before they actually occurred. I invariably had an intuition that such and such a thing would happen before it actually took place. It was considerably past twelve when the mysterious countess came home; the charms of the opera and the Floral Hall must have detained her until the last moment, unless she had met with some entertaining companion who beguiled the hours by soft speeches and tender phrases, such as lovers alone know how to invent and utter. I began to unrobe her, but after I had divested her of her cloak, she called for her dressing-gown, and told me to go and bring her some coffee. The cook was gone to bed, and I found some difficulty in making the water boil, but at last I succeeded in brewing the desired beverage, and took it upstairs. The countess was, on my return, industriously making calculations, at least so it seemed to me, in a little book bound in morocco leather, and smelling very much like a stationer's shop. She might have been making poetry, or concerting the plot of a drama, but she stopped every now and then, as if to "carry" something, after the manner of mathematicians who do not keep a calculating machine on the premises.

After I had put down the coffee, she exclaimed -

"You can go. Good night."

I replied in suitable terms, and left her, but not to go to my room or to sleep. I hung about the corridor in a stealthy way, for I knew very well that no one else was likely to be about, and I wanted to watch my lady that night, which I felt convinced was going to be prolific of events of a startling nature. The night was a little chilly, but I did not care for that. Sheltering myself as well as I could in the shadow of a doorway, I waited with the amount of resignation and patience that the occasion required. In about half an hour's time the door of the Countess of Vervaine's apartment opened. I listened breathlessly, never daring to move a muscle, lest my proximity to her should be discovered. What was my surprise and astonishment to see a man issue from the room! He held a light in his hand, and began to descend a flight of stairs by its aid.

I rubbed my eyes to see whether I had not fallen asleep and dreamed a dream; but no, I was wide awake. The man must, I imagined, have been concealed somewhere about the apartment, for I saw no trace of him during the time that I was in the room. He was a person of small size, and dressed in an odd way, as if he was not a gentleman, but a servant out of livery. This puzzled me more than ever, but I had seen a few things in my life which appeared scarcely susceptible of explanation at first, but which, when eliminated by the calm light of reason and dissected by the keen knife of judgment, were in a short time as plain as the sun at noonday. I thought for a brief space, and then I flattered myself that I had penetrated the mystery. I said to myself, *It is a disguise.* The Countess of

Vervaine was a little woman. She would consequently make
a very small man. The one before me, slowly and with careful
tread going down the staircase, was a man of unusually small
stature. You would call him decidedly undersized. There was a
flabbiness about the clothes he wore which seemed to indicate
that they had not been made for him. The coat-sleeves were
especially long. This gave strength to the supposition that the
countess had assumed male attire for purposes of her own.
She could not possibly have had herself measured for a suit of
clothes. No tailor in London would have done such a thing.
She had probably bought the things somewhere - picking
them up at random without being very particular as to their
size or fit. I allowed the man to reach the bottom of the staircase before I followed in pursuit. Gliding stealthily along
with a care and precision I had often practised in the dead of
night at home in order that I might become well versed and
experienced in an art so useful to a detective, I went down
step by step and caught sight of the man turning an angle
which hid him from my view, but as he did so I contrived
to glance at his features. I started and felt inclined to shrink.
Every lineament of his face was concealed by a hideous black
mask. My sensations were not enviable for many a long night
afterwards; that dark funereal face-covering was imprinted
in an almost indelible manner upon my mind, and once or
twice I awoke in bed shivering all over in a cold perspiration,
fancying that the black mask was standing over me holding a
loaded pistol at my head, and threatening my life if I did not
comply with some importunate demand which I felt I could
not pay the slightest attention to. Recovering myself, as best
I could, I raised my dress, and stepping on my toes, followed
the black mask. He descended to the lower regions. He held

the light before him, occasionally looking around to see if any one were behind him. I contrived whenever he did this to vanish into some corner or fall in a heap so that the rays of the lamp should not fall upon my erect form. We passed the kitchen, from which the stale cabbage-watery smell arose which always infests those interesting domestic offices after their occupants have retired to rest. I could hear the head cook snoring. He slept in a small room in the basement, and was, I have no doubt, glad to go to bed after the various onerous duties that he had to perform during the day, for the office of cook in a good family is, you know, no sinecure. Aristocratic birth does not prevent the possessor from nourishing a somewhat plebeian appetite which must be satisfied at least four or five times a day. A plain joint is not sufficient, a dozen messes called *entrées* must accompany it, composed of truffles and other evil smelling abominations, such as are to be met with at the shop of a Parisian epicure. I had not searched the rooms on the basement very closely, but during the cursory investigation I had made, I noticed that there was one which was always kept locked. No one ever entered it. Some said the key was lost, but none of the servants seemed to trouble themselves much about it. It was an empty room, or it was a lumber room. They did not know, neither did they care. This being the state of things existent respecting that room I was astonished to see the man in the black mask produce a key well oiled so as to make it facile of turning, put it in the lock, turn it, open the door, enter and disappear, shutting the door after him. It did not take me long to reach the keyhole, to which I applied my eye. The key was not in it, but whether the Black Mask had secured the door inside or not, I could not tell. The time had not then arrived at which it was either necessary or prudent to solve the riddle. I could see inside the room with the greatest ease. The lamp was on the floor, and the Black Mask was on his knees engaged in scrutinizing the flooring. The apartment was utterly destitute of furniture, not even a chair or a common deal table adorned the vacant space, but a few bricks piled on the top of one another lay in one corner. Near them was a little mound of dry mortar, which, from its appearance, had been made and brought there months ago. A trowel such as bricklayers use was not far off. While I was noticing these things the man in the black mask had succeeded in raising a couple of planks from the floor. These he laid in a gentle way on one side. I could perceive that he had revealed a black yawning gulf such as the entrance to a sewer might be. After hesitating a moment to see if his lamp was burning brightly and well, he essayed the chasm and disappeared in its murky depths, as if he had done the same thing before and knew very well where he was going. Perfectly amazed at the discoveries I was making, I looked on in passive wonderment. I was, as may be supposed, much pleased at what I saw, because I felt that I had discovered the way to unravel a tangled skein. Queen Eleanor, when she found out the clue which led her through the maze to the bower of fair Rosamond, was not more delighted than myself, when I saw the strange and mystic proceeding on the part of the Black Mask. When I had allowed what I considered a sufficient time to elapse, I tried the handle of the door - it turned. A slight push and the door began to revolve on its hinges; another one, and that more vigorous, admitted me to the room. All was in darkness. Sinking on my hands and knees, I crawled with the utmost caution in the direction of the hole in the floor. Half a minute's search brought me to it.

My hand sank down as I endeavoured to find a resting-place for it. I then made it my business to feel the sides of the pit to discover if there was any ladder, through the instrumentality of whose friendly steps I could follow the Black Mask. There was. Having satisfied myself of this fact, I with as much rapidity as possible took off the small crinoline I wore, for I considered that it would very much impede my movements. When I had divested myself of the obnoxious garment, and thrown it on the floor, I lowered myself into the hole and went down the ladder. Four or five feet, I should think, brought me to the end of the flight of steps. As well as I could judge I was in a stone passage. The air was damp and cold. The sudden chill made me shudder. It was evidently a long way under ground, and the terrestrial warmth was wanting. It had succumbed to the subterraneous vapours which were more searching than pleasant; a faint glimmer of light some distance up the passage, showed me that the Black Mask had not so much the best of the chase. My heart palpitated, and I hastened on at the quickest pace I considered consistent with prudence.

CHAPTER III

BARS OF GOLD AND INGOTS

I COULD see that the passage I was traversing had been built for some purpose to connect two houses together. What the object of such a connexion was it was difficult to conceive. But rich people are frequently eccentric, and do things that those poorer and simpler than themselves would never dream of. The Black Mask had discovered the underground communication, and was making use of it for the furtherance of some clandestine operation. The passage was not of great length. The Black Mask stopped and set the light upon the ground. I also halted, lest the noise of my footsteps might alarm the mysterious individual I was pursuing. I had been in many perplexities and exciting situations before, and I had taken a prominent part in more than one extremely perilous adventure, but I do not think that I was ever, during the whole course of my life, actuated by so strong a curiosity, or animated with so firm a desire to know what the end would be, as I was on the present occasion. In moments such as those which were flitting with the proverbial velocity of time, but which seemed to me very slow and sluggish, the blood flows more quickly through your veins, your heart beats with a more rapid motion, and the tension of the nerves becomes positively painful. I watched the movements of the Black Mask with the greatest care and minuteness. He removed, by some means with which he was acquainted, half a dozen good-sized bricks from the wall, revealing an aperture of sufficient dimensions to permit the passage of a human body. He was not slow in passing through the hole. The light he took with him. I was in darkness. Crawling along like a cat about to commit an act of feline ferocity upon some musipular abortion, I reached the cavity and raised my eyes to the edge, so as to be able to scrutinize the interior of the apartment into which the Black Mask had gone. It was a small place, and more like a vault than anything else. The light had been placed upon a chest, and its flickering rays fell around, affording a sickly glare very much like that produced on a dark afternoon in a shrine situated in a Roman Catholic Continental church. The sacred edifice is full of darkening shadows, but through the bronzed railings which shut off egress to the shrine, you can see the long wax tapers burning, emitting their fiery tribute to the manes of the dead. The Black Mask had fallen on his knees before a chest of a peculiar shape and make; it was long and narrow. Shooting back some bolts, the lid flew open and disclosed a large glittering pile of gold to my wondering gaze. There was the precious metal, not coined and mixed with alloy, but shining in all the splendour of its native purity. There were bars of gold and ingots, such as Cortez and Pizarro, together with their bold followers, found in Peru, when the last of the Incas was driven from his home, his kingdom, and his friends, after many a sanguinary battle, after many a hard-fought fray. The bars were heavy and valuable, for they were pure and unadulterated. There were many chests, safes, and cases, in the vault. Were they all full of gold? If so, what a prize had this audacious robber acquired! He carefully selected five of the largest and heaviest ingots. Each must have been worth at least a thousand pounds. It was virgin gold, such as nuggets are formed of, and, of course, worth a great deal of money. After having made his choice, it was necessary to place the bars in some receptacle. He was evidently a man of resources, for he drew a stout canvas bag from his pocket, and, opening it, placed them inside; but, as he was doing so, the mask fell from his face. Before he could replace the hideous facial covering, I made a discovery, one I was not altogether unprepared for. The black mask - ungainly and repulsive as it was - had hitherto concealed the lovely features of the Countess of Vervaine. With a tiny excla-mation of annoyance she replaced the mask and continued her task. I smiled grimly as I saw who the midnight robber was, whose footsteps I had tracked so well, whose movements I had watched so unerringly. It would take but few visits to this treasure vault, I thought to myself, to bring in a magnificent income; and then I marvelled much what the vault might be, and how the vast and almost countless treasure got there. Questions easy to propound, but by no means so facile of reply. At present my attention was concentrated wholly and solely upon the countess. It would be quite time enough next morning to speculate upon the causes which brought about effects of which I was the exultant witness. Having stowed away the ingots in the canvas bag, the mysterious countess rose to her feet, and made a motion indicative of retiring. At this juncture I was somewhat troubled in my mind. Would it be better for me to raise an alarm or to remain quiet? Supposing I were to cry out, who was there to hear my exclamation or respond to my earnest entreaty for help and assistance. Perhaps the countess was armed. So desperate an adventuress as she seemed to be would very probably carry some offensive weapon about her, which it was a fair presumption she would not hesitate to use if hard pressed, and that lonely passage, the intricacies of which were in all probability known but to herself and me, would for ever hide from prying eyes my blanching bones and whitening skeleton. This was not a particularly pleasant reflection, and I saw that it behoved me to be cautious. I fancied that I could regain the lumber room before the countess could overtake me, because it would be necessary for her to shut down and fasten the chest, and when she had done that she would be obliged to replace the bricks she had removed from the wall, which proceeding would take her some little time and occupy her attention while I made my escape. I had gained as much information as I wished, and I was perfectly satisfied with the discovery I had made. The countess was undoubtedly a robber, but it required some skill to succeed in bringing her to justice. In just that species of skill and cunning I flattered myself I was a proficient. Hastily retreating, I walked some distance, but to my surprise did not meet with the ladder. Could I have gone wrong? Was it possible that I had taken the wrong turning? I was totally unacquainted with the ramifications of these subterranean corridors. I trembled violently, for a suspicion arose in my breast that I might be shut in the vault. I stopped a moment to think, and leaned against the damp and slimy wall in a pensive attitude.

CHAPTER IV

IN THE VAULT

WITHOUT a light I could not tell where I was, or in which direction it would be best for me to go. I was in doubt whether it would be better to go steadily on or stay where I was, or retrace my steps. I had a strong inclination to do the latter: whilst I was ruminating a light appeared to the left of me. It was that borne by the Countess of Vervaine. I had then gone wrong. The passage prolonged itself, and I had not taken the right turning. The countess was replacing the bricks, so that it was incumbent upon me to remain perfectly still, which I did. Having accomplished her task, she once more took up her bag, the valuable contents of which were almost as much as she could carry. I was in the most critical position. She would unquestionably replace the planks, and perhaps fasten them in some way so as to prevent my escaping as she had done. My only chance lay in reaching the ladder before her, but how was it possible to do so when she was between myself and the ladder? I should have to make a sudden attack upon her, throw her down, and pass over her prostrate body, all very desirable, but

totally impossible. I was defenceless. I believed her to be armed.
I should run the risk of having a couple of inches of cold steel
plunged into my body or else an ounce of lead would make
a passage for itself through the ventricles of my heart, which
were not at all desirous of the honour of being pierced by a
lady of rank. I sighed for a Colt's revolver, and blamed myself
for not having taken the precaution of being armed. Although
I wished to capture Lady Vervaine above all things, I was not
tired of my life. Once above ground again and in the house
I should feel myself more of a free agent than I did in those
dreary vaults, where I felt sure I should fall an easy prey to the
attacks of an unscrupulous woman. Lady Vervaine pursued
her way with a quick step, which showed that she had accomplished her object, and was anxious to get to her own room
again, and reach a haven of safety. As for me, I resigned myself
to my fate. What could I do? To attack her ladyship would,
I thought, be the forerunner of instant death. It would be like
running upon a sword, or firing a pistol in one's own mouth.
She would turn upon me like a tiger, and in order to save herself from the dreadful consequences of her crime, she would
not hesitate a moment to kill me. Serpents without fangs are
harmless, but when they have those obnoxious weapons it is
just as well to put your iron heel upon their heads and crush
them, so as to render them harmless and subservient to your
sovereign and conquering will. I followed the Countess of
Vervaine slowly, and at a distance, but I dared not approach
her. I was usually fertile in expedients, and I thought I should
be able to find my way out of the dilemma in some way. I was
not a woman of one idea, and if one dart did not hit the mark
I always had another feathered shaft ready for action in my
well-stocked quiver. Yet it was not without a sickening feeling

of uncertainty and doubt that I saw her ladyship ascend the ladder and vanish through the opening in the flooring. I was alone in the vault, and abandoned to my own resources. I waited in the black darkness in no enviable frame of mind, until I thought the countess had had sufficient time to evacuate the premises, then I groped my way to the ladder and mounted it. I reached the planks and pushed against them with all my might, but the strength I possessed was not sufficient to move them. My efforts were futile. Tired and exhausted, I once more tried the flags which paved the passage, and cast about in my mind for some means of escape from my unpleasant position. If I could find no way of extrication it was clear that I should languish horribly for a time, and ultimately perish of starvation. This was not an alluring prospect, nor did I consider it so. I had satisfied myself that it was impossible to escape through the flooring, as the Countess of Vervaine had in some manner securely fastened the boards. Suddenly an idea shot through my mind with the vivid quickness of a flash of lightning. I could work my way back through the passage, and by feeling every brick as I went, discover those which gave her ladyship admittance into the vault where the massive ingots of solid bullion were kept. I had no doubt whatever that so precious a hoard was visited occasionally by those it belonged to, and I should not only be liberated from my captivity, but I should discover the mystery which was at present perplexing me. Both of these were things I was desirous of accomplishing, so I put my shoulder to the wheel, and once more threaded the circumscribed dimensions of the corridor which led to the place in which such a vast quantity of gold was concealed. I took an immense deal of trouble, for I felt every brick singly, and after passing my fingers over its rough surface gave it a push to see if it yielded. At last, to my inexpressible joy, I reached one which "gave;" another vigorous thrust and it fell through with a harsh crash upon the floor inside. The others I took out more carefully. When I had succeeded in removing them all I entered the bullion vault in the same way in which her ladyship had, and stopped to congratulate myself upon having achieved so much. The falling brick had made a loud noise, which had reverberated through the vault, producing cavernous echoes; but I had not surmised that this would be productive of the consequences that followed it. Whilst I was considering what I should do or how I should dispose myself to sleep for an hour or so - for, in nursery parlance, the miller had been throwing dust in my eyes, and I was weary - I heard a noise in one corner of the vault, where I afterwards found the door was situated. A moment of breathless expectation followed, and then dazzling blinding lights flashed before me and made me close my shrinking eyes involuntarily. Harsh voices rang in my ears, rude hands grasped me tightly, and I was a prisoner. When I recovered my power of vision, I was surrounded by three watchmen, and as many policemen. They manacled me. I protested against such an indignity, but appearances were against me.

"I am willing to come with you," I exclaimed, in a calm voice, because I knew I had nothing to fear in the long run. "But why treat me so badly?"

"Only doing my duty," replied one of the police, who seemed to have the command of the others.

"Why do you take me in custody?" I demanded.

"Why? Come, that's a good joke," he replied.

"Answer my question."

"Well, if you don't know, I'll tell you," he answered, with a grin.

"I have an idea, but I want to be satisfied about the matter."

"We arrest you for *robbing the bank*," he replied, solemnly.

My face brightened. So it was a bank, and the place we were in was the bullion vault of the house. The mystery was now explained. The Countess of Vervaine had by some means discovered her proximity to so rich a place, and had either had the passage built, or had been fortunate enough to find it ready-made to her hand. This was a matter for subsequent explanation.

"I am ready to go with you," I said; "when we arrive at the station-house I shall speak to the inspector on duty."

The man replied in a gruff voice, and I was led from the vault, happy in the reflection that I had escaped from the gloom and darkness of the treasure house.

CHAPTER V

HUNTED DOWN

"GLAD to see you, Mrs. Paschal," exclaimed Colonel Warner when I was ushered into his presence. "I must congratulate you upon your tact, discrimination, and perseverance, in running the Countess of Vervaine to earth as cleverly as you did. Rather an unpleasant affair, though, that of the subterranean passage."

"I am accustomed to those little dramatic episodes," I replied: "when I was taken to the station-house by the exultant policeman, the inspector quickly released me on finding who I was. I always carry my credentials in my pocket, and your name is a tower of strength with the executive."

"We must consider now what is to be done," said the colonel; "there is no doubt whatever that the South Belgravia Bank has been plundered to a great extent, and that it is from that source that our mysterious countess has managed to supply her extravagant habits and keep up her transitory magnificence, which she ought to have seen would, from its nature, be evanescent. I am only surprised to think that her depredations were not discovered before; she must have managed everything in a skilful manner, so skilful indeed as to be worthy of the expertest burglar of modern times. I have had the manager of the bank with me this morning, and he is desirous of having the matter hushed up if possible; but I told him frankly that I could consent to nothing of the kind. One of the watchmen or policemen who took you into custody must have gone directly to a newspaper office, and have apprised the editor of the fact, because here is a statement of the circumstance in a daily paper, which seems to have escaped the manager's notice. Newspapers pay a small sum for information, and that must have induced the man to do as he apparently has done. The astute Countess of Vervaine has, I may tell you, taken advantage of this hint, and gone away from London, for I sent to her house this morning, which was shut up. The only reply my messengers could get was that her ladyship had gone out of town, owing to the illness of a near relation, which is, of course, a ruse."

"Clearly," I replied, "she has taken the alarm, and wishes to throw dust in our eyes."

"What do you advise?" asked Colonel Warner, walking up and down the room.

'I should say, leave her alone until her fears die away and she returns to town. It is now the height of the season, and she will not like to be away for any great length of time."

"I don't agree with you, Mrs. Paschal," returned the colonel, testily.

"Indeed, and why not?"

"For many reasons. In the first place, she may escape from the country with the plunder. What is to prevent her from letting her house and furniture in London, and going abroad with the proceeds?"

"There is some truth in that," I said, more than half convinced that the colonel took the correct view of the case.

"Very well, my second reason is, that a bird in the hand is worth two in the bush."

Proverbial, but true, I thought to myself.

"Thirdly, I wish to recover as much of the stolen property as I can. A criminal, with full hands, is worth more than one whose digits are empty."

"Do you propose that I shall follow her up?" I demanded.

"Most certainly I do."

"In that case, the sooner I start the better it will be."

"Start at once, if your arrangements will permit you to do so. Servants are not immaculate, and by dint of inquiry at her ladyship's mansion, I have little doubt you will learn something which you will find of use to you."

"In less than a week, colonel," I replied, confidently, "the Countess of Vervaine shall be in the hands of the police."

"In the hands of the police?" What a terrible phrase, full of significance and awful import. Redolent of prison and solitary confinement. Replete with visions of hard-labour, and a long and weary imprisonment, expressive of a life of labour, disgrace and pain. Perhaps indicative of summary annihilation by the hands of the hangman.

"I rely upon you," said Colonel Warner, shaking my hand. "In seven days from this time I shall expect the fulfilment of your promise."

I assented, and left the office in which affairs of so much importance to the community at large were daily conducted, and in nine cases out of ten brought to a successful issue.

Yet the salary this man received from a grateful nation, or more strictly speaking from its Government, was a bare one thousand a year, while many sinecurists get treble that sum for doing nothing at all. My first care was to return to the Countess of Vervaine's house. It was shut up, but that merely meant that the blinds were down and the shutters closed in the front part. The larger portion of the servants were still there and glad to see me. They imagined that I had been allowed a holiday, or that I had been somewhere on business for her ladyship. I at once sought the housekeeper. "Well, Paschal," she said, "what do you want?"

"I have been to get some money for the countess, who sent me into the City for that purpose, ma'am," I boldly replied, "and she told me I was to come to you, give you ten pounds, and you would give me her address, for she wished you to follow her into the country."

"Oh! indeed. Where is the money?"

I gave the housekeeper ten sovereigns, saying - "You can have five more if you like, I dare say she wont miss it."

"Not she. She has plenty."

The five additional portraits of Her Majesty were eagerly taken possession of by the housekeeper, who blandly told me that the countess would be found at Blinton Abbey, in Yorkshire, whither she had gone to spend a fortnight with some aristocratic acquaintance. I always made a point of being very quiet, civil, and obliging when in the presence of the housekeeper, who looked upon me as remarkably innocent, simple, and hardworking. After obtaining the information I was in search of I remained chatting in an amicable and agreeable manner for a short time, after which I took my leave. When, ho! for the night mail, north. I was accompanied by a superintendent, to whom I invariably intrusted the consummation of arduous enterprises which required masculine strength. He was a sociable man, and we might between us have proved a match for the cleverest thieves in Christendom. In fact we frequently were so, as they discovered to their cost. There is to me always something very exhilarating in the quickly rushing motion of a railway carriage. It is typical of progress, and raises my spirits in proportion to the speed at which we career along, now through meadow and now through woodland, at one time cutting through a defile and afterwards steaming through a dark and sombre tunnel. What can equal such magical travelling? It was night when we reached Blinton. The Abbey was about a mile and a half from the railway station. Neither the superintendent or myself felt inclined to go to rest, for we had indulged in a nap during the journey from which we awoke very much invigorated. We left our carpet bags in the care of a sleepy railway porter who had only awaited the arrival of the night mail north, and at half-past one o'clock set out to reconnoitre the position of Blinton Abbey. The moon was shining brightly. We pursued a bridle path and found little difficulty in finding the Abbey as we followed the porter's instructions to the letter. All was still as we gazed undisturbed upon the venerable pile which had withstood the blasts of many a winter and reflected the burning rays of innumerable summer suns. I was particularly struck with the chapel, which was grey and sombre before us; the darkened roof, the lofty buttreses, the clustered shafts, all spoke of former grandeur. The scene forcibly recalled Sir Walter Scott's lines,

> "If thou would'st view fair Melrose aright,
> Go visit it by the pale moonlight;
> For the gay beams of lightsome day
> Gild but to flout the ruins grey,
> When the broken arches are black in night
> And each shafted oriel glimmers white;
> When the cold light's uncertain shower
> Streams on the ruined central tower;
> When buttress and buttress alternately
> Seem framed of ebon and ivory -
> Then go, but go alone the while,
> Then view St. David's ruined pile."

We halted, inspired with a sort of sacred awe. The chapel, the turreted castle, the pale and silvery moonlight, the still and witching time of night, the deep castellated windows, the embrasures on the roof from which, in days gone by, many a sharp speaking culverin was pointed against the firm and lawless invader, all conspired to inspire me with sadness and melancholy. I was aroused from my reverie by the hand of the Superintendent which sought my arm. Without speaking a word he drew me within the shadow of a recess, and having safely ensconced me together with himself, he whispered the single word, "Look!" in my ear. I did as he directed me, and following the direction indicated by his outstretched finger saw a dark figure stealing out of a side door of Blinton Abbey. Stealthily and with cat-like tread did that sombre figure advance until it reached the base of a spreading cedar tree whose funereal branches afforded a deathlike shade like that of yew trees in a churchyard, when the figure produced a sharp pointed instrument and made a hole as if about to bury something. I could scarcely refrain a hoarse cry of delight for it seemed palpable to me that the Countess of Vervaine was about to dispose of her ill-gotten booty. I blessed the instinct which prompted me to propose a visit to the Abbey in the night-time, although I invariably selected the small hours for making voyages of discovery. I have generally found that criminals shun the light of day and seek the friendly shelter of a too often treacherous night. In a low voice I communicated my suspicions to the superintendent, and he concurred with me. I suggested the instant arrest of the dark figure. The lady was so intently engaged that she did not notice our approach; had she done so she might have escaped into the Abbey. The strong hand of the superintendent was upon her white throat before she could utter a sound. He dragged her remorselessly into the moonlight, and the well-known features of the Countess of Vervaine were revealed indisputably.

"What do you want of me, and why am I attacked in this way?" she demanded in a tremulous voice as soon as the grasp upon her throat was relaxed.

I had meanwhile seized a bag, the same canvas bag which had contained the ingots on the night of the robbery. They were still there. When I heard her ladyship's inquiry, I replied to it. "The directors of the South Belgravia Bank are very anxious to have an interview with your ladyship," I said.

She raised her eyes to mine, and an expression of anguish ran down her beautiful countenance. She knew me, and the act of recognition informed her that she was hunted down. With a rapid motion, so swift, so quick, that it resembled a sleight-of-hand, the Countess of Vervaine raised something to her mouth; in another moment her hand was by her side again, as if nothing had happened. Something glittering in the moonlight attracted my attention. I stooped down and picked it up. It was a gold ring of exquisite workmanship. A spring lid revealing a cavity was open. I raised it to my face. A strong smell of bitter almonds arose. I turned round with a flushed countenance to her ladyship. She was very pale. The superintendent was preparing to place handcuffs around her slender wrists; he held the manacles in his hand and was adjusting them. But she was by her own daring act spared this indignity. A subtle poison was contained in the secret top of her ring, and she had with a boldness peculiar to herself swallowed it before we could anticipate or prevent her rash act. The action of the virulent drug was as quick as it was deadly. She tottered. A smile which seemed to say, the battle is over, and I soon shall be at rest, sat upon her lips. Then she fell heavily to the ground with her features convulsed with a hard spasm, a final pain; her eyes were fixed, her lips parted, and Fanny, the accomplished, lovely, and versatile Countess of Vervaine was no more. I did not regret that so young and fair a creature had escaped the felons' dock, the burglars' doom. The affair created much excitement at the time, and the illustrated papers were full of pictures of Blinton Abbey, but it has long since passed from the public mind, and hundreds of more sensation have cropped up since then. The South Belgravia Bank recovered its ingots, but it was nevertheless a heavy loser through the former depredations of the famous Countess of Vervaine.

THE SECRET BAND

CHAPTER I

A COMPLICATED CASE

THE postman's knock sounded at the door with its usual sharp rifle-like crack, crack; and shortly afterwards my servant entered the room, saying, "A letter for you, ma'am." The official seal quickly informed me that it was on business. Nor was I sorry to receive the information that it contained. I had been idle lately; that is to say, I had given myself a holiday for a fortnight, and I was anxious to be on active service again. I felt that I was becoming rusty and inert, not to say obese and stupid. The letter was from Colonel Warner. He wrote: -

"My dear Madam, - I have a little affair to propose to you which I think will be congenial to your feelings. There is nothing so efficient and time-saving as plunging into the middle of a thing when you happen to have business of a serious nature under your consideration, so I will, without further preface, let you know what I wish to have done. There is in existence in London a society called the 'Secret Band.' It consists of men who have banded themselves together after the manner of the famous 'Carbonari.' The members are to a man Italians and political refugees. What their oaths and ultimate objects may be I am unable to say, but this I know, they are dangerous men, unscrupulous men, who have neither the fear of Heaven or of their fellow-men before their eyes. One of their members came to me yesterday imploring my protection. His name is Felice Mantuani. It would appear from his statement that he has broken his oath. He would tell me no more. The penalty of the infraction of that which he had sworn to keep inviolate is, according to the laws of their association simply *death*. Mantuani declared most solemnly to me, with tears in his eyes, that he went about in fear of his life, which he was certain would soon be forfeited. He appealed to me as chief of that secret force which exists for the special purpose of protecting life and property to render him some assistance. He is now hiding away in obscure lodgings in Soho, but he does not feel secure there, he is constantly apprehensive of a stab in the dark, or some other vengeful proceeding. Such a state of things ought to be put a stop to, and I am determined that I will do what I can to assist this unfortunate foreigner. I have always disliked secret societies, and nothing would please me better than to deal one of them a severe blow such as they are likely to remember for a long time to come. The man whom Mantuani appears to dread more than the others is named Zini. He is a man of gigantic stature, and immense determination. His watch cry is 'The Regeneration of Italy,' for the achievement of which object the 'Secret Band' has been formed by him. Owing to the dereliction of duty on the part of Mantuani, Zini has taken an especial dislike to him, and as I before observed, his life is not safe. I wish to discover who and what this man Zini is, and to find out whether the representations of Mantuani are worthy of credence. You will find the latter at the following address. [Here followed a certain number in a low street.] By all means seek an interview with him without delay. Use your superior sagacity, and unravel the secrets of this nest of secret assassins. If they have killed one man they will not hesitate to kill another, and Mantuani assures me that more than one member of the 'Secret Band' has mysteriously disappeared without leaving the slightest clue to his fate. Mantuani expects you. I have told him that you will call, therefore do not fail to do so without delay."

After reading this letter I foresaw a difficult task before me. The secret society of the Italians that Paul Feval and Alexandre Dumas have so often celebrated in their romances were well known to me by repute. I had heard of their existence in London and of the terrible power which they exercised over one another. I was commanded by my superior to unravel their plots and watch over the life of a proscribed member. I knew at once intuitively that Mantuani was a coward and perhaps a traitor. About Zini I had a different opinion, but I deferred giving a definite judgment upon either until I had seen them. I supposed that Colonel Warner imagined that a service of so delicate a nature would stand more chance of success if confided to a woman than it would if put in the hands of the regular police. Men are less apt to suspect a woman if she play her cards cleverly, and knows thoroughly well how to conduct the business she is instructed to bring to a successful termination. I proceeded after breakfast to the temporary lodgings of Signor Mantuani. It was a squalid abode such as political exiles are often compelled to put up with. In many cases they have neither money or friends and are obliged to shift for themselves. Mantuani received me blandly, pressed me to drink some brandy which I declined, and finding that his efforts of conciliation were without avail, said, "It is rather unusual for ladies to be employed about matters connected with the police, is it not?"

He spoke very good English and there was a certain grace about his manner, but I did not like the man. Perhaps I allowed myself to be prejudiced against the man through knowing that he had incurred the displeasure of his friends and compatriots. His narrow retreating forehead, his small piercing eyes, his long dark black hair, his thin quivering lips all set me against him; but I nevertheless resolved as in duty bound to do my best for him. In reply to his remark, I said, "I don't know how it is in Italy, but in this country it is not so uncommon a thing."

"Indeed, you surprise me, but I have seen many astonishing things since I have been in England."

"In that case, why do you not return to your own country?"

"Because I should be in danger of arrest and imprisonment," he replied.

"Are you really afraid that Zini will kill you or have you killed?" was my next question.

As the name of Zini passed my lips I could see a shudder convulse his attenuated frame. He trembled visibly and turned as white as any sheet. Approaching me with a cautious tread, he whispered in my car, "He will kill me; the knife is already sharpened."

I laughed at his fear; but the man was reduced to a state of abject terror such as I never before witnessed. After some more conversation of a trivial nature, I went away with a very bad opinion of Mantuani, and having an innate conviction that a dreadful fate was really in store for him; he had done something at least to deserve the retributive justice of those who were formerly his companions. It was a case full of perplexity. The vendetta had been launched against Mantuani. He felt positive that his days on earth were numbered. He even knew who his murderers were to be. The plain and simple course under such circumstances would have been to go before some magistrate and denounce the conspirators; but although Colonel Warner had strongly recommended him to do this he steadily refused, because he declared it would not assist him at all. He had no material evidence upon which a magistrate could issue a warrant. If threats had been used towards him, as he alleged, the sitting magistrate had the power to bind those uttering such threats over to keep the peace for a certain period; but Mantuani laughed at the idea of Zini being bound over in any way by an empty legal process to do that which he had no inclination for. He said to me when I spoke to him of Zini, "He is a terrible man, one of the most remarkable of modern times. He is a demi-god. His patriotism is pure and unalloyed, while I am a wretch in comparison with him; but it is hard to die because one is naturally weak. Zini is here to-day and gone to-morrow. There is a price upon his head in Naples, Italy, Rome, Venice, and Hungary. It is worth thirty thousand francs to any one who would betray him. But in spite of the persecution of foreign Governments, in spite of their hatred and their vigilance he comes and goes as he likes. He is like the wind, he wanders where he lists and no one can so much as hold him in their hand for an instant. Oh, he is a great man, but he is cruel and unforgiving."

It was strange that Mantuani should preserve a feeling of affection and veneration for his chief, although he knew the immutable decree had gone forth against him. Like a French criminal condemned to the scaffold, he knew he was to die, but he did not know when or on what day. The executioner might call him up any morning, waking him from his last sleep. He would not tell you in what way he had offended Zini. Although I tried on several occasions to break down the barriers of his reticence, I could not succeed in doing so. I did not imagine for an instant that Mantuani had even had sufficient courage and determination to dispute with Zini for mastery; that his puny spirit aspired to control the members of the band, and that worsted in the combat he had, like Lucifer and his lost seraphs, been signally defeated. I could not fancy that one was Rome the other Carthage, and that they waged a sort of Punic war together for supremacy and conquest. Mantuani went about, when he did venture abroad, with his head hanging down, for he felt that he was doomed. Colonel Warner and myself held more than one animated colloquy about this singular case. The unfortunate Italian had heard much of the skill, cleverness, and sagacity of the London Detective Police, and he applied to us as the only chance of safety that occurred to him. We could not see in what way we could help him except by having him constantly watched, so that any evil intentions on the part of his enemies might be nipped in the bud and frustrated at the very commencement. I contented myself with playing the spy on Zini. Having been directed to the house in which he lodged, I found, to my great satisfaction, that there was an attic to be let, which I instantly engaged, and at once took possession of it. It was not much of a place to live in, but I represented myself as a servant out of place, and I did not mind undergoing privations when I was required to hunt down noble game worthy of much care, trouble, and endurance. In tracking Zini, I felt that I was not in pursuit of a commonplace man; from all I heard of him I was sure that he was a man amongst men. Hitherto I had chased game of less grandeur and importance. Now I had before me the monarch of the forest, with whom to play was dangerous, and in fighting with whom one false step would be destruction. Zini occupied the second-floor. He was not a studious man. His habits were restless, and he was frequently out of doors. Now and then he would be closeted for hours writing long letters on thin transparent paper. These he would allow no one but himself to post. What surprised me more than anything was he had a wife. Zini a married man! to me it was incredible. A patriot I thought had no time for domestic joys, or to waste in amorous dalliance with a woman. His mind should be otherwise employed, and for ever bent upon the coming of that glorious awakening and moral resurrection which he was endeavouring to stimulate and bring about amongst his persecuted and down-trodden countrymen. I saw her one day on the stairs. She was a thin, pale, fragile-looking little thing. A toy - a child - a baby. He must have loved her for her very emptiness. I could see at a glance that she had no mind, and was frivolous to a degree; but then she was pretty and engaging in her manner, which will in the eyes of some men cover a multitude of sins. Her long fair hair was very glossy and silken; it was a pleasure to look at it. Her eyes were soft and melting; her lips rosy and small, but there was nothing to love about her except her personal appearance. I had expected to see the wife of Zini a commanding woman, with dark flashing eyes, an erect figure, with her whole soul beaming on her face and trembling on her lips. Dark as the night and terrible as an enraged Pythoness. I had begun to take an interest in Zini. I knew that he was perfectly

disinterested; that he was a man of simple mind and gener-
ous impulse, and I was shocked and dispirited when I saw
the doll-like creature he had made his wife. I had met him,
and his form was impressed indelibly upon my memory.
His stature was large; that is to say, he was at least one inch
and a half taller than most men; and he excelled them in
physical strength and size; so he did in his moral attributes.
He was a man to admire. There was a calm dignity and self-
possession about him which prepossessed you in his favour
the moment you came in contact with him. His brain, vast
and comprehensive, appeared always to be revolving gigantic projects fraught with immense moment to the whole
human race. His kindling glance and quivering nostrils
spoke volumes of the exalted schemes which this remarkable man was ever cherishing. A week had elapsed since
I received the letter which brought Signor Mantuani
under my notice, and yet he was not dead. No hostile demonstration had been made against him, and everything
remained in a state of the most complete quiescence. It
happened one evening that I descended the stairs from
my attic, for the prolonged captivity was rather irksome,
in order to hang about the passages, talk to the landlady,
and see if I could overhear any conversation between Zini
and his wife. I halted just outside his door and listened. All
was still within. I placed my ear to the keyhole; not a very
dignified proceeding, but one I thought justified by the
peculiar circumstances of the case, which I had been com-
missioned to investigate. Luckily a footstep warned me to
withdraw, or I should have been detected in a despicable
act, for Zini himself suddenly opened the door. I had not
time to withdraw. Seeing me he spoke. This was the first

time I had heard his voice, a deep melodious voice, bearing command in its very accent; a sweet sounding and a thrilling voice, such as men are moved and governed by.

"Are you living in the house?" he said. "If so, would you mind doing me a favour?"

"With pleasure," I replied. "What can I do for you?"

"If you do not mind doing so I should like you to buy me a bottle of brandy - I am not well tonight."

"Certainly," I said.

He placed a sovereign in my hand, thanking me for my courtesy and kindness, and I went to execute his mission. When I returned I found his door standing open. I knocked; he immediately made his appearance. He was writing, but he rose as he saw me.

"Will you not come in?" he exclaimed.

I wished nothing better than such an invitation. I laughed in my sleeve when I thought that he little knew who he was entertaining. I accepted his offer, and sat down by his request near the fire-place. The gas in the room was alight, so that I had a better view of him than I had ever had before. There was an expression of agitation, anxiety, and suspense about his face which I was at a loss to account for. He himself dispelled my wonderment, and explained the cause to me. He offered me some brandy, which I declined. Raising a glass to his lips he quaffed the contents, and placing it down empty upon the table, said -

"I am glad I have met you. I like to be friendly with my neighbours, especially with those living in the house. I am very anxious to-night about my wife. She went out early this morning, saying she should not be gone more than an hour, and now the day is spent. I do not know what to think.

I shall really esteem it a great kindness if you will keep me company for a short time. I do not like to leave the house and seek diversion elsewhere, because she might return during my absence, and I should only prolong my uneasiness. I tried to read, but I was compelled to throw down the book. Boccaccio and Petrarch usually have some interest for me, and Dante is not wholly unentertaining, but to night I could not fix my eyes upon the page. I have tried to write; but for the wealth of a bank I could not write more than one line in five minutes, though I am not generally considered slow at composition. My friends call me a ready writer. It is horrible to be kept in suspense when one you love is the object of your solicitation.'

He took up a cigar, and having asked my permission to do so, lighted it, and began to smoke. As the thin clouds of bluish vapour eddied and circled through the denser air of the room, Zini seemed to derive some solace and relief from the soothing qualities of the narcotic weed. His speech to me had opened up a new vista of ideas in my mind. I had not previously imagined it possible that he could be susceptible of tender emotions, or that his stern and inflexible nature could so far descend as to be capable of loving a woman altogether unworthy of such love in the pure and fervid way in which it was evident that he loved his wife. This fact was another evidence to the power of Cupid, the son of Venus. A noise came at the door; Zini started up, saying, "What was that?"

I made no reply; holding my breath with expectation I awaited a recurrence of the sound which had aroused our attention. Zini walked up to the door with the intention of turning the handle and making an investigation.

CHAPTER II

THE DEATH OF MANTUANI

ZINI opened the door with a frantic haste which plainly indicated to what an extent he was agitated. His lip quivered, and his jaw fell. Certainly he must have had a prognostication of evil; if so, his anticipations were mournfully realized. A silent crowd stood without upon the landing. They held between them a shutter, hastily torn down from its hinges, upon which lay the mangled form of his once lovely baby-wife. For a moment a pale flush of hope illumined his face, but as he approached the extempore bier, he saw that she was dead. As if a leaden bullet had pierced his breast and stopped the action of his heart, he recoiled, falling heavily against the jamb of the door. A sympathizing bystander caught him in his arms, and held his head up, so that he might take breath in a readier manner. Poor fellow, how I pitied him! I forgot his exquisite talent for desperate intrigue, his remorselessness of purpose, his determination, his cruelty, and all his other faults. I only looked upon him now as the bereaved husband, sorrowing for the wife of his bosom, whom he loved beyond all else in this world of fleeting joys and transitory pleasures. They brought her into the room and laid her upon a bed, with the same cruel thoughtlessness which had prompted them in the first instance to bring her there at all. It would have been kinder of them to have taken her to the nearest dead-house, and have come to him afterwards, breaking the news gently; but some people are born without tact, and nothing can ever teach them the amenities of civilized life. In this manner they are what their ancestors three thousand years ago were - savages. There are people who will, without meaning it, insult you in the most gross manner, wound your feelings, and hurt your pride; yet if you asked them to do you a service they would run a mile to be of use to you. It is to be regretted that perfection is not to be found in those born of a woman. I listened attentively to the random chatter of the throng upon the staircase, and I heard certain scraps of information which I shaped into a connected tale. The unhappy lady had walked some distance, and, owing to the heat of the weather, had fainted in the street. An officious policeman, with the insolent demeanour and reprehensible rashness peculiar to the race, had picked her up, accused her of being intoxicated, and carried her forthwith to the station-house. She was placed in a cell, in unpleasant proximity to a woman of bad character, a thief, and a costermonger who had been taken up for endeavouring to gain an honest living! Really, civilization is a parody on creation. When she came to herself, Mrs. Zini demanded an interview with the inspector, which was, incredible to state, granted her. On finding that she was not tipsy he liberated her, fearful perhaps of an action for false imprisonment. But she had been confined some time. She was weak and ill. On her way home she had to cross a notoriously dangerous thoroughfare. In the act of going from one side to the other, she was knocked down by a Guardsman's drag. The four horses, whom he held in hand, trampled upon her body, and trod out the life-spark. Horribly mutilated, and so cut about as to be almost unrecognisable, she was picked up and conveyed to the shop of the nearest surgeon. He could do nothing for her. She was *dead!* So, with a grim smile and a solemn professional shake of the head, he advised her being taken home to her friends.

A letter found in her pocket indicated the locality, and so the melancholy procession was formed which startled Zini from his propriety, by its sudden and unexpected apparition. Whilst I pitied Zini, I thought that this dreadful calamity would ultimately be for his advantage. The object of his life would then be exclusive. He would have no narrow-minded unsympathizing doll to distract him from the grand plan of Italian Unity, with Rome for its capital, and the Adriatic for its maritime extremity. I derived a morbid satisfaction from seeing this strong man in an agony of grief, but the paroxysm did not last long. His pride, his mind, and his character soon came to the rescue. He recovered himself from his state of stupefaction by the exercise of an heroic effort. He could not bend down and kiss his wife's brow, for in its entire state it did not exist. He caught up one of her hands and pressed his lips with an action indicative of the most intense devotion against the cold flesh. Then he walked slowly downstairs, first of all giving me a bow so elaborate as to be almost studied. The landlady met him at the door. He spoke to her, and then went away. But that was not the last that I saw of Zini. I retired to my room, thinking of the uncertainty of human life and the mutability of human affairs. I sat down and tried to write a letter, but -

> "Sweet inspiration softly wooed,
> Replied in tones so very rude,
> That straight I broke the fragile quill,
> And vainly forced the stubborn will."

The events of the evening had upset me; and seeing that I should not recover my equanimity until the next morning, I went to visit a friend who lived within an easy distance, and endeavoured amidst the friendly pleasure of social intercourse to dissipate the clouds of care that had gathered about me.

The next morning I went to Whitehall. Colonel Warner received me with, I thought, a slightly reproachful air.

"Do you know what has happened?" he exclaimed.

I replied that I did not.

"Mantuani is dead," he said, solemnly.

"Dead! is it possible?"

"In spite of all my efforts to the contrary he was found dead in his bed this morning with three stilettos buried up to the hilt in his body."

"Then he died by the hand of an assassin?"

"Assassinated beyond doubt," replied Colonel Warner; "he could not have killed himself in that treble manner; he is the victim of the conspiracy; he asked me to protect him against that which has been too powerful for me. I can make every allowance for you, because it was one of those difficult enterprises which are so difficult to bring to the desired issue; but there is one thing which must be done. The murderers are at large, and we must let these Carbonari know that blood is not to be shed in this country with impunity, nor is human existence to be cut short and sacrificed without quick and even-handed justice following quickly in the wake of the offender. You know something about them, make it your business to bring them to the scaffold."

"You think that more than one man is implicated in this assassination?" I said.

"Yes I do, because of the three daggers that were found in the body."

"My impression is totally different."

"What do you think?"

"I believe that Zini is the assassin."

"Without an accomplice?"

"Yes; my impression is that he committed the crime single-handed."

"Then the three daggers are a ruse?"

"Precisely so."

"It is rather perplexing," exclaimed Colonel Warner.

"Very much so," I replied.

"Well, Mrs. Paschal," resumed the colonel, "I put the matter in your hands."

"I will do my best, though no one can be infallible."

"That is all I expect. I think a woman is more likely to be successful in a thing of this sort, because men are thrown off their guard when they see a petticoat."

"You may depend upon it that Zini is the culprit," I said. "There was something in his manner last night that indicated he was in a fit state for the commission of any crime, however heinous."

"You think he is our man?"

"Unquestionably!"

It was arranged between us before I left the office that I should exert myself to the utmost to prove that Zini was the perpetrator of the crime which had deprived Mantuani of his life. I have been engaged in more complicated affairs, and have been tolerably successful in my endeavours; but there was something about Zini which made me think I should come off second best in the encounter. He was one of those subtle, fox-like men, who are continually on the alert. In addition to this he possessed great determination, and was a man of unlimited plans and experiences. He had baffled the entire police force of the Continent. The reward offered for him in some cities would have made any individual man rich for the rest of his life, could he have made good his right to its possession. He could have retired from business upon it, and have given up the irksome duties of his office; but Zini had defied them. He had patrolled their streets and haunted their crowded and public places, so well and thoroughly disguised, that detection was out of the question. This morning he would be an old man; to-morrow, a young one, bearded like the pard. To-day, a professor in spectacles; the next, a drivelling dotard, hanging on a stick. Zini was acquainted with many noblemen and gentlemen who held positions of trust in the country, and who were wealthy. Their mansions were always, to a limited extent, at his command; but he preferred to live with Spartan simplicity, believing that self-denial and perseverance brought about the achievement of great deeds sooner than an indulgence in luxury and an abandonment to the pleasures of sense. Nor was he wrong. Thermopylæ was not defended by men who lived upon the fat of the land, but by those who ate coarse bread and spring onions - rather objectionable in feminine eyes, but conducive to physical development; men who punished uxoriousness, and held that the whole duty of man was a love of his country and self-abnegation. *Dulce et decorum est pro patriâ mori*, was their shibboleth, as it should be of every nation which is not utterly lost in the lust of gain. Goldsmith says, "Where commerce long prevails, honour dies;" and it is certainly true that a primitive state of partial simplicity is more productive of virtue than any other condition of life. Hannibal's soldiers at Capua forgot their precedents of bravery, their toil in crossing the Alps - forgot Cannæ, and neglected the advantages which they had gained. Rome was before them almost undefended, but the Cyprian delights of a luxurious capital delayed their march, and so the winter passed away, during which they lost the golden opportunity which was never destined to be regained. Opportunity must be seized when it is close to you. If you look and gaze and wonder at it, you miss your chance, and a life-long regret will not bring it within your reach again.

Zini's only weakness had been his wife, and he was not the first man who had succumbed to the charms of a woman. Moses showed his perception and intimate acquaintance with human nature when he made Eve tempt Adam. With all the difficulty fairly mapped out before me, I undertook the capture and condemnation of Zini the patriot.

CHAPTER III

THE OLD MILL

THE meeting-place of the Secret Band was a strange one. Strange in many ways. It was only by dint of perseverance that I was enabled to discover it. I tracked Zini to his lair, and found out the place where the most desperate political refugees were wont to assemble. It was far away in the extreme east of London, in a locality known as the Isle of Dogs, a low, swampy, marshy place, exposed to the pestilential vapours emitted by the Thames, and in the midst of a rough seafaring population. There were houses upon it, and streets formed of those houses; there were a few factories, and other erections of bricks and mortar. But it was a poor place at best. Near the river, close to where the hurrying current rushed by with tidal impetuosity, was a ruined mill.

At least you would have taken the dilapidated structure for something utterly useless. It was constructed of wood, and reared its ungainly head amidst slime and mud and sedges. The huge wheel was most of its time motionless. Now and then it was made to revolve, because it gave an appearance of activity to the gloomly-looking mill. This mill was the property of Zini and his compatriots. It was some distance from any other habitation, and stood out gray and desolate in the moonlight: you could approach it either by land or water. The Secret Band usually travelled by land. Water was all very well, but except you went in a steamer the journey was a very long and tedious one, for wherries, although manned by jolly young watermen from Wapping Old Stairs, are proverbially slow. During the absence of the Secret Band the mill was tenanted by an old woman, who did not appear to know much about her employers. She was satisfied if she obtained her wages every week, and a slight gratuity into the bargain transported her with delight. She knew nothing about political refugees, conspiracies, and murders, and assassinations. She could not read, and therefore she was dependant for her information on passing events upon the kindness and garrulity of her neighbours. These were few and not only far between, but far away. She had to leave her place of bondage to go and talk to them, which she always did in fear and trembling, for she never knew when the Secret Band would come and hold their frequent conclave. Or else she had to bribe a private messenger, and beg some old crone to come and keep her company for half an hour or more until the good man came home from his work.

I discovered all these particulars by making searching inquiries, and I exulted in this old woman. To me she was invaluable. Lonely as she was, she would only be too glad of my society; so one day I went to the Isle of Dogs, and walked boldly up to the mill. The tide was running down with great velocity, carrying ships and steam vessels upon its bosom. But the sun was shining brightly and illuminating all around with a red glare. It was three o'clock in the afternoon. I had started early, but the blocks in the city traffic had impeded the progress of my cab. I had experienced the miseries of Temple Bar, and the horrors of Ludgate Hill, while the terrors of Cheapside afforded me much food for rumination upon the municipal bodies who had control over the thoroughfare, and the Board of Works, whose duty it was to regulate the traffic of much-enduring but still liege citizens.

The dust, composed of crisp sand and dried mud, rose up in a cloud at every step I took. The old mill was not without a certain picturesqueness. It was very much like the stock mill of drawing masters, such as they produce by an infinity of black lead pencil marks, and a dash or two of white chalk here and there. The planks which formed its sides had some years before been tarred over so as to defy the action of the weather and the wear and tear of time, but the sun had blistered the tar, and the wind and the rain had broken the blisters, so that the structure was blotched all over with unsightly patches, something like a huge green wave flecked with foam. The water wheel overhung the river, but it did not exist in its entirety. It had lost a spoke, and a nail had come out here, a piece of iron was missing there, and I am strongly of opinion that the water rats used to deride and make fun amongst themselves of that once formidable wheel, which was now rotting away for want of a little care and attention. I myself saw one long-tailed gentleman sitting unconcernedly upon it, looking very impudently at me. When I reached the door of the mill, I knocked boldly upon it with my knuckles, doing some damage to my skin, for the surface was rough and jagged. Some time elapsed, and then an antediluvian woman made her appearance and looked at me curiously.

"You'll be coming from Mrs. Goodman, for her glasses," she said in a cracked tone. "Say I'll send them back to-morrow."

I replied with great truth that I had not the honour of Mrs. Goodman's acquaintance, although I should feel proud to be acquainted with one of the old lady's friends.

"What is your want then?" she demanded testily.

"I want a sack of flour," I said innocently, as if I did not know very well that no corn had ever been crushed into powder since the old woman first took up her tenancy within its hospitable walls.

"Sack o' flour! God bless the woman," she cried, laughing heartily. "Why, we have not had such a thing this ever so long. The business is given up."

"That's tiresome, for I have walked some distance to get it."

"Have you? You'll be feeling tired."

"A little." This was said with an affectation of fatigue.

"Step inside, my dear," said the old woman, "and sit thee down a bit. And I to think it was Mrs. Goodman sent for her glasses, but lor' - there, I am getting old and silly I suppose. It is not much of a place to ask you into, but I am a poor creature, and I find it good enough for me. I've neither kith nor kin to care for me, and it isn't surprising if I do sometimes feel a bit lonesome."

She carefully dusted a chair with her apron, and gave it me to sit down upon. She had some tea in a cupboard, and she cheerfully made some, apologizing in her old-fashioned way for not having anything better to offer me. Before an hour elapsed we became very friendly, and she asked me as a great favour to come and see her again. I made the old woman talk about her youth, and scenes of long ago in which she had figured, listening to her twaddle with well-simulated attention. I did not at once accept her invitation, but I eventually gave way to her urgent solicitation.

"What day would be most convenient to you?" I asked.

"On Friday I shall be a little busy."

"I am sorry for that," I said immediately, "because I am engaged on every other day."

"Oh, well, I must make it Friday then. You see, my dear, the master is coming, and he always brings some friends with him, and they sit and talk and smoke, and I thought perhaps they wouldn't like to be disturbed in any way, for they always tell me to have no one here. No more I ever do; but it is so lonesome without a soul to speak to. So you'll come on Friday, dear, will you? and I'll get a little green snuff. Lor', what am I a-saying of - I mean tea, just to make a social cup with."

I left the antediluvian old woman, considerably gratified by my visit. I had not expected to be so successful as I had been. I sought an early interview with Colonel Warner, and we made the best arrangements we could think of. I was to listen to the conversation of the members of the secret band, and see if I could not get hold of some evidence upon which we could reasonably hope to base a conviction. A galley, filled with police armed to the teeth, was to be in waiting under the shadow of the mill; at a preconcerted signal it was to dart to shore. The police were to land, and take possession of the ruined structure, and hold in safe custody those of the secret band whom I should point out to them. If nothing occurred which I could make any use of, I was to postpone the capture until next week, when perhaps the conspirators would be less cautious, thinking all danger had passed away. I trembled a little as I set out on the appointed day for the old-world tumble-down mill, the antediluvian occupant of which was for the time being my most particular friend. I knew how unscrupulous Zini and his friends were. The theory of the dagger was fully understood by them, and they supplemented theory by practice. But owing to frequent acquaintance with peril, I had become unusually hardened for a woman. I made up my mind to brave the danger as well as I was able, and do my best to bring a desperate criminal to justice. I never had much sympathy, even in my younger days, with secret bands or societies who resort to violence and intrigue to establish an impossible state of things. Patriotism in the abstract, on paper or in a speech, was not so bad; when backed up by the steel of the assassin, to me it was intolerable. It was growing dark when I reached the mill. Dark shadows were stealing around everything. Gloomy clouds skimmed swiftly over the surface of the horizon, showing by their appearance that their black bosoms were heavily charged with rain. There was a deathlike stillness in the air - not a sound was to be heard. The atmosphere was hot and sultry. The slight breeze which had prevailed to a limited extent during the day had now altogether subsided, and an electric heaviness seemed to have usurped its place. The harsh barking of a dog now and then disturbed the stillness, but nature, animate and inanimate, for the most part was enjoying that state of quiescence which is known as a calm before the storm. When old Dorothy opened the door to me, I asked in a low tone of voice if the conspirators had arrived. I wished them to have done so, because Zini might have noticed me in the old woman's room, and with his usual tact and sagacity have recognised me as the person who had been engaged in conversation with him on the night when his baby wife died. This would at once have aroused his suspicions, and my plans would have been frustrated, if not altogether annihilated. Dorothy replied that they had. She said they were upstairs in the room where the grinding-stones were.

"How many are there?" I ventured to ask.

"Just eleven."

The death of Mantuani had prevented that twelfth apostle from being present, so that their number was incomplete.

"What do they do to amuse themselves in this out-of-the-way place?" I said.

"Oh, speechify, and that."

"Do they? It is a strange place to come to."

"It is that. Would you like to get a peep at them?"

"I should not mind."

"Well, there is a hole I found out in the boarding, and through that you can see everything fine."

"Can you? I should like to try."

"Hear them speak, and all," added Dorothy.

"I will have a cup of tea, and then you can take me up," I replied, "if it won't be giving you too much trouble."

"No trouble, my dear. It's always been a pleasure with me to oblige a friend, and you're a good sort to come a long distance to see a body who's lonesome," exclaimed Dorothy, who bustled about to get the tea ready.

I watched her slow movements with considerable impatience, because I was extremely anxious to be at once on the watch. Time was valuable, I groaned inwardly and fretted when my amiable but tardy hostess forgot where she had last put the sugar, or wondered why the tea-caddy was not where her feeble mind imagined it to be. At last tea was made. I refused to have more than one cup, and that I drank while it was scalding hot, because the quantity of milk was limited, and was even not kept on the premises.

"Now, my dear, I'll take you up," said Dorothy; "but don't make no more noise than you can help, because the master and his friends might not like it, and you wouldn't wish to get me into trouble, I'm sure."

"Certainly not," I answered. My heart palpitated with more than its usual quickness as we ascended the creaky steps of the rickety staircase which led into the rude apartment in which the important business of the Secret Band was transacted. As we reached the landing I heard the sound of voices, and as a gleam of light flashed through many a chink in the dilapidated wooden walls, which in their best days had never been able to boast that close connexion which defies wind and weather, Dorothy pointed out to me a small hole in the wall, of an oblong shape, and looking through which I could gain an admirable view of those within, and, by placing my ear to the cavity, catch every word they said. The door leading into the room was situated in the middle of the partition. The hole was to the left of the door, on the side opposite the staircase. Pursuing the passage in which I was standing I should have reached a lumber-room where sacks were kept in the palmy days of the mill, when corn was ground and flour was sold to such as were willing to buy it. When looking through the hole I was in the dark; had the door been suddenly opened I should have been more effectually concealed than ever, because its broad surface would have shielded me from observation altogether. Dorothy pointed out the hole in the wall to me, and having told me to come downstairs again as gently as I could when I had satisfied my curiosity, she expressed a desire to finish a cup of tea, and so left me. She had not been gone more than half a minute before I heard a loud noise, as of a heavy body bumping from stair to stair. My first impulse was to rush forward and see what it was, but prudence restrained me. The Secret Band must have been aroused by the sound, and would most probably make their appearance directly, to find out the cause. If I were at the bottom of the stairs I should infallibly be discovered but by remaining where I then was I should be safe. I stood still, listening anxiously.

CHAPTER IV

THE HOLE IN THE WALL

A HALF-UTTERED, smothered cry arose, and then all was still. My impression was that Dorothy had fallen down the stairs. She held no light in her hand, and without some guiding rays she was as likely as not to lose her footing. I could think of no other explanation of the phenomenon. The Secret Band were alarmed, for the door of the room in which they were assembled opened, and some one with a lamp issued out upon the landing. Through the chink of the door I could tell from his commanding figure and erect bearing that this was Zini. He was in his way a brave man, and if any danger was to be encountered he always preferred taking the risk upon his own shoulders to allowing any other member of the band to do so. He cast a keen and vigilant glance around, and then descended the stairs with a loaded pistol in his right hand. I could see its gleaming barrel, the sight of which did not suffer any of my apprehensions as to the termination of my adventure to decrease. I tried to fancy how the passage of a bullet through anybody would affect me if it avoided the cardial region and chose some less fatal spot. I did not then know that there were weapons more effective than bullets in the hands of the conspirators. The Secret Band did their work in a surer way, and firearms were only resorted to as a means of defence when dangerous aggressors could not be disposed of in any other way. My acquaintance with that delectable body of men, who were now in solemn council assembled, was destined to enlighten me on more than one point. In the course of two minutes Zini slowly ascended the stairs. He carried something in his arms. Passing into the room, he shut the door after him. I applied my eye to the hole in the wall at once and with alacrity. The conspirator's burden was none other than Dorothy. The unfortunate creature had, I concluded, missed a step and fallen with great force from the top to the bottom of the flight of stairs. This was enough to stun her, if not to kill her. Zini advanced to the middle of the room and laid her on a table; he then felt her pulse, and exclaimed, in his usual self-possessed manner, "She is dead!"

A murmur of astonishment ran through the members of the Secret Band, who were surprised at so extraordinary an occurrence. They imagined that she must have been coming upstairs to communicate something to them, and that she had come to a sudden and melancholy end in the way I have already described. Zini, always practical, and since his wife's death utterly devoid of the minutest vestige of sentiment, said, "Since her spirit has departed, it is useless to discuss the matter when subjects of more importance are before our notice. She is dead. There is nothing else to be said. If we are religious in our way, we are not formalists, we are not desirous of saying prayers for her. She was nothing to us; we looked upon her and used her as a tool. Now she is gone; well, there is an end of it."

He took her up in his arms once more, and conveyed her to a corner of the room, laying her upon the bare boards with a reverent motion. These men looked upon death as some unreal phantom which possessed no terrors for them. Their lives had often been in danger, and they laughed at Death because they did not fear him.

Poor Dorothy! a tear unbidden started to my eyes. I could not help feeling grieved that the old woman had met her fate through her efforts to befriend me; but I, too, was somewhat callous, through experience and contact with a hard world, so I dashed away the tear which was the apotheosis of the deceased woman, and applied myself with renewed ardour to the task before me.

The room in which the conspirators were assembled was as nearly square as could be. A long table was placed in the middle, and around it, seated upon common cane-bottomed deal chairs, were grouped the eleven members of the Secret Band. They were dark, sinister-looking men, who appeared prepared for the commission of any crime which would further the ambitious ends they had in view. Some of them were drinking and smoking, others, forming the more sedate portion, refrained from doing either one or the other. After depositing the body of Dorothy in its temporary resting-place, Zini returned to his chair, and continued a speech he was engaged in delivering when the noise on the stairs put an end for a time to his eloquence. He did not speak in an impassioned tone, for he deprecated all appeals to the passions. He spoke quietly, but with emphasis. Nor was action wanting to his oratorical display. He did not wish to captivate and lead away his auditors. He was more like a Chancellor of the Exchequer expounding his budget than an agitator. There was not the least approach in anything he said or did to the stump orator. He was the calm, collected man of genius, who relies more upon the nature of what he is saying, than the manner of his delivery. Yet with such clearness and perspicuity was every word that fell from his lips uttered, that it sank deep down into the hearts of his hearers, and convinced them that they were listening to a man of talent and not to the empty verbiage of a charlatan and an impostor.

"We met here this evening," he exclaimed, "to consider what steps we should take to supply the place of the traitor Mantuani. He paid the full penalty of his offence. He died by my hand, for as his offence was committed principally against me, it was meet that I should be his executioner."

I made a mental note of this incautious declaration, which the crafty Italian would not have made had he imagined me within hearing. Just at this juncture I fancied I heard a strange rumbling without, resembling the sound of distant thunder. It appeared to me ominous of some catastrophe.

Zini resumed, after a momentary pause -

"When the cowardly wretch gave information to the Austrian police of my intended visit to Venice, it was for the sake of securing the magnificent reward which the faint-hearted House of Hapsburg - the members of which are the slaves of the infamous Concordat - have been pleased to offer for my apprehension; but so well am I served abroad, and especially in dear Venice - dear from old associations - dear from the unutterable sufferings of a patriotic people - dear because its citizens are brave - and dear for its heroic efforts in former times to throw off the odious yoke of the tyrant conqueror - and dear, above all things, for the many precious friends who there love me - that I was informed of the arrangements made in the queenly city of the Adriatic for my arrest, and fortunately able to defeat the machinations of my enemies; but one sigh of regret escaped my lips whilst I plunged my stiletto up to the hilt in the quivering heart of the treacherous Mantuani. He had broken his oath, and by that act he had forfeited all claim to mercy and to pardon. When a man becomes so far demoralized as to love money better than honour and glory, he is unfit for the society of true patriots. He knew our secrets, or else he might have lived until the poignancy of his remorse killed him. He was dangerous; therefore I slew him."

A murmur of applause ran round the room as this terrible announcement was made with all the calmness of a man who believes he has done an enviable action. Zini had drawn himself up to his full height, and looked as if no stain of sin, no blot of a heinous crime sat upon his soul. It was part of his code and his philosophy, that a man should die who broke his oath and betrayed his country by betraying one of its most ardent champions.

A desultory conversation now ensued between the members of the Secret Band, which became animated as it proceeded. I remained in the same position, with my eye to the hole in the wall. I did not take much notice of the other conspirators; my attention was chiefly riveted upon him. I was a keen sportsman, and he was my quarry. I was only waiting till I could get my rifle to bear, and then I intended to draw a barrel upon him. The time, it appeared to me, had nearly arrived when it was advisable for me to give the signal to the police, who were patiently awaiting my summons in the galley outside. I was about to move downstairs for that purpose, when I saw Zini - who had been casting restless glances in my direction for some time past, but to which I had attached no great importance - raise his hand as if to enjoin silence, which instantly reigned in its most profound state. I was a loss to account for this pro-ceeding until I saw Zini take stealthy steps towards the door. Is it possible, I thought, that he has caught sight of my eye at the hole in the wall? With such a man you can never be too much on your guard, and I began to fear that I had been rash and imprudent in exposing myself too much. I did not venture to run down the staircase, because I felt sure I should be inter-cepted in my flight before I could reach a haven of safety. The door opened, was partially closed again, and Zini and myself stood face to face. I noted well his cold, cynical glance, which appeared cruel and remorseless as he was standing in the faint light emitted from the room through the half-opened door.

CHAPTER V

LIFE OR DEATH

"So I have caught you," exclaimed Zini, remorselessly.

I was unable to speak.

"You are a spy," he continued. "But come here, we will talk afterwards."

I obeyed him mechanically. Just then I was incapable of action, I felt as if I had been deprived of all power of volition. The shock emanating from so sudden a discovery completely prostrated me. I had fallen into the hands of the conspirators, and I was not at a loss to imagine what fate awaited me when in the toils of such men as those composing the Secret Band. The signal that had been agreed upon between myself and the police was a whistle of a particularly shrill description. I had had one made on purpose for me; in point of fact, it was my own idea and my own unaided invention. It could be heard some distance, and while unintelligible to those not in the secret, very significant and full of meaning to those for whose edification it sounded. But I was afraid to use the means at my command, because had I done so I should at once have aroused the suspicion of my captors, and they would in all likelihood have dealt out summary vengeance. I entered the room after Zini, and stood awaiting his further orders. I saw that my only chance was to be submissive and obedient. I was determined if necessary to assume a bold front, but my first care was to tell them some plausible story through means of which I could effect my liberation. Zini beckoned me on. Every eye was fixed upon me, and I thought that more than one regarded me loweringly. Zini resumed his seat with his accustomed placidity, and told me to take up a certain position in front of his chair, where the light of the lamps would fall upon my features and reveal the play of my countenance, and respond to each question he thought fit to put to me. I saw what his intention was, and I resolved to preserve a passive immobility which should indicate nothing; or if I did allow my features a play, I would call all my versatility into action, and bring my histrionic powers into prominence, so that he should discover nothing but innocence, or at least the meritorious affectation of it: I even refrained from looking at the corner in which Dorothy lay. I longed to cast one pitying glance upon her senseless form, but

I restrained my inclination and concentrated all my thoughts upon what most nearly concerned me - my present liberty When Zini had placed me as any photographer might have arranged some client who wished to have his portrait taken, he turned his large eyes full upon - those lustrous searching orbs, whose power was immense. If ever mesmerism, fascination, animal magnetism, odic force - call it what you will - dwelt in a look, it did in his. I cast my eyes down, for I feared to encounter his gaze longer than I could help. I had need of all my faculties, and I did not wish to be thrown off my guard by any of the arts which it was evident he had cultivated to perfection. Suddenly his eyes flashed; he exclaimed, "I have met you before!"

As before, I said nothing.

"Is it not so? Answer me."

"It is," I replied. I had my own reason for saying so.

"Tell me when."

"Do you not remember?"

"I remember perfectly well, but I wish to be told by you."

"I first saw you when your wife died."

"Yes. What brings you here?"

"I came to see a friend."

"A friend! Any one in this room?"

"No," I replied, laconically.

"Speak then. Do not prevaricate."

"She is dead."

"Do you intend to signify that the woman who is in that corner of the room - a corpse - was your friend?"

"I do," was my reply.

"Have you known her long?"

"Some years." This of course was not true, but it was necessary to say so.

"And you came to see her?"

"Yes; or I should not be here."

"By her invitation, or in obedience to your own inclination?"

"She invited me."

"What was her name?"

As Zini asked me this question, he fixed his searching glance upon me with an expression of triumph, which seemed to say, "I think I have hit you hard."

Fortunately for myself, I had seen a sampler downstairs worked by the old woman years ago, upon which was the name Dorothy Drake. So I answered his query satisfactorily.

"Why did you not go to your friend's assistance, when you either heard or saw her fall down the stairs?" asked Zini.

"Because I was otherwise engaged."

"In what way?"

"I was listening to your speech; and I was so carried away by my admiration, that I did not think of my friend."

"A bad answer," exclaimed Zini; "because it carries the impress of falsity on the face of it."

"I tell you the truth."

"That is a matter of opinion."

"I did not know that she was mortally injured, or indeed seriously hurt, until you brought her into the room," I continued.

"I must congratulate you upon the warmth of your friendship."

More than one member of the Secret Band smiled secretly at this home thrust.

"Do you know my name?" demanded Zini.

"I have heard you addressed as Mr. Fower," I replied; and

this was strictly matter of fact, for he went by that name at his former lodgings.

"By no other?"

"Never by any other."

"Did you know Mantuani?"

"Certainly not. You mentioned the name just now."

"You remember that?" he said.

I did not think it an incautious admission, because, as I had acknowledged that I had been listening for some time outside the door, I must necessarily be familiar with the name of Mantuani. So I replied in the affirmative.

"Where is he now?" asked Zini, cautiously.

"Who?" I replied.

"Mantuani."

For a moment I forgot my assumed part, forgetting that Zini was interrogating me, and that the assembled men would, if they discovered me to be a spy upon their proceedings, dispose of me in some dreadful way, if only to preserve their secrets intact and their meeting-place inviolate. I only thought of the horrible way in which the Italian had been murdered; and I said, in answer to Zini's question -

"He is dead, and you know it better than any one; for it was by your hand that he fell."

"How do you know that?" cried Zini, by a commanding gesture suppressing the indications of hostility which were to be perceived on all sides.

In an instant I collected myself, and replied, with equanimity -

"I heard you say so yourself a short time ago."

"Tolerably well answered," said Zini. "But I cannot divest myself of the idea that you are a spy. I have heard of the Lady

Detectives of London, and you may be aware that old birds are not easily limed, nor are they fond of that food which consists of the husk after the corn has departed from it. Political foxes are often as cunning as their brethren of the field. Even if you are not a spy, you know a great deal too much. You have heard me say that I slew Mantuani. It is a deed I revel, glory, and rejoice in; but, nevertheless, it would be prejudicial to my interests to have the trifling circumstance published in your newspapers. Therefore it is necessary, without any further delay, that sentence should be passed upon you."

"Sentence!" I cried. "What sentence is it in your power to pass upon me? This is an anomalous tribunal, and you have no jurisdiction over me. What offence have you proved me guilty of?"

"That of knowing too much."

"How can I help that? You should have been more cautious in your remarks."

"You talk wildly, and like a silly woman who is afraid," remarked Zini. "I will put it to the gentlemen who are sitting round this table, whether you are more worthy of life than death."

"Let me be tried by a jury of my *own* countrymen," I said, frankly.

"In their absence, I dare say we shall do as well. Now, gentlemen, what do you say - life or death?"

In solemn tones the ten Italians replied, "Death!" They were unanimous, and I could see from the determined aspect of their countenances that they were frightfully in earnest.

"You are nothing better than assassins!" I cried.

"You are condemned to death," said Zini, with his cold and merciless look.

"I appeal from your conviction to a higher Power, whom I trust will deliver me from your jurisdiction."

"If that one is your only chance," replied Zini, "you had better make your peace with it, for in five minutes you will be there."

I fancied myself in a dream. I could not bring myself to believe that I was to be cut off in my prime, and that death was treading so closely upon my heels; and yet it was so! When I thought matters over, with the rapidity that extreme danger engenders, I began to see that I was indeed in the power of eleven men who were longing and thirsting after my blood, and who would not hesitate in a specified time to take it.

But five minutes to live!

It was a brief space - a very brief space!

I had declared that I appealed from their decision to the even-handed justice of Heaven, but I was not prepared for the manifestation that was about to take place. It did not instantly follow my appeal, but the storm was brewing, nevertheless, and ready to burst at the most opportune moment.

What is man's puny power in comparison with that which guides the destinies of man, and rules the universe?

CHAPTER VI

THE FLASH OF LIGHTNING

At the end of the room was a ladder which led down into a lower room. You were not likely to remark it unless you had strayed to that part of the apartment and come unexpectedly upon it. I was soon to make acquaintance with this ladder in a manner far from pleasant. Zini spoke once more: -

"I have yet to decide in what manner your death shall take place; but as it has been decreed without one dissentient voice that you are to die, it is unnecessary that that particular question should be put to the meeting, and its sense taken about it."

The Secret Band approved of this remark by affirmatory nods and exclamations.

I held my peace.

"In the corner of this room there is a flight of steps. It conducts to a room below this, in which is situated the water-wheel, which puts the machinery in motion. It does not matter whether the tide is running up or down, because the stones will revolve either way, so that the mill can work by night as well as by day. That wheel has long been idle; but if a chain is loosened it will instantly commence going round. When it is revolving with a velocity corresponding to that of the tide, it is very formidable. If any one were by chance to fall within its compass, life would soon be extinct, and a mangled corpse would before long be floating down the river. No trace, no clue could be found, and it seems to me an admirable way of disposing of a troublesome person."

Vehement applause followed this diabolical and ingenious suggestion.

"To the wheel - to the wheel!" cried the Secret Band.

"Your doom has been pronounced," said Zini to me.

"Why am I to be thus treated?"

"Because you are dangerous, and it is incumbent upon me to remove you from our path."

"Are you in earnest?" I pleaded.

"Very much so. I never jest about such a subject as death."

"You dare not do as you say you will"

"Then you are in error."

"You have no adequate motive for such a crime."

"It is not a crime. It is an execution," said Zini, grandly.

"I assert the contrary."

"Without a vestige of foundation. If you were liberated our lives would not be secure. You might retard the regeneration of Italy. You might, by cutting us off, throw back the cause of Italian unity for many years, and the acquisition of Naples, Rome, and Venice, is more precious to me than your life."

A glow of enthusiasm overspread his face as he spoke, and I saw that at least he was sincere in his opinions.

"Prepare for death," he added, abruptly.

An awful silence ensued for the space of one minute. No one moved, no one stirred, no one spoke. It was that I might commune with Heaven. But one chance remained for me, and that was to summon those without to my rescue. "Oh, if I could only make them hear me!" I mentally exclaimed. I thought that I should stand some chance of attracting their attention as I went down the ladder. Anyhow I resolved to try it. My hands were not bound, and if I succeeded in blowing the whistle my captors could not aggravate the punishment they had declared that they were fully prepared to mete out to me. This reflection consoled me somewhat, although drops of perspiration as big as beads hung on my forehead, and I was greatly agitated. Who in such a terrible situation would not be? The silence of the conspirators was broken by a loud clap of thunder which sounded just over our heads, and by its awful clamour shook the mill to its very foundation. The Secret Band paid no attention to this evidence of a storm raging outside. They were accustomed to, and thought nothing of, natural phenomena. Through a crack here and there in the walls the vivid lightning flashes could be perceived cleaving the heavy air and illumining the profound darkness.

"Are you ready?" inquired Zini.

I refused to answer him.

"If you do not reply we shall presume that you are ready, and act on that presumption."

"I dispute your authority to deal with me in this hasty manner," I said, impetuously.

"That doesn't matter; we make our own laws."

"They are infamous."

"Possibly they are so in your opinion. Walk by my side, or I shall be compelled to use force."

He put himself by my side. I did as he told me, because I wished to conciliate him to a certain extent. If he allowed me to descend the ladder first, or by myself, I should be able to sound my whistle, and so attract the attention of those without.

It was a moment of great expectation. Although I was boiling over with anger and suppressed passion I endeavoured to conceal my emotion. We walked to the corner of the room. It was the opposite one to that in which Dorothy Drake was lying. Notwithstanding my own perilous position, I stole a glance at her. She was very quiet, and still, and motionless, and I wondered whether I should soon be like her, out of the turmoil of the world, in that region where the weary were at rest. If the truth must be told, I did not think I should. I thought that something would happen which would enable me to defeat the machinations of my unscrupulous enemies. Such a feeling only shows how drowning men catch hold of straws, and how condemned criminals, for the due and legal abridgment of whose career judges have put on the black cap, cling to the remote and slender chance of a reprieve, which they think - poor creatures! - may reach them at the last moment, at the foot of the scaffold even.

When we reached the ladder, Zini said -

"I shall descend first; you will follow me."

I made an inclination of the head to signify consent. I dared not trust myself to speak, because my exultation was so great. I allowed Zini to touch the bottom before I set my foot upon the first step. He held up a lamp to guide me. When I had reached what I considered to be the middle, I raised my whistle to my lips, and turning my face in the direction of the river, blew loud and shrilly upon it. So prolonged was the signal that I only desisted when Zini sprang up the steps, and with one energetic blow dashed it out of my hand. He conveyed me to the foot of the ladder in an iron grasp, uttering curses and exclamations which I should not have thought could have emanated from him: he was ordinarily so self-possessed.

"Quick! quick!" he cried. "She has accomplices without."

The Secret Band rushed with rapidity down the ladder, and Zini dragged me to the part of the room in which the huge mill was situated. It was a terrible instrument. As an implement of torture and of death it was unequalled: it evidenced that Zini had a mind fertile in fiendish ideas, if it was at the same time patriotic - a strange mixture of virtue and ferocity. When we were close to it, I peered down into the murky depths and I could see the murky waters gliding with still rapidity through the submerged spokes. Giving me into the charge of one of the Secret Band, Zini mounted on a block of wood and let down the chain which held the wheel. In an instant the rush of the water was heard, the huge wheel revolved with great speed, and the noise of the wheels and the other machinery upstairs sounded harshly and gratingly upon the ear. I shuddered. I gave myself up for lost, and for the first time the courage which had hitherto supported me went away. I felt faint and ill. Zini caught me in his arms. Exerting all my strength, I struggled and broke from his grasp, falling heavily on the floor. A vivid, blinding flash of lightning darted through the open space above the wheel, and sought a victim. Zini, from his proximity to the metallic construction of the substantial part of the wheel, offered the most prominent mark, and it struck him, reducing him to a scathed mass of charred humanity. He had not time to utter a cry or a groan; he was completely prostrated, and my appeal to a Higher Power had not been so disregarded as he had been pleased to think it would be. The fall of their leader appalled the rest of the Secret Band. Dismayed and wonder-stricken, they gazed upon his blackened remains, from which the vital spark had been so rudely snatched. He had lately been instinct with the breath of life. Now what was he? A melancholy spectacle. I had indeed been saved by a miracle. In one moment more I should have been launched into eternity. I rose to my feet, and encountered the startled glances of the surviving members of the Secret Band. They might and probably would have carried out the sentence Zini had passed upon me when they had recovered from their consternation; but at present they were incapable of doing so. Whilst I was hesitating what to do, I thought I heard a noise like the battering down of a door. The conspirators looked at one another, as if they too heard what filled me with agreeable sensations. Presently footsteps were heard overhead, then dusky forms descended the ladder. These were the police who had heard my signal, and who had responded to it with the greatest quickness they were capable of. The Secret Band at first stood upon the defensive; but seeing they were outnumbered by at least half-a-dozen, they surrendered at discretion. When I found myself amongst friends and freed from the great danger which lately menaced me, I showed that I was a woman and swooned away. When I came to myself, the storm was over, the moon was shining brightly, and the police with their captives exhibited quite a theatrical appearance. The moonlight streamed in at the aperture above the mill-wheel, and illumined the prostrate form of Zini, whose restless soul was now at peace. The Secret Band were taken to town; but we were unable to prove their complicity in the detestable murder of which their chief had been guilty, so they were liberated.

I followed Zini to the grave; for if his moral nature was warped, and some of his finer senses deadened, he still possessed some fine qualities, amongst which the most transcendent was the almost insane love of his country which he cherished through good and evil report.

THE LOST DIAMONDS

THE DUKE OF RUSTENBURGH

EVERY one knew the Duke of Rustenburgh. He was a celebrity in all the European capitals, not on account of his position, or anything that he had ever done to make himself conspicuous, but because he had in his possession the most famous precious stones in the world. They were extremely rare and valuable; the duke had been a collector of these glittering pebbles from his boyhood, and at the death of his father, the thirteenth Duke of Rustenburgh, he inherited all the heirlooms of the family, among which were several tiaras and bracelets formed of stones of great price. He had no territorial possessions; what land he had acquired a title to at the death of his father he had long ago sold to provide money for the furtherance of his favourite hobby, and so he carried his fortune about with him wherever he went; and a splendid fortune it was. With it he could have bought up many petty German states and principalities; but he preferred dwelling in seclusion, except when he sallied forth into society to display his wonderful diamonds. He always wore as many as decency and propriety would allow him; but he had found out at a very early age that only a woman can display jewellery as it ought to be exhibited. So he married the first woman he met, not because he loved her, but because he wanted a sort of barber's-block upon which he could show his jewels. She was the daughter of a Paris banker, and brought him a large sum as her dowry, which he spent before a week was over in buying the wonderful Blo-y-nor diamond, which had for centuries been in the possession of the kings of Delhi, but which, owing to those vicissitudes which affect monarchs as well as plebeians, was now in the Parisian market. This acquisition made him inexpressibly happy for many weeks, and he undertook a trip to Russia in order to parade his new purchase before the *virtuosi* of St. Petersburg. Whenever anybody met him, they always used to say, "Well, duke, have you bought any more diamonds?" And the ladies would beg as an especial favour that they might come to his hotel and have a peep at the famous Blo-y-nor, which was turning the heads of half the diamond merchants in Europe. Some people can tell you the pedigrees of illustrious families, some are great at the pedigrees of horses, but the duke's favourite study was the genealogy of precious stones; he knew the names of all the wonderful stones in existence, where they came from, and in whose possession they were; how many hands they had passed through, and whether they were of the first and purest water. He had compiled an essay, which he called the "History of Precious Stones," more for his own edification and pleasure than anything else; but the public had taken it up, and the Duke of Rustenburgh was favourably known for his little and unambitious treatise, which, in spite of its faults of style and grammatical errors, was entertaining. Its blemishes were to be corrected in the second edition by a gentleman who was a member of the *Société des Gens de Lettres*, and his name, widely known in connexion with the

Paris press, was a sufficient guarantee for the accuracy of the contemplated corrections.

It cannot be said that the duchess was happy. She was a woman of extravagant tastes and habits, which the parsimony of the illustrious husband would not allow her to gratify. If a relation died and left her some money he spent it all immediately in buying diamonds - such was his almost insane passion for these glittering baubles. He loved a scintillation from one of these glittering bits of glass more than he did his wife's whole body, and she, poor thing, knew it. When she went out, she literally blazed with diamonds; but that was not what she wished for. She did not care about so much empty show, and so her heart was driven back upon its own resources; she pined for an affection which was denied to her ardent longing, and to avoid distraction, she plunged recklessly into a search for excitement. Where was the wished-for stimulation to be found so well or so effectually as at the gambling table? So the Duchess of Rustenburgh, through her husband's folly, became a confirmed gambler. Wherever the fashionable vice obtained in London, Paris, or Vienna, there was she a constant visitor. All the money she could scrape together was devoted to the gratification of her hobby, which the duke had himself created. Sometimes she won, and at other times she was unsuccessful. Fortune was fickle, and like Janus, exhibited two faces alternately, showing them now to the delight of the beholder, afterwards to his unutterable confusion and dismay. At Hamburgh there is a private entrance to the gaming-house, and a private staircase leading to a private box in which the gamester is concealed from view. Many times has a small exquisitely gloved hand obtruded itself through the narrow aperture in the box, and laid on the surface of the table a rouleau of bank-notes. This was the Duchess of Rustenburgh. The duke took little or no notice of this proclivity of his wife's. If any one spoke to him about it, he would reply, "Poor child, *Elle s'amuse*," and this answer he considered a good and sufficient reason for the terrible plunge she had taken headlong into the dangerous ocean which sooner or later engulfs all its rack and ruin-bent votaries. The duke adhered to the old style of dress because he could wear shoes with diamond buckles, and he took snuff because it gave him an excuse for having the box set most profusely with jewels, and he offered a pinch to all his friends, so that they might admire the splendour of the receptacle for the pulverizing mixture. And so the world wagged and laughed at the foolish old Duke of Rustenburgh, but behind the smile lurked a secret admiration of his incomparable diamonds.

CHAPTER II

A FALSE SCENT

"Have you heard the news?"

"I can't say I have. What is it?"

"The Duke of Rustenburgh's lost his diamonds."

"Has he, indeed?"

"It will break his heart, I should think."

"So I should imagine. Lost his diamonds, has he? Poor fellow!"

I happened to be posting a letter at the General Post-office when this information fell upon my ears. The speakers were two friends who had come with the same object in view as myself, and having accomplished it they walked away. I pondered their words over carefully as I went home, because any loss or robbery was in my way. It was my business to discover the perpetrators of theft, and so I immediately began to think how I could turn the information to account. I never did things in a hurry. I always deliberated, so that by reflection I should be able to hit upon the right path, which would lead me eventually to success, if such a consummation were to be achieved by mortal means. After dinner the same day I sallied forth; I went to head-quarters, where I obtained all the necessary information. The robbery, for such it was, had been committed in London, where the duke and duchess happened to be staying, as usual. They were staying at an hotel. The duke was beside himself with mortification and rage. His vexatious passion knew no bounds, and he frantically offered prodigious sums for the recovery of his stolen treasures. The priceless Blo-y-nor was among the missing stones, and that alone was worth a king's ransom. On the day upon which the loss was discovered, it appeared that one Karl Fulchöck had decamped. This man was the duke's valet, the only son of the man who had held the same position of trust for very many years. On the death of the elder Fulchöck, his widow entreated his grace to take her son into his employment. Thinking he might safely do so, he consented to her urgent wishes, and the young Karl, not quite twenty-three years of age, entered the duke's service as *valet de chambre*. A photograph of the man had been sent to the police-office, and faithfully copied. I secured one of the imitations, as did most of the detective police, who embarked upon the chase on speculation. Many detectives have more than one piece of employment on their hands at one time, because they are tempted by the rewards; and this cupidity and grasping after money is very often the cause of their failure. I never in my life attempted more than one thing at a time, because I know very well that if my hands were overloaded I should get confused, and fail in my endeavours, which, however strenuous, could not possibly be complete. I was aware that in engaging in this matter I was undertaking a contest with the keenest wits and most fertile brains in the force; but I was rejoiced at this, for if I proved myself cleverer than they turned out to be, it would redound to my credit and give me a higher position than the one I now occupied. The Rustenburgh diamond robbery was a *cause célèbre*, and I applied myself to it with all diligence. Whenever I happened to be in company with birds of my own feather I found that they were unanimously of opinion that Karl Fulchöck, the absconding valet, was the actual culprit; so they one and all devoted themselves to his capture. If he was not the guilty person, or in some way connected with the robber or robbers, why should he run away? At first sight this seemed to be an unanswerable argument, and I remarked that the oldest officers in the force shared the general opinion. I, however, thought differently. I was as positive as one can be, about anything uncertain, that they were all on a false scent. I had fortified myself with all the information I could glean respecting the Duke and Duchess of Rustenburgh; and I did not join in the hue and cry for Karl Fulchöck, who up to the seventh day after the commission of the robbery remained undiscovered.

This led me to believe that he had powerful protectors, and was in safe keeping. I paid a visit one day to the room in which he had slept when at the hotel. Casting my eyes carefully round, I perceived all the evidences of a hasty flight. I deduced an important inference from this fact. If Karl Fulchöck really planned such a sophisticated robbery of such magnitude, he must have been a man of some calculation - he would not have left letters, clothes, and papers scattered about in the way he had done. I was an indifferent German scholar, so I brought a lady with me who faithfully translated some letters in a woman's handwriting. They were from a German girl, with whom Karl had been in love before he left his fatherland. A half-written reply to one of her epistles was found in a desk, and a locket lay beside it. I did not hear that he was a young man of immoral habits or loose character; on the contrary, every one with whom he had come in contact gave him an excellent character for sobriety, honesty, and chastity. He was not extravagant in his habits. He was in the receipt of a liberal salary from the duke, his master, and he had placed away a small sum every month which he faithfully transmitted to his father. Certainly, if he had been a cool, calculating man of mature age, he might have left all his traps and effects in rude disorder, so as to baffle and confuse his pursuers; but nothing transpired to give one the idea that he was cool or calculating. The opinion I formed of Karl Fulchöck was that he was a plain, honest, straightforward, hardworking young man; that he loved his mother and loved his German sweetheart, that he was proud of being in the duke's service, and had always striven to do his duty in the state of life in which he had been placed. The conclusion I came to after leaving his bed-chamber was that he had been *suddenly and unexpectedly abducted*, and that he was at the present time in the hands of the real perpetrators of the audacious outrage upon the duke's property. But who were these perpetrators? I made a shrewd guess as to the identity of one of them, and that was no less a personage than the Duchess of Rustenburgh herself. Whether she was the instigator of the robbery or not I did not pretend to say, but that she had a hand in it I would have sworn in any court of justice in Great Britain. It behoved me to go very carefully to work, because to denounce so powerful a lady as her Grace without full and adequate proof would be to make oneself ridiculous, and to cause the important accusation to recoil against its originator. Of course I did not say a word about my suspicions to any soul living. If I ever achieved a triumph, which I sometimes did, I did not like my laurels shared by any one else. Such as they were I approved of wearing them myself without any partnership in the wreath. The propensity of the Duchess of Rustenburgh for gambling was almost as well known as the duke's passion for diamonds. She was reported to have been a heavy loser on more than one occasion lately, and I, in conjunction with others, wondered, where she obtained the money from to satisfy her debts of honour. Who so likely to accommodate her as a money-lender? Her security was good; in point of fact, it could not have been better. Now, my theory was that her Grace had lost large sums of money over the fatal and unpropitious green-baize, upon whose alluring surface she so often played her favourite game of Baccarat - the most fashionable of all gambling games in polite circles. Having lost the money, it was absolutely necessary, for the sake of her credit, that she should pay it. But she had not the money to satisfy her creditors. The duke would not trust her with a single halfpenny. She was then, perforce, driven to the Jews, who would, according to my own experience of the amiable and accommodating Israelites, be only too glad to do her paper to any amount. A time, however, must come when even a money-lending Jew requires payment of sums advanced, for although sixty per cent is very fair (or unfair) interest, it is gratifying to handle one's principal occasionally. Not having the money to satisfy the Jews, her Grace had, I surmised, listened too readily to their pernicious counsels, and had lent herself to the plundering of the unsuspecting husband. Karl Fulchöck had been hastily removed and kept in durance so that suspicion might be diverted from the actual channel, and turned into another and fallacious current, which was sure in the end to lead to nothing. These were not random thoughts. I had made minute observations, and deduced, as I have before said, the inferences I have stated. I was convinced that the duchess was the culprit, and it was towards her that I now turned my attention. It was clear that she had not done what amounted to a felony of a serious nature without having an able accomplice at her elbow - a man of tact and of experience, who knew how to conduct matters in a scientific manner. So I began to watch her movements to see if I could trace her to any particular house. This once discovered would be equivalent to gaining half the battle. I set to work in a very cautious manner, so as not to rouse the faintest shadow of suspicion in the mind of her Grace, and I did not allow a syllable to fall from my lips which might indicate to those engaged in the same enterprise as myself that they were on a false scent. All the efforts of the police were ineffectual to discover the remotest trace of Karl Fulchöck. This strengthened my opinion, which was further encouraged owing to no signs of the missing diamonds having been seen. The man who had supplied the Duchess of Rustenburgh with money must, I felt assured, be a capitalist of extensive means. Having once got the diamonds in his possession he could afford to wait a year or two before he realized them. He wasn't a vulgar thief who was pushed for immediate supplies of petty cash. He was the man to lock up the precious stones in his strong box and keep them there until the excitement had cooled down and the vigour of the search was somewhat abated. The unfortunate Karl was, I apprehended, a thorn in his side, for he must have been at a loss to know what to do with him. I hoped sincerely that I should be able to prevent any violence being used which would tend to shorten his life, for I was persuaded that the poor fellow was a victim and not the rascal it was the intent of them to make him appear.

CHAPTER III

CHAINED TO THE WALL

I INVARIABLY employed a boy to discover minute and petty details which it was inconvenient for me to investigate myself. It was imperative that I should be apprised of the movements of the Duchess of Rustenburgh. I could not stand outside her hotel and watch her go out, and then rush round the corner, spring on the back of a horse ready saddled and bridled, and follow in pursuit, but I could send my factotum and let him make his observations; no one would take any notice of him, and even a policeman would, out of pity for his ragged attire, refrain from moving him on. I picked up Jack Doyle one day with his hand in a gentleman's pocket; in another instant the handkerchief would have been gone, and the boy with it, but I seized him by the arm, and led him whining and sobbing into a quiet bye-street, where

I could talk to him more at my ease than I could in a crowded thoroughfare. I did not begin my harangue by telling him that he had been guilty of a serious offence against the law of the land, for which any sitting magistrate at the nearest police-court would send him to a reformatory - a mild term for rigorous imprisonment and hard work.

He was already perfectly well aware of the fact, but the following dialogue ensued between us.

"You were picking that gentleman's pocket."

"Yes, mum," he replied, with his knuckles in his eyes.

"What did you do it for?"

"Cos I was hungry, mum."

This declaration was followed by a remarkably fine whine and a puerile sniff.

"You did not expect to find anything eatable in a pocket, did you?"

"Didn't know, mum."

"Oh yes, you did. How long have you been a thief? Tell me the truth, and it will be better for you."

"Going on three year, mum; ever since father was killed falling from a scaffold, and mother was took and died with the fever."

"To whom do you take what you steal, and what does he give you for them?"

"Don't like to say," he replied, doggedly.

"Well, I won't press you. Of course you don't care to betray your employer. Do you like the life you are leading?"

"Can't do nothing else."

"Have you ever tried?"

"Not as I know on."

"How can you tell then?"

Dead silence for a brief space, followed by whines, grunts, groans, and sniffs.

"Would you like to lead an honest life?"

The boy's face brightened, and he replied, "I should indeed, mum."

"Would you like to be my servant?"

"You wouldn't take me," he said, sceptically.

"I will, if you'll promise to behave well."

"I'll promise, mum, if you'll try me."

"What's your name?"

"Jack Doyle."

I put Mr. Jack into a cab, took him home and had him washed and dressed. I treated him kindly, gave him a certain weekly sum for wages, so that he might not be tempted to return to his own way of living from absolute want of pocket-money, and I found that my investment was not such a bad one after all. The boy served me well and faithfully, and I could rely upon him. If I gave him a commission to execute, he would do it, notwithstanding it might cost him an infinity of trouble. He always avoided his old haunts, and when I had the time to spare I taught him to read and write, and inculcated high moral precepts in his fertile mind. He improved under my tuition, and I looked upon him as a brand snatched from the burning.

It was Jack that I employed to watch the Duchess of Rustenburgh. I took lodgings in a mews close by, so that he could run and tell me directly he saw her going out. He could not mistake her, for I had pointed her out to him on a previous occasion. We remained on the alert for three days, during which time she never so much as stirred out of the house. I supposed that the duke was so excessively annoyed and put out by the loss of his diamonds, that he required her dutiful allegiance, and would not let her leave him. When she contrived to escape this despotism, she did not order her carriage, but walked down the street. As soon as Jack saw her issue from the hotel, he came and told me. I had a cab in readiness, and I jumped into it. Jack got on the box, and away we went, overtaking her just as she was getting into a hack vehicle; we followed it, and tracked it to a house in Bloomsbury. The duchess stayed there for at least two hours, and then went straight home, dismissing her cab at the bottom of the street, close to the spot where she had first entered it. Her not driving to her hotel was a suspicious circumstance in my eyes. I went to the neighbourhood of her friend's house to make inquiries respecting the inmates. It was as I had imagined: a notorious money-lender lived there. Armed with this information, I at once called upon Colonel Warner, and asked for a select body of police. He wished to know why I wanted them.

"Have you found the Duke's diamonds?" he said, in a bantering way, never supposing for one moment that I had obtained, as I thought, a clue to them.

"I believe I have," I replied.

"What! are you in earnest?"

"Perfectly so. Can I have the men?"

"As many as you like; choose them yourself."

I wrote down on a piece of paper the names of several officers with whose worth I was well acquainted, and desired that they might be told to hold themselves in readiness for me at six o'clock that evening.

"Upon my word, Mrs. Paschal, we shall have you at the top of the tree soon," remarked the Colonel; "I was just beginning to think that you were not so clever as people think. All our fellows have been at fault, and I shall think more than ever of the Lady Detectives if you accomplish what you lead me to suppose you can."

"You may depend upon my doing my best."

"That I don't doubt for a moment. Well, don't let me keep you; you shall have these men at six o'clock."

I did not tell the police that I wanted them to help me to capture the state diamonds of the Duke of Rustenburgh, nor did they ask any questions; they only knew that they were ordered on special duty, and it was no business of theirs to inquire its nature. I left some outside the house; two I took with me for personal protection and to assist me when I had effected an entry. I knocked boldly at the door, and asked for Mr. Lupus, which was the name of the money-lender whom I suspected to be in league with the duchess, who liked gambling better than diamonds.

The servant said he had just finished dinner, but she had no doubt he would see us if we would wait a short time.

I replied that we should be glad to do so, as we came on important business connected with a loan and was desirous of seeing her master that evening.

With my attendant satellites, who were attired in undress, and resembled well-to-do tradesmen, I was ushered into a waiting-room.

The minutes that elapsed before the appearance of Mr. Lupus were passed by me in great anxiety and suspense. If I were right in my conjectures, I should in a small way make my fortune. I should gain a large access of reputation, and a considerable sum of money, which the duke, in the first agony of his loss, had offered. But if

I were wrong, I should be overwhelmed with ridicule and confusion.

When the servant came back, she desired me to follow her, as her master would receive me in his study. That was what I wished for. I had instructed the three policemen to take advantage of the first opportunity that offered, and search the house to see if they could find a young man whom I imagined was confined upon the premises. I could keep the money-lender engaged in conversation, whilst I had the satisfaction of knowing that my work was being effectually done in my absence. I left my coadjutors sitting in an unconcerned attitude, with a stolid and indifferent look upon their faces. They never allowed their faces to betray what was passing within them, and it was for their wonderful self-possession and their carriage that I had chosen them from amongst their "confrères." Mr. Lupus was a tall, thin man, with a profusion of hair upon his face. He looked steadily at me, and certainly showed no indication of being the guilty man I took him for.

"Sit down, my dear madam," he exclaimed politely. "Take this chair. Do you come on your own account, or are you the emissary of another?"

"I come for another," I replied.

"And those gentlemen my servant told me were waiting with you - "

"Are no friends of mine. I know nothing about them. I suppose they are waiting to see you on business."

"Possibly; but allow me to ask from whom you come?"

I lowered my voice, and replied, "From the duchess."

"Rustenburgh?" he queried.

"Yes," I replied.

"Are you her servant?"

"I am one of them - not the one she usually sends on confidential missions, but in the absence of that one she has selected me."

"Imprudent; but I think I begin to understand you. What do you want?"

"As usual, money," I replied.

"Money! always money," he cried, holding up his hands; "why, she would drain the bullion vaults of the Bank of England in a year."

"She is sadly extravagant, but you must remember she is unlucky."

"She should not play so high."

"I agree with you; but what can you do for her?"

"To-night?"

"Yes, at once."

"Absolutely nothing."

"Her Grace anticipated this, and told me to say that if you would send her a diamond she could dispose of it."

"What do you mean?" he replied, eyeing me with great acuteness.

I assumed an air of innocence, and replied - "I mean nothing in particular. I am only delivering a message with which I was charged."

"I know nothing of any diamonds. Tell her Grace she must be mistaken."

"Certainly. I was instructed to say that her Grace was very hard pressed; in fact, it was almost a matter of life and death with her."

"If she sends me such messages, and is so pertinacious in her demands, I may as well shut up my house and run away, for I cannot stand such a perpetual drain upon my resources."

"What shall I say when I return?"

"Say I refused."

"In that case, sir, I have only three words more to utter, and then I can go back, having fulfilled the commands of the duchess to the letter."

"What are they?"

I went close to him, and said in a distinct voice - "Blo-y-nor!"

He started, and exclaimed - "Her Grace must indeed be in a dilemma since she sends me that signal. Stay, I will see what I can do for you."

He went to a safe which stood in a corner of the room, opened it with one of those patent keys belonging to locks that defy picking, and opening a drawer, took out a roll of notes. As he did so, I fancied I saw the glitter of diamonds. Going to a table, he carefully took down the number of each note, and then gave them to me, saying, "Excuse the remark, but I know the numbers of these notes, and if they do not in their entirety find their way to the duchess, they will be stopped at the Bank."

"If her Grace trusts me, I do not see why you should object to do so," I replied, with dignity.

"I trust nobody," he said, with a cynical smile. "I meant no offence, however. I was merely taking a precautionary measure, which every business man is justified in doing."

As I was folding up the notes, a servant rushed precipitately into the room, exclaiming -

"Oh! sir, I do think there's thieves in the house."

"What?" vociferated Mr. Lupus.

"Thieves, sir. They're going on anyhow!"

"Who - when - can't you speak?"

"Downstairs, sir - the cellar, sir, and - oh! the young man, sir."

Uttering a wild exclamation, Mr. Lupus ran to the safe, closed it, and put the key in his pocket, then he hastily followed his servant. I left the room with him. We descended to the lower regions, where I saw my men. They had forced open the door of a cellar, and were gazing with a puzzled expression upon what they saw. The cellar was of limited dimensions, probably eight feet by three. The wine-bins had been removed, and nothing remained but its plain white-washed walls. On the ground, upon a heap of straw, a young man was lying. The sickly glare of the candle fell upon his upturned countenance which was ghastly pale.

In an instant I recognised Karl Fulchöck. The poor fellow seemed beside himself with terror. He did not know what new torture or what fresh imprisonment awaited him.

Mr. Lupus glared at the men who had invaded the privacy of his house in a demoniac manner.

"Shut the door," he cried; "what right have you here?"

I gave them a rapid sign, and they seized him. He struggled desperately, but although a strong man, what was he in the arms of three men equally as powerful as himself? In less than three minutes from the commencement of the struggle, the result of which was not for one moment doubtful, Mr. Lupus was a prisoner. The handcuffs were around his wrists, and he was subdued and helpless.

It was now time to turn my attention to Karl Fulchöck. He had risen to his feet during the contest, and now that he was standing up I noticed what I had not remarked before. He was chained to the wall. A chain constructed of formidable links surrounded his waist, and was fastened to a staple driven into a brick. A loaf of bread lay upon the straw, together with a pannikin of water.

I thought it was now time to assume my authority.

"Liberate that man," I said to one of the officers.

He drew a chisel and a hammer from his pocket, and sinking down on his knees upon the straw, began his task; half a brick sufficed him for an anvil, and in a short time one link of the chain was severed, and Karl was free. He ran forward and sank on his knees before me, saying in very good English -

"What do I not owe you?"

"Nothing, Karl Fulchöck," I replied. "Your sufferings are over now."

Overcome by his emotions, he fell forward on his face and swooned away. Leaving one of the policemen in charge of him, I told the other two to conduct Mr. Lupus upstairs.

This gentleman had been a silent spectator of these exciting events up to the present time, but he now exclaimed in a bitter voice, - "Done, by Heavens!"

I smiled sardonically, and we went upstairs.

Once more in the study, I felt in Mr. Lupus's waistcoat-pocket for the key of the safe. I found it. When the safe was opened I ransacked it, and to my great satisfaction found a quantity of the missing diamonds. Amongst them was the Blo-y-nor.

"I seize them in the name of the Queen," I exclaimed, triumphantly.

As I was securing them about my person, Mr. Lupus recovered his equable demeanour, and throwing himself into a chair, said, with an unconcerned laugh -

"When you have finished your apparently interesting occupation, listen to me."

"I am ready to do so now."

"What do you intend to do with me?"

"I shall take you to the nearest police-station."

"You will do nothing of the sort."

"Indeed! Why not?"

"Because if you do, you expose the Duchess of Rustenburgh, as well as me."

This was a difficulty I had not thought of.

I hesitated before I replied.

"Shall I tell you what you had better do?" continued Mr. Lupus.

"If you like."

"Very well. There is nothing like judgment in times like these. Take me to the duke's hotel; confront me with himself and his duchess, and let them deal with me."

"Why so?"

"Is not the reason apparent? The Duke of Rustenburgh will never allow me to be prosecuted, because he knows that such a course would only disgrace his wife."

"There is something in that."

"Of course there is."

"Are all the jewels here?" I demanded.

"All but a few trifling ones that I have disposed of."

After considering for a time, I concluded that it would be better to do as Mr. Lupus suggested, so I ordered Karl Fulchöck to be brought upstairs. He had recovered his temporary weakness, and could walk without any assistance.

I sent for two cabs, and having embarked in them, we travelled to the duke's hotel. When we arrived there, and I sent in word that I brought news of his precious diamonds, we were at once admitted. On seeing Karl, the duke ran forward, crying -

"That's the wretch; that's the one. Send him to prison! *Scélérat*, where are my diamonds?"

"They are here, your grace," I exclaimed, handing those I had rescued to him.

He caught hold of them. Scanned them eagerly, and then pressing them to his bosom, burst into tears. The reaction was too painful to be borne without this natural vent.

The duchess was in the room engaged in eating some olives when we arrived. Directly she cast her eyes upon the man Lupus, she turned pale as death, and would have flown from the apartment but I detained her, forcing her mildly into a chair.

The whole circumstances were at length explained to the duke, and he hurled his ducal anathema at Lupus, who did not seem to be much affected by the demonstration. Having regained his diamonds, Rustenburg did not care particularly to revenge himself when he knew that if he did so he would cover his wife with confusion and disgrace. So he consented to the affair being hushed up, and Mr. Lupus escaped with a whole skin, although he did not deserve the clemency he met with. He was however out of pocket through his dealing with her grace. He had advanced her large sums of money, and, as I had supposed, which she had never paid him. He had not had time to sell the diamonds, although had I been two days later, they would have all been sent to Australia.

Turning to me, after all had been explained, the duke said, "I cannot express my gratitude to you, madam."

Karl Fulchöck next engrossed his attention. He spoke to him in German, and said, as well as I could understand, "that he would endeavour to make him all the reparation which lay in his power."

To Mr. Lupus he exclaimed, "Go, sir; you escape the life-long imprisonment you have earned; but you will, like Cain, carry with you a heavy weight arising from a consciousness of crime."

"Oh dear no," replied Mr. Lupus calmly. "I am rather proud of the whole transaction. I certainly have failed in the end, and that failure I shall regret. Another time when I essay a similar affair I shall be more on my guard against female detectives."

This last part of his speech was accompanied by a vicious glance out in my direction.

I never knew what became of Mr. Lupus; but I have been informed that the countess left off gambling from that day. Nothing would induce her to touch cards or dice; while the duke treated her, as he ought to have done at first, with greater consideration and kindness, and thought less of his diamonds. I received the reward, and was much complimented by all who knew me and who were acquainted with the affair upon the sagacity I had displayed in recovering the lost diamonds.

STOLEN LETTERS

_____

CHAPTER I

EAVESDROPPING

THE post-office is one of those institutions where scrupulous honesty is required, where very inadequate pay is given, a man is expected to slave like a mule or a camel for something under a pound a week, and to resist temptation. Some do it, others do not - they fall. Possibly these latter have wives and children, and cannot help thinking of them as a letter passes through their hands with a half-sovereign inside. It is not a large sum, but it is more than half a week's wages to them, and would enable them to do something for the "young ones." The post-office, or more correctly the public, is robbed to a large extent annually, and it is impossible to put a stop to these depredations, for although the offenders are detected in some instances and brought to justice, others escape and become hardened in crime. During the year of the last Great Exhibition these robberies became so frequent that it was found necessary to adopt some extraordinary means to check them. The utmost vigilance was exercised by the officials, but they found their efforts unavailing. The thefts continued, and the authorities were deluged with letters stating that money, notes, cheques, and valuables of all descriptions had never come to hand. In the dilemma in which they found themselves placed they had recourse to the police, and Colonel

Warner recommended the case to my notice. I undertook it; for it was a task of some difficulty which I fancied would occupy a week or so most agreeably. I was always happier in harness than out of it. I do not mean to say that I despised reasonable relaxation, but I depreciated any great waste of time. I petitioned to be allowed to learn the business of a letter-sorter, which request was granted at once. A few days initiated me in this branch of the business, and I was then drafted into the room in which the latest operations were carried on. Large bags of letters were continually being shunted down shafts. When they reached the floor they were eagerly pounced upon and sorted for transmission to all parts of the kingdom. I carefully watched every man, which would seem a useless proceeding on my part, because a spy appointed for the express purpose is continually looking on. He is concealed from view, and gazes through a pane of glass at those who are at work in the room, and of course he detects frauds when they are very frequent. This man maintained, for his own credit's sake, that the robberies were perpetrated at some other place and not in the General Post-office, but I did not agree with him. It required something more searching than the sleepy vision of a hired spy to detect the skilful thieves who were making a large income out of his carelessness and inefficacious efforts. The quickness with which experienced men perform their duties is inconceivable to those who have not witnessed their exertions. I found it very difficult to keep my attention sufficiently fixed upon one in particular to be able to remark the peculiarity of his manner. The hands of all of them were here, there, and everywhere at once. For the sake of appearances two other women had been introduced at the same time, but we were not by any means regarded favourably.

The men scowled, and looked upon us as if we intended to take the bread out of their mouths. I took no notice of their hostile glances. I pretended to be absorbed in my occupation, although I was in reality remarking everything - one man especially attracted me. There was something so restless in his manner, that from the first time I set my eyes upon him I singled him out as the most likely fellow in the room to be a thief. I remarked that he every now and then raised his hand to his mouth. But so rapid were his motions that they resembled sleight-of-hand, and I could not discover what he was doing. This man looked as if he had known trouble, and was thoroughly acquainted with that painful process which is known as being in hot water. Perhaps he had been born with ideas above his station. There are people who move in a very humble sphere in life who think that they ought to have been born peers of the realm, and nothing but monarchical great men will content others, though the majority of aspirants draw the line at nobility. Luxurious notions may have entered this man's head. He may have had a fancy for asparagus, or new potatoes, or lamb and duck and green peas, and his own beggarly salary not "running to it," as the phrase goes, he may have thought it no great sin to help himself when the occasion presented itself in a favourable manner. He was not of full habit of body. There was something hollow and unsubstantial about him, although he was not much more than thirty years old, if you could judge from his outward appearance, which was not prepossessing. I determined, when work was over to follow this man to his lair, and see what he was like at home. The domestic hearth is something like wine. It shows men in their true characters. The public-house is not a bad interpreter, but the hearth is the best of all. Work was over at six. At that time the right man came on. I afterwards ascertained that the man's name was John Brown. He walked with a quick step along the street, looking behind him occasionally without seeing anything to arouse his suspicion, and entered a public-house, which was situated about half-way up a small court whose obscurity must have prevented it from being generally known. Standing at the bar was a young man of gentlemanly but dissipated appearance, well dressed, and wearing some jewellery which, if real, must have been expensive. When he perceived Brown, he exclaimed -

"Johannes, my man, otherwise John, I am glad to see you."

Brown responded by a nod and a grunt.

I followed, unnoticed by either party, and placed myself in a convenient position for eavesdropping.

Brown sat down by the side of his acquaintance, and said -

"Rather later than usual to-day, Mr. Wareham. The bags were rather heavy."

"Never mind that. Have you worked the oracle properly?" replied Wareham.

"About the same as usual, I think; my pocket's pretty well lined."

"Turn them out; there is no one here to notice us."

"I shouldn't mind something to drink first," growled John Brown.

"You shall have it, my pippin. What tap's most to your liking?" replied Mr. Wareham.

Brown expressed an opinion strongly in favour of beer such as is brewed by Bass on the Banks of Trent, which was promptly brought him by an obsequious waiter. After quenching his thirst, he said -

"Now, sir, I feel better."

Putting his hand in his coat pocket, he produced several pieces of money together with little scraps of paper. He had, I imagined, first of all felt the letters that passed through his hands, and if he detected the presence of gold, he raised the envelope to his mouth and bit off the corner in which the coin had fallen, afterwards placing it in his pocket. He appeared to have about twelve pounds to show as the result of his day's work.

Mr. Wareham examined the spoil, counted it, and having divided it equally, gave Brown one half as his share of the plunder. Brown uttered an exclamation of discontent.

"What are you growling at?" exclaimed Wareham.

"I ought to have the whole of it. I run the risk," he replied.

"So you do. But you are obliged to bring all you get to me, because I know your secret. I need not give you anything if I did not like. You ought to be grateful for the generosity with which I treat you; upon my word, Brown, you are a fortunate fellow."

"More of a fool than that," grumbled Brown, who seemed inclined to retaliate and kick over the traces.

"I can't agree with you, then."

"It don't much matter whether you do or not. I am pretty well sick and tired of this little game. I have a good mind to leave England and go to Australia."

"At the expense of the government," sneered Wareham.

"If I went, you'd go with me," said John Brown, fiercely.

"Think so? Well, you have a right to form your own opinion."

"I, however, don't suppose that such a thing is even remotely possible. I am very well satisfied with my native

country; I have found you, and you are a source of profit
and of income to me. You are what I may call a pearl of great
price; I am unwilling to relinquish you. If I did so, I should
be like the man who killed the goose that laid the golden
eggs. My dear Johannes, you are necessary to my existence."

"You always think of yourself."

"Of course; egotism is the primary duty if not the whole
duty of man."

"I don't know anything about that, but I'm tired of the
way we're going on. I would rather be in a prison than lead
this sort of life."

"Have you ever been in a prison?" exclaimed Wareham,
with a searching glance.

"No, but the time may come, for all that. I'm going the
right road to be shut up in gaol," returned Brown savagely.

"As we are friends," said Wareham, "I don't mind telling
you that I have."

"You!" said Brown.

"For a year and a half I enjoyed that pleasure."

"I wish you were there now."

"Very possibly, my friend, but I really cannot join you in
your amiable desire. I am unable to say in the spirit of the
song, 'I have been there and still would go,' for it is anything
but a little heaven below."

"So you had had your hand in before you met me," said
Brown, with a malicious grin.

"Certainly I had; a man must live, and I can declare that
I was never any burden to my respectable parents; from my
earliest infancy I had a talent for appropriating the property
of other people, and I have lived upon my wits ever since
I first knew I had any."

"What got you into trouble?"

"An inordinate passion for riding. I always envied people I saw on horseback; and one day as I was loitering about the best part of the town, a gentleman asked me to hold his horse for him, while he entered the house of a friend; I looked upon the request as an insult, and while I held the bridle I ruminated as to the best method of revenge upon the aristocrat who had laid himself open to my resentment. It occurred to me that the best way to punish him would be to rob him of his horse. So seizing an advantageous opportunity, I sprang lightly upon the animal's back. I did not know how to ride. The horse found at once that he had a light weight upon him, and he soon discovered, with equine instinct, that I had never been on a horse before. Setting back his ears, the beast bent his legs under him and set off at a quick pace. John Gilpin going to Edmonton must have felt very much as I did. The horse galloped recklessly and furiously from street to street, and at last landed me in the paternal arms of a blue-coated policeman, who looked after me with the care of a father. I was committed for trial, and engaged Mr. Earwig, the celebrated Old Bailey counsel, who did his best for me, and moved the court to tears as he recounted the sad position of this well-connected young man (my father was at the time in Lancaster gaol for debt, and my mother at Norfolk Island owing to a little matter of manslaughter), whose parents were highly respectable. The misguided youth had given way to a sudden impulse of temptation which led him into the commission of a sin, the enormity of which was regretted by none so much as himself.

"At this juncture of the learned barrister's speech the prosecutor got up and said he hoped the court would deal leniently with the prisoner.

"He was willing to make all the reparation which lay in his power.

"The horse had subsequently run up against an omnibus, broken his neck, and damaged sundry pedestrians in his dying struggles, so it may be imagined that I was not able to make much reparation.

" 'The unhappy boy (sobs audible in various parts of the court) narrowly escaped with his life. When he in an unguarded moment leaped upon the saddle he had no idea that the horse would go on. He had never been in a similar position before, and was so ignorant of the first principles of horsemanship that a donkey on Hampstead Heath would lead him to destruction. No felonious design lurked in my client's head. Steal the horse! Why, gentlemen of the jury (this with a persuasive simper), you might just as well and with equal propriety accuse me, me - Mr. Earwig - of wishing to run away with the box in which you are at this moment sitting. (A murmur of incredulity arose from the body of the court, which was instantly suppressed by the energetic efforts of the usher.) No, no, my lord. The poor young man whose prospects in life are already partially ruined, owing to his having been placed in the ignominious position in which he is by the precipitancy of the sitting magistrate who committed him for trial: whose character has been aspersed, and whose prospects have been blighted through a strange perversion of the truth, and a misconception of actual facts, never - I say it emphatically, never - contemplated an offence against the common law of the land. (Applause, and 'hear, hear' from a juryman). Acquit him, gentlemen. You are not the slaves of prejudice. Do your duty as is meet and proper for men of standing and position. Why should you wreak an imaginary vengeance upon an innocent man, for innocent he is, in spite of the allegations that have been made to the contrary? Let him go his ways, gentlemen of the jury, and none of you will sleep the worse for it.'

"Mr. Earwig sat down in a state of moisture arising from perspiration and exertion, but his arguments were not so availing with the jury as I would have wished them to be; they found me guilty, and I made acquaintance with the interior of Holloway Prison. Profit by my experience, my dear Johannes. If you are of an ascetic turn of mind, and wish to mortify the flesh, by all means step within the pale of the criminal law, and get brought up before the assistant judge. You will not forget your interview with that terrible functionary in a hurry. I have seen him once, and I do not want to renew my acquaintance with him. Since that delightful period of my existence I have played the part of the monkey who made use of a cat's-paw to pull the chestnuts out of the fire for him. You, my accommodating Johannes, are my cat's-paw. The sovereigns you bring me from the G. P. O. are the chestnuts. My heart overflows with gratitude to you. I regard you as my benefactor, and I wish I could promote you in some way. The days in which Jack Sheppards and Dick Turpins flourished have gone by, but you might be a Redpath or a Dean Paul; I think you have talent enough for a Redpath, and I don't think you would make a bad Roupell."

"When you have ended your nonsense I shall be glad if you will tell me," exclaimed Brown, who had been fretting and fuming during this lengthy speech.

"My good, my excellent Johannes," replied Mr. Wareham, "I have scarcely commenced."

"What I want to know is, how much longer this game is to last?"

"I can tell you," said Wareham. "If you can manage to nail a certainty - by that I mean something worth having - we will divide the swag, and you can go to America when you like. I shall not endeavour to stop you. Can't you rob the Californian mail; get yourself put on night duty; do something. If you go on like this you will get bowled out at last, and we shall have to throw the sponge up."

"I'll try," replied John Brown, moodily.

"Think it over, Johannes, and do your best."

"I wish I had never given way to your temptation," muttered Brown, in a low voice, but Wareham did not overhear the remark.

"I must tear myself away from your fascinating society, Johannes," continued Wareham; "I have an appointment with a fly flat (*i.e.* a clever fool), and he has some superfluous cash which I covet. See if you cannot do something worth talking about. I shall meet you to-morrow at the usual time."

Wareham lighted a cigar, and nodding to his accomplice, strutted leisurely out of the place.

Brown allowed his face to sink upon his hands, and I heard him say, "Curse him, may God in Heaven curse him." He remained sunk in a lethargic despair for more than an hour, then he raised himself and left the tavern. I returned home to ponder. It was necessary to put a stop to the nefarious practices that Brown carried on with such skilfulness, and I considered how I should best take action in the matter.

PNEUMATIC DESPATCH

I HAD not the remotest conception how Mr. Wareham became acquainted with John Brown's secret, but one thing I was sure of, and that was, that the aforesaid gentleman was a consummate scoundrel. In order to understand his character better, and to see with whom I was contesting, I applied to an intelligent officer who was acquainted with almost all the thieves, vagabonds, and rogues in the metropolis. The reply I received confirmed my suspicions. Wareham was well known to the police under a dozen of aliases. He had been convicted, and I resolved that he should be so again if there was any virtue in an indictment for conspiracy to defraud. I watched the two men carefully for some days, and at last I gained some information upon which I determined to act. They had planned an elaborate robbery between them, and Mr. Wareham's habitual prudence was so far overruled that he consented to take an active part in it. Those letters which were registered on account of their containing valuables were always placed in a bag by themselves. Of course there were different bags for different places, but the Birmingham bag was always a bulky one; they determined to appropriate the contents of that one. It was Brown's duty to take certain bags to the lower regions of the Post Office for transmission through the tubes of the Pneumatic Company, which had just been laid down. Having overheard all their plans, and made my arrangements accordingly, I concealed myself, with one of the watchmen connected with the establishment, in an angle of the wall, where I was free from observation, but able to spring out on a moment's notice. Wareham accompanied Brown from above, and assisted him to carry the bags. No one asked him any questions; it was supposed that he had been told off on the same duty. The room in which the opening to the tube was situated was unoccupied by anyone except the workmen connected with the machinery requisite to put the valves in motion. Brown and Wareham, thinking themselves alone, commenced the execution of their nefarious project. They hastily untied the neck of the small sacks, and plunging their hands in drew out as many letters as they could conceal about their persons. They had taken the precaution to have pockets ingeniously sewn on inside their coats and waistcoats, so that the plunder might be more easily distributed about their bodies. If they had crammed and stuffed the two ordinary pockets that every coat possesses, they would have bulged out, and most likely have betrayed them. I allowed them to satisfy their rapacity, and waited patiently to see what they would do next.

The mouth of the pneumatic tube was very like the opening of a boiler or a furnace. The bottom part resembled a miniature railroad, and the idea was strengthened by the car or small waggon which was driven along at an immense pace by atmospheric pressure. The waggon was in readiness for the bags, and when the two thieves had robbed the Birmingham bag of as much of its precious contents as they thought they could safely carry away with them, Brown raised it up and placed it in the waggon. I considered this a good opportunity to make my presence known and make a captive of Brown and his dangerous accomplice. Stepping from my place of concealment I appeared unexpectedly before them. Brown uttered a terrified cry and stood pet-rified with fear and apprehension. To be detected when success seemed most certain was very mortifying. He had made his arrangements to leave the country that very night. I could see by the aid of the gaslight that he was ghastly pale. Wareham did not exhibit the symptoms of terror and consternation that characterized the bearing of his less hardened confederate, but he was a little thrown off his guard, nevertheless.

"Well, mother, what do you want?" he exclaimed in a voice he vainly endeavoured to render calm.

"What are you going to do with all those letters?" I asked.

"Letters - what letters?" he replied with well-affected astonishment.

"Those you have in your pockets."

"I don't know what you mean."

"Don't you, really? That's a pity," I said in a bantering tone. "Unfortunately I saw you put them away."

"And suppose you did, what then?" he cried boldly; "I suppose you want something to keep your mouth shut?"

The watchman had remained in his hiding-place up to the present time, but now turning half round I beckoned him to show himself. He did so.

"Take that man into custody," I cried, "for robbing the Post Office."

Brown was too much alarmed to make any resistance, and in half a minute the handcuffs were glittering on his wrists.

Wareham looked on at this with blank amazement; then when it was finished and his friend secure, he burst into a loud laugh and exclaimed, "Sold, by Heavens! a female detective."

The watchman now came to my assistance and we advanced to Wareham, who retired until he came to the mouth of the pneumatic tube. I made sure of catching him, and was already congratulating myself upon having apprehended the prisoners without any bloodshed, when I was unpleasantly forced to remember that there was such a thing as a slip between the cup and the lip. Just as our hands were upon him Wareham courageously gave a spring and entered the tube, taking a recumbent position upon the waggon by the side of the Birmingham mail-bag. Seizing the handle he pulled the door to after him. This, I afterwards found, was the signal for the workmen to put the machinery in motion. The bird had escaped from my hand just as I was about to seize it. I do not think that Wareham imagined the waggon would be at once propelled through the tube; it is more probable that he wished to gain a temporary asylum; but a loud rumbling soon informed us that something was taking place inside. Leaving John Brown in charge of the watchman I ran hastily upstairs and asked where the tube discharged its contents. I was told at King's Cross. I went hastily into the street and got into the first cab I could see and drove to King's Cross at the utmost speed of which the cab horse was capable. On arriving there I proceeded to the post-office department, and found to my inexpressible chagrin that the waggon had duly arrived with its human freight ten minutes before. The workmen were surprised to see a man travelling in charge of the bag; but Wareham, elated at his narrow escape, told them that he had done it out of curiosity, and they asked no further questions. As may be imagined, he took the earliest opportunity of leaving the office, and I was too late to apprehend him. That, however, did not annoy me very much. I had a satisfactory clue to Mr. Wareham, and by twelve o'clock the next day he was in custody. Neither money nor letters were found upon him, so he must have been associated with some gang to whom he had handed over for the better concealment thereof the quantity of letters he had stolen. He was afterwards induced to relate his sensations when in the tube. "The air," he said, "felt cold and refreshing, but the darkness was appalling. The waggon was about four feet long by two wide. He disposed his legs as well as he was able, so as to avoid contact with the sides of the tube or any foreign body he might encounter. He was surprised beyond measure when he found the waggon in motion, but being somewhat of a philosopher, he resigned himself to his fate. The speed at which he was driven along took his breath away, and he was not at all sorry when he arrived at his journey's end." Brown and Wareham were arraigned side by side at the Old Bailey - I was the principal witness against them. Brown, at the last moment, finding he had no chance of escape, having been taken *in flagrante delicto*, turned Queen's Evidence, so that his punishment was comparatively trivial to that of Wareham, who was for a term of years removed from that busy sphere in which he had so greatly distinguished himself, and of which he was so promising a member. He was much missed by the school to which he belonged, and many of the thieving fraternity went into deep mourning for what was almost equivalent to the death of their versatile friend.

THE NUN, THE WILL, AND THE ABBESS

<hr />

CHAPTER I

EXPLANATORY

IN order to render my share in the eventful drama I am about to describe explicit it is necessary that I should relate the following particulars: -

Evelyn St. Vincent was an heiress, belonging to a most bigoted Catholic family, the members of which could no more tolerate a Protestant than an Evangelical minister can a Romanist. Her father died when she was very young, but her mother survived, and turned her attention exclusively to the cultivation of the daughter's mind. When she came of age, it was popularly supposed that she would inherit personally to the amount of a hundred thousand pounds, and real property, consisting of estates in Norfolk and Essex, of the value of five thousand a-year. These sums were slightly exaggerated, but rumour was not so far wrong in her calculation as she generally is. Evelyn was very lovely at the age of sixteen; she resembled a fragile flower, for the austere life her mother compelled her to lead made her weak and delicate: getting up at six in the morning, and praying for two hours before breakfast; fasting on saints' days and holy days, and observing all the ceremonies of the Church in the most rigorous manner, is scarcely conducive to the health of a growing girl, but Evelyn had no will of her own. She loved her mother dearly, and was of a religious and devotional disposition. She felt a positive pleasure in executing the penance that her father confessor inflicted upon her, because she imagined that mortifying the flesh was acceptable in the eyes of the Deity. Father Romaine, the priest of the family, who lived in the same house with the St. Vincents, was one of those simple-minded, earnest old men, who adorn the faith they profess. He was very strict - he carried his severity to the verge of asceticism - but he was animated by a sublime conviction that he was treading in the narrow way which would lead him to eternal life. Mrs. St. Vincent greatly resembled the priest. She regarded all pleasures and amusements as sinful. Theatres she avoided as she would have done a lazar or a pesthouse. Balls and parties were to her but specious devices of the arch fiend. Evelyn's education had been confided entirely to Father Romaine, who instilled his own peculiar views of things in general into her mind on every occasion. She was taught to look forward to a conventual life from her earliest childhood, and she longed for the time when she would serve Heaven, as she thought, more thoroughly and effectually in the seclusion of a cloister. The turmoil and the giddy whirl of the busy world were not to her taste. She thought it only productive of vanity and vexation of spirit. She, poor child, was in truth a verification of honest Robert Owen's theory, that children are what you make them, and that the man is but the result of education. You may educate him for the gallows as surely as you can educate him for the woolsack.

Mrs. St. Vincent was well off and independent of her daughter; when she married she had been liberally endowed by her father, and she lived upon the interest of her jointure. Although she loved her daughter tenderly and dearly, she made no opposition to her entering a convent. When Father Romaine first mooted the idea, she was a little reluctant, but she soon gave way to the energetic reasoning of her spiritual adviser, and it was finally decided, when Evelyn was but two years old, that she should retire from the world at the completion of her eighteenth year. She was like a lamb going to the slaughter. She was tortured by no regrets at leaving the fair world which was created for man's enjoyment. She thought that she should be happier in her lifelong imprisonment than in the polite circles in which her birth, fortune, and position entitled her to move. To those of a more practical creed it is melancholy in the extreme to witness such self-immolation, and yet the sacrifice has its sublimity nevertheless. Single-mindedness and disinterestedness must always command admiration even when the fact of their being misplaced raises a sigh of pity and commiseration.

Evelyn St. Vincent was related to the Wrinikers, a famous Catholic family in the West of England. Her cousin, Alfred Wriniker, was a frequent guest at her mother's house, and Alfred, who had reached the susceptible age of nineteen, fell desperately in love with his pretty and delicate relation. He longed to be able to make her his own, and carry her off beyond the seas to some country where there were no priests and no convents, where he could restore the roses to her cheeks, and bring a smile to lips that were assuming a Puritanical rigidity. Mrs. St. Vincent did not discountenance the intimacy that she saw plainly enough was springing up between the young people; she never dreamed for a moment that it would lead to anything more serious than a passing friendship. Such a thing as love between them was, in her opinion, so supremely ridiculous that, supposing that they were gifted with the most fertile, elastic, and vivid imaginations, they would not think even remotely of such a preposterous thing. In a short time Evelyn would take the veil, and then the pomps and vanities of a wicked world would be to her as if they did not exist. But, as often happens in such cases, Mrs. St. Vincent was wrong in her calculations - Alfred loved Evelyn, and, lover like, endeavoured to inspire a reciprocal flame in her breast; in this attempt he was unhappily too successful; the unhappy girl returned his attachment and so destroyed her peace of mind for ever. She could not resist the promptings of nature; they were stronger than the trammels of art. She broke through all restraint, and amidst tell-tale blushes, which in an unwonted manner suffused her ordinarily pale cheek, confessed her love. Alfred Wriniker was beside himself with delight. Transported with joy he covered her with kisses utterly oblivious of the troublous times that were in store for him and for the miserable girl whose heart he had carried by storm. The lovers were seated upon a rustic bench one evening in summer. The spreading branches of an aged beech-tree sheltered them from the rays of the setting sun now turning the western horizon into a sea of gold. Evelyn was dressed with charming simplicity. A plain white muslin dress of fine texture encircled her body. Her skirts were not puffed out and made voluminous by the modern invention of crinoline. A band of plain blue ribbon cinctured her waist. Her hair, of a rich auburn colour, hung down her back. A straw hat was upon her head. Her eyes were cast upon the parched grass, which was covered with beech mast. The appearance of her face seemed to indicate that she was listening to some conversation the nature of which alarmed her. Alfred had fixed a burning gaze upon her Grecian features, which were partly shaded by the broad brim of her hat. He spoke in low but thrilling tones.

"If you love me, Evelyn, which you say you do."

"How can you ask me, Alfred," she replied, reproachfully, "when you know so well I do."

"If so, why not leave your home and come with me to a foreign country? Never mind your fortune, let the priests have that. It is not your money, but your darling self I am anxious to obtain."

"I ought not to listen to you when you speak like that."

"Is our happiness to be destroyed because you were destined for a conventual life before you were old enough to know what the world is like and what it requires of all those who live and move in it? You should remember the man who wrapped his talent up in a napkin."

"Oh! Alfred, pray do not tempt me," she murmured tearfully, in reply to his passionate appeal. "I may not listen to you."

"But you *must*, my gentle Evelyn. Those words have long been trembling on my tongue, and I shall know no peace until you have heard what animates me night and day. We love one another. If you enter a convent we shall be separated, and so our passion, which would otherwise conduce to our mutual happiness, will only doom us to a lifelong regret - an existence of misery and despair. For I can never forget you, and I flatter myself that you are just as unalterably attached to me. You may seek the waters of oblivion in prayer, fasting, and meditation, but will you find them? I venture to say you will not. I am of opinion that like the unhappy Heloise you will ever find my image 'stepping between thy God and thee.' You will see me at the altar, and you will see me in your cell. I shall sit by you in the refectory, and kneel at your feet in the chapel. I shall pervade your thoughts by day, and haunt you in your dreams by night. Be guided by me, my sweet child, refuse to obey your mother and the priests."

"Disobey my mother!" echoed Evelyn, in horror. "Oh, no! It would be a heavy sin - you do not know what you ask me to do."

"Well well," replied Alfred, testily, "gain her consent if you prefer it better. But all I can say is that if she withholds her consent to our united solicitations you will not be violating the fifth commandment by using your own discretion. Fly with me, Evelyn; fly with me."

He pleaded earnestly, but Evelyn was too well tutored to yield to his urgent entreaties. She owed her first duty to Heaven and her religion, and she - poor foolish little bird - began to look upon Alfred as some incarnation of satanic cunning sent to earth to tempt her from her allegiance; so, like some persecuted saint of old when weary of the harsh monastic rule, and longing for admission to the forbidden world, she mentally said, "Retro Sathanas."

"Gain my mother's permission to marry me, and you may lead me to the altar to-morrow," replied Evelyn. But, dear Alfred, you must not urge me to the commission of what my whole nature rebels at, and which my conscience tells me is very sinful."

"You will not?" he said, in accents of despair.

She raised her eyes devoutly to heaven, and murmured slowly, -

"There is the bright abode in which all my hopes are fixed. I would not jeopardize my salvation for worldly happiness, which at best is brief and fleeting."

"She speaks like a priest," said Alfred, to himself. "This religious thraldom is awful. Evelyn, will you listen to me?"

She made no answer. With her fingers she rapidly traced the sign of the cross upon her forehead.

"Oh! Evelyn," he continued, "you do not know how I love you!"

"I am sorry, Alfred, that we ever met," she replied, sadly.

"Do not say that; we may yet be very, very happy - ineffably happy!" he cried; but as he spoke his mind misgave him. The shadow of the black clouds which were gathering around their young lives was already falling upon them and bathing all in a funeral gloom.

"You must not urge me any further, Alfred," said Evelyn, with firmness and decision; "I am very much perturbed. I must seek solace and guidance in prayer."

So wrapped up in themselves were the lovers, that neither had remarked the dark and sombre figure of Father Romaine, who had stolen upon them unawares, and overheard their conversation. His face was puckered up with displeasure, and there was an unkind gleam in his eyes which was unusual with him. As Evelyn uttered the words, "I must seek solace and guidance in prayer," the priest exclaimed, in measured accents, "That is well said, my daughter."

Alfred Wriniker started to his feet and glared savagely upon the priest; his brow darkened, and his lips trembled with suppressed passion.

"I was not aware," he said, sarcastically, "that it was part of a priestly avocation to play the part of eavesdropper, and listen to conversations the tenor of which is not intended for their ears!"

The priest smiled grimly.

"Come, child," he said, to Evelyn, "let us to the confessional. It is meet that we should leave one who, like a man of Belial, takes advantage of my sacred character to insult me."

All at once it struck Alfred that it was exceedingly impolitic of him to offend and make an enemy of Father Romaine, so with contrition openly displayed upon his ingenuous countenance, he advanced a step or two, and said, -

"Father Romaine, I spoke hastily."

"My son, you have done more than that: you have abused the hospitality of this child's mother; you have striven to wean her soul from Heaven, to which it has been dedicated. You have done our family grievous wrong."

"Forgive me, father!" pleaded Alfred, whose conscience told him that the priest spoke truly.

"On thy knees!" cried Father Romaine, with asperity.

Alfred instantly dropped on his knees, uncovered his head, and bent it down in humiliation.

The priest advanced to him, raised his clasped hands in the air, and appeared engaged in prayer for the space of a minute; then his hands descended upon Alfred's head, and there rested, whilst Father Romaine muttered a monkish benediction. He could not say, "*absolvo te fili*" - that form of expression is reserved for the confessional alone.

It was a strange scene. The spacious garden bathed in a flood of ebbing sunlight; the shrinking, timid, wonder-stricken form of Evelyn; the contrite body of Alfred; the solemn attitude of the aged priest - it was almost melodramatic in its striking reality.

When the priest had ended his ceremony, he took Evelyn by the hand and led her gently and unresistingly towards the house. Alfred remained in his penitent position for some time, then he threw himself upon the ground and burst into an agony of tears.

TAKING THE VEIL

THE result of the discovery which Father Romaine had made may be easily guessed. Alfred Wriniker was forbidden the house, and the unfortunate Evelyn was, by her spiritual advisers, exhorted perpetually to religious exercises and an increase of piety. They endeavoured to drive Alfred's image from her heart, but it was too closely shrined there down in its lowest and most sacred depths to admit of their efforts being successful. She remembered but too well his fervid, burning words, and she shed many a tear in private over her blighted affection. They led her into the oratory, but they could not make her pray. She thought of Alfred, and then her religious enthusiasm became obscured and vanished. She entertained worldly wishes, and sighed a protest against being shut up in a convent. So the seeds of the canker which was to consume her heart's core were sown, and although both her mother and the priest could see plainly enough that she was gradually wasting away, they would not take compassion upon her, but relentlessly pushed on the preparations for the sacrifice. They sent Evelyn to a convent to commence her noviciate; at the end of the six months during which this was to last it was settled that she should take the veil. The convent was dedicated to St. Ursuline, and it was celebrated in certain circles for the severity of its discipline.

Evelyn shuddered when she saw that Alfred and herself were separated for ever. A death-like chill stole over her as she contemplated her position: she was doomed to be enclosed in a living grave.

Alfred was equally disconsolate. He made several ineffectual attempts to see the mistress of his heart, but Father Romaine was a jealous guardian, and like a dragon of old watched well over his ward. The boy was a good Catholic, but his religion was not so pure as Evelyn's, and he did not derive much consolation and support from it. In his wilder moments he felt tempted to rebel against a Providence which remained quiescent whilst his enemies were working their wicked will upon him.

Wearily the time passed on until the day appointed for the ceremony which was to make two people miserable for life was very near.

When a Chinese soldier goes into action he is well primed beforehand by bhang, a spirit distilled from hempseed; for the time being this maddens them and they fight like infuriated demons. Acting upon his principles Father Romaine so worked upon Evelyn's young, innocent and susceptible spirit that she began to think she was making a sacrifice acceptable in the sight of heaven and she prepared for her fate with an insane fanaticism. The priest imagined that he was doing that which was right, proper, and praiseworthy, instead of lending himself to a deed of shame. The order of St. Ursuline would be benefited by the acquisition of Evelyn's vast property, and in his opinion it was better that it should be so bequeathed than fall into the possession of some worldling, who would not spend one stiver of it for the good and the benefit of Mother Church.

Father Romaine was indissolubly wedded to his faith. He had embraced the life of a priest and a celibate at an early age purely from the force of conviction. He was a conscientious man, but he was not free from the faulty prejudices and superstitions of his Order, and which the teaching of the Church of Rome does so little to dispel. He had once made a solemn pilgrimage to Rome barefooted, and with the staff and scrip of a pilgrim. He had his own ideas about several matters, for his character was original. He was a man of small means, but he did not take any money with him. He literally begged his way from door to door, and from the time of his leaving the convent in London in which he was domiciled, he lived and slept how and when he could. The Superior of a religious house at Dover passed him over in the steamer, and then he walked through France and Italy until he reached his Mecca. The Pope received him with a kindly smile of welcome, and more than one cardinal, when they heard his story, prophesied great things of him; but Father Romaine was of a humble and unassuming turn of mind. He did not show that ambitious craving for rank, power, and universal dominion which characterizes the Jesuits. He was content to work as well as he could, in a comparatively insignificant sphere, as a poor but honest labourer in the vineyard. Others might wear the purple and fine linen which it was necessary for the government of the Church that some one should don; but he was very well satisfied with his habit of serge and his horsehair shirt. His mind when young had received a strange twist. Had it not been so perverted, Father Romaine might, in a healthy mental state, have shone in society, adorned a profession, and deserved well of the State, instead of wasting a valuable life in cruel penances for imaginary sins and petty intrigues, amongst the most notable of which was that of shutting up a helpless girl in the deathlike seclusion of a strict convent.

Alfred with tears in his eyes besought the inexorable father to grant him an interview with Evelyn; but the priest, judging that a meeting between them would only tend to agitate the girl and undo the work of months, calmly refused; and Alfred left him without a word of farewell. There was a fierce fire of passion surging and boiling in his breast, and he feared to speak because he could not trust his treacherous tongue. He sought the convent, hung about its walls like a prowling midnight robber. He wished that he was some powerful monarch and could march an army against it to liberate his darling Evelyn. He could play a little on the flute, and imitating the example of Blondel, the minstrel of Richard Cœur de Lion, he dressed himself in shabby attire, and played beneath the windows of the convent. He selected those airs with which he knew Evelyn was acquainted. He thought that she would be attracted by the familiar strains, and rush to the window of her cell, so that he might know in what part of the building she was confined, and let his eyes feast upon the loved spot. Finding this attempt ineffectual, he derived a slight solace from standing under the walls of the chapel. He fancied that he could detect the sound of Evelyn's voice, amidst the swelling and glorious diapason of the choir. Evelyn's voice was not powerful, but for a mezzosoprano she was a splendid soloist, and the poor fellow on several occasions had the melancholy satisfaction of hearing her sing. The rich clear clarion-like tones of her melodious voice rose up in varied cadences to the roof of the chapel, and, floating through the open windows, descended in a heavy shower of melody upon the entranced ears of her enraptured lover.

There was a garden attached to the convent, in which the nuns for the sake of their health were allowed to walk. The novices also promenaded in the small space which was their world. When Alfred discovered this, he made friends with the policeman on the beat, and fraternized with him, and gave him money, telling him that he wished to mount the wall, and look at a girl he loved, who was confined in the convent. He would shelter himself behind the branches of a tree.

Whilst making his simple confession he blushed like a woman. The policeman looked at him, and not finding any external evidences of burglarious purpose about him, granted the request that he might scale the wall. It was a difficult thing to do, but lovers are like cats, they can climb anywhere, and you cannot kill them. They may fall down from a dizzy height that would break every bone in the body of an ordinary man, but they are only a little shaken. You may run them through with a sword and not touch any vital part, and as for pistols, when directed at them the caps invariably snap and refuse to go off.

Alfred reached the top of the wall amidst the half suppressed exclamations of admiration which arose from the policeman's mouth. Crawling cautiously along, he came to the protecting shade of a hawthorn-tree, and there took up his position. The garden was not of great extent, but it was richly wooded. The forms of nuns in their sombre attire were to be seen here and there employed in various avocations, some reading, some sewing, some walking about engaged in melancholy musing. Alfred had eyes for one alone amongst the homogeneous throng, and that was Evelyn. She was not far from where he was ensconced. Her eyes were red and her face flushed, as though she had been keeping some painful vigil. Her manner was pensive. A piece of moss, a stone, a twig from a bough, would each have roused her attention.

How ardently Alfred longed to make her aware of his proximity, but he refrained. He felt that such a proceeding on his part would not be productive of any good to either of them. His heart palpitated quickly, and a sensation of madness took possession of his brain. He had the greatest inclination to throw himself headlong to the ground, and die at her feet. Presently a bell rang, and they all walked into the convent again - the nuns silent and solemn, most of them with an innocent expression of countenance almost amounting to something resembling idiocy, or at least imbecility; the novices talking together in a subdued tone, as if everything natural and genial were by the edict of the Lady Superior banished from the walls of the Convent of the Ursulines.

In this manner did Alfred pass his time, until the day arrived - the fatal day on which the mistress on his heart was to be torn from him for ever. He attended in the chapel amongst a crowd of people who were nothing better than eager sightseers. They had no feeling for the bride of Heaven. *They* could not sympathize with the true heart the fanatical folly of her friends was breaking. With a look of heavenly resignation upon her face, she went through the various forms appointed by the rubric on such occasions. From the passive gentleness of her manner and the sadness of her demeanour, she might have been ascending the Hill of Calvary, in the footsteps of her Great Master. When it was all over, and the irrevocable vows were taken, Evelyn fell back in the arms of Father Romaine, and fainted away. With the assistance of a sacristan, the priest carried her behind the altar. A great commotion took place in the sacred edifice. A man was pushing people about in all directions, in defiance of order and decorum. He sprang from seat to seat, and cleared the altar-rails at a bound. Everyone cried "Sacrilege!" but their fierce exclamations did not deter him. What did Alfred Wriniker care for the scandal he was creating? What were the wild tumult and hubbub to him? Less than nothing! He had seen his darling Evelyn fall prostrate upon the cold stones - carried away in the arms of a cynical priest, and it was more than he could bear. So he dashed furiously behind the altar, and in his frantic eagerness he dealt Father Romaine a heavy blow on the chest, and sent him reeling over the mosaic. Sinking on his knees, he pressed his lips to the pallid face of Evelyn, and wept like a child. He raised up her hand, and wrung it passionately, but she was insensible alike to his agitation and his caresses. The first alarm over, the constabulary were sent for, and, marching up the aisle with heavy tread, they laid violent hands upon Alfred, and dragged him, quivering like an aspen, from the chapel.

And Evelyn was never, never conscious of that grand heroic effort which celebrated their eternal parting.

CHAPTER III

CONVERTED

IT was some time after the event recorded in the last chapter that Alfred Wriniker sought the assistance of the police. He imagined that the abbess of the Ursuline Convent was interested in Evelyn's death, and that she would treat her with harshness and severity in order that her property might accrue to the Order of which she was the head. What he alleged was that, in all probability, undue influence was being used - such influence, in fact, as would render a will invalid in the Court of Probate. It was not, however, the money that he was anxious about, although he said he should not like them to make so rich an acquisition, if it were in his power to prevent it. He wished to save Evelyn St. Vincent's life, which his intuition told him was in danger. This was vague evidence to go upon; but as Mr. Wriniker did not ask us to interfere in our official capacity, Colonel Warner told him that, in his opinion, it was just the case for a Lady Detective, and he gave him my address. The young man called upon me, and gave me all the particulars I have recounted in the two preceding chapters. Misery and disappointment had, I could see, made great ravages in his once fine and handsome countenance. He was but the wreck of his former self, he intimated to me, and I could readily believe his assertion. He placed the case entirely in my hands: he did not stint me for money, and made me the most extravagant promises, the fulfilment of which was to be contingent upon Evelyn's restoration to his arms. "You see, Mrs. Paschal," he said, "we shall have a hold upon them if we can prove that they have been tampering with the girl or treating her badly. We can threaten them with exposure, and in order to compromise the matter they will be glad enough to let her go. Oh, my God! the very thought of so much happiness maddens me. Do you know, I could run up against the convent walls and dash my brains out. I believe I should have done it, if this idea had not entered my head. It has saved me from doing something desperate, because it has given me hope. What do you think, now? Is there any chance of success for us?"

"Frankly, I think there is," I replied.

"Pray let there be no reservation in the matter of money, Mrs. Paschal," he observed. "I am not what the world calls a rich man, but I have more than enough to live upon, and

I would spend my last shilling in the endeavour to recover the lost one. I was a staunch Catholic before this happened; now I have my doubts about a religion which countenances the severing of hearts and the breaking-up of homes. May I ask in what way you propose to proceed?"

"I have not arranged my plan of action as yet."

"I suppose you have a hazy sketch in your mind?"

"Yes, I have the bare outline, which you shall hear if you like."

"It would give me much pleasure."

"In the first place, I must introduce myself within the walls of the convent."

"Capital!" he exclaimed.

"Having once achieved that, half the battle would be won."

"Quite so. How do you intend to manage it?"

"That is what I have to plan."

"You would not take the veil?" he remarked, with a laugh.

"It would not be necessary to do that."

"And why not?"

"Simply because it is usual to commence what is called a noviciate. The nuns and novices are in a manner distinct from one another, occupying different parts of the building, but they are perpetually brought in contact. The nuns teach the novices, and prepare them mainly for the sacrifices they are about to make. It is a sort of mental fattening of the sacrificial calf. Do you understand?"

"Perfectly," he replied.

"It occurred to me," I resumed, "that if I could obtain admittance to the Ursuline Convent as a novice, I might meet Sister Evelyn, or whatever name she has assumed, and under the guise of receiving spiritual instruction and advice from her, extract the history of her conventual life. When I had collected sufficient materials to support a charge against the abbess, and obtained a little documentary evidence if possible, I could strike my colours and desert the strongholds of Catholicism. You must remember that I am reasoning upon the presumption that some underhand work is going on within the convent, the object of which is, as you suggest, the death of Miss St. Vincent and the speedy acquisition of her property."

"I think so; because I have dreamt lately the most horrible things respecting Miss St. Vincent. I am not superstitious; but I belong to a Scotch family; and you know the Scotch are celebrated for their wonderful power of second sight. My nocturnal visions have seldom deceived me. I like your plan very much. It is a clever conception, and worthy of a Lady Detective."

"You think so?" I replied, with a smile.

"It is one of those cases that a man could not manage for any one whatever."

"Certainly not. The appearance of a man in a convent would be like that of a wolf amongst a flock of sheep, or a hawk in a dovecot."

"So it would. How long do you think your investigations will last?"

"It is impossible to say. I may be detained within the convent a month, or even two; but I have one thing to ask."

"What is it?" replied Mr. Wriniker.

"Something may go wrong, and I may be detected. If so, some terrible punishment may be inflicted on me."

"I trust not."

"So do I; but we must always be prepared for contingencies."

"What can I do to prevent such a catastrophe?"

"I should like you to call and ask for me once a week. I shall go under my own name. If all goes well, I shall be allowed to see you. If some excuse is made, you must instantly take steps for my liberation; for, having taken no vows, they cannot legally detain me."

"I will make it my especial care to do so."

"Our conversation will be purely upon common-place topics. For instance, you must tell me my mother is well, and I will ask after your wife. It will be best for you to be my brother. These subterfuges are necessary, because I have reason to believe that during an interview like the one we propose, a nun is always placed in a convenient position for overhearing the conversation that takes place."

"You are prepared for everything!" he remarked, in a tone of admiration.

"If I were not, I should be unfit for the position I hold, and unworthy of the confidence that Colonel Warner places in me."

"You must be courageous beyond the average run of women."

"Habit is second nature," I answered, carelessly.

Mr. Wriniker left me with his spirits encouraged and his hopes raised. I felt quite interested in his sad case, and would have done and risked much more than I had mapped out in my rough sketch of operations, if I thought that by so doing I should restore his lost Evelyn to his arms. He told me before he took his departure that he loved her more than ever, and if she were indeed separated from him for ever, he could not survive the blow - the severity of the shock would kill him. The tears sprang to his eyes as he spoke. It was evident that he was painfully in earnest. In order to carry out my design, I made the acquaintance of a Catholic priest, and went through a hypocritical farce which I hope was not wrong; because I firmly believe the end justified the means, and detectives, whether male or female, must not be too nice. The unraveling of crime is always a conflict of wits. It was so in the present instance. I pitted myself against the abbess of the Ursuline Convent, and those who I imagined, according to the instructions I had received, were in league with her to deprive a defence-less girl of her fortune and patrimony.

I told the priest - who was no other than Father Romaine - that I doubted whether the Protestant religion was calcu-lated to make me happy. Since the death of my husband I had doubted much, and I wanted his advice. Seeing the chance of making a convert, the good and unsuspecting father took great pains with me. I met him half-way, and soon became a renegade. I selected Father Romaine because I knew he was intimately connected with the authorities of the Ursuline Convent, and would at once gain me admittance there in preference to any other, should I evince any liking for a life of seclusion, which after my questions I soon did. I affected a distaste for the frivolities of the world, and declared that I did not think I could be happy except in the calm and quiet seclusion of a convent; but I had heard so much of the strict discipline of convents that before I took the irrevocable step, I should like to have an insight of the inner life of a convent. Father Romaine told me that nothing was easier; I could enter as a novice as soon as I liked.

It was necessary to pay a small sum to defray the expense of my noviciate, and that was speedily forthcoming. When a woman takes the veil, or a man assumes the cowl, they endow the house they enter with all their worldly goods, because they are supposed to leave the world, and to have no further use for their money, which is held in trust for them by their Superior, and defrays the expense of their board and lodging; but in the first instance, that is, during the preliminary noviciate, you must give a certain sum which is dependent upon your means.

At the expiration of a week, I entered the convent as a lay-sister, and was much struck by the calm, inoffensive piety displayed by those with whom I came in contact. The nuns were exceedingly kind to me, but I fancied that their amiability was somewhat studied and forced. They were always representing the happiness of their life, and the sweet reward that followed their self-abnegation in assuming the character of a nun, an example they were perpetually exhorting me to follow. I had been a week in the convent without seeing or hearing anything of Miss St. Vincent.

CHAPTER IV

IN SHEEP'S CLOTHING

I ASSUMED a harmless character, which recommended me to the nuns. I was always very docile and obedient. I would run about the house for them and bring them books from the library, for it sometimes happened that although they had "put on the new man," the old one would give unmistakable signs that he was not utterly banished. The prevailing sin of the sisters I found was listlessness and laziness, including a disinclination to work. The abbess or Lady Superior of the convent was a stern-looking woman of fifty, with a forbidding face like a vinegar plant. There was a bad expression about her eyes which denoted inherent cruelty of disposition, and I took a dislike to her from the first moment I saw her. The nuns dreaded her, for she was very strict with them; she used to punish them most severely for the most trifling offences. It was a common thing for her to shut them up in a damp cell for two days and nights without food, light, or water, and not a soul to come near them from the commencement of their imprisonment until the expiration of the sentence. Her favourite punishment for a disobedient or an idle novice was to make her sit for hours with her face opposite a newly white washed wall. Fortunately, I did not incur her displeasure. One day the abbess, to my great gratification, asked me if I should like to be her servant. It was, of course, a mark of a special favour for which any of the novices, or nuns either for the matter of that, would have been very grateful, but it was contrary to the rules of the convent for a nun to serve any one but her Creator. Perhaps the abbess selected me because I appeared of a mature age, and on that account more likely to be demure and discreet. The novice who had hitherto served her had lately taken the veil, and it was necessary for her to look around so that her place might be supplied. I accepted the offer gladly, because it would give me such wonderful opportunities of watching her actions, and spying out the interior of the convent. When the proposition was made me I at once sank on my knees, reverently bowing my head, and kissing the hand of the abbess in token of gratitude and submission to her sovereign will. I was now removed from the part of the convent in which I had formerly boarded, and occupied a bed in a small room adjoining that of the abbess. My duties were not light. I had to dress her every morning, make her breakfast, and attend her on her peregrinations through the building. On the evening of the second day after I had entered on my new employment, after vespers I was told to bring a loaf and a jug of water. I did so, and followed the abbess along several corridors, until we came to a spiral staircase. This we descended, and in time reached the basement. Here another long passage displayed itself to my view. The abbess lighted a small hand-lamp which stood upon a bracket, and we pursued our way, coming at length to a series of cells: at one of these the abbess stopped. The atmosphere of these vaults, cells, or cellars - I hardly know which name is most appropriate for them - was damp and heavy. It struck a chill to my bones, as I stood still with the scanty fare in my hand. Had the abbess observed me narrowly, she would have perceived that my face was flushed with expectation. It was difficult to say what I anticipated; but I had a vague presentiment that I should shortly look upon the face of Evelyn St. Vincent. What made me think so I cannot imagine, except the fact of my having been all along impressed with the idea that the poor girl was the victim of foul play. The abbess produced a bunch of keys, and regarded them with her old relentless look, until she discovered the particular one she was in search of. This inserted in the lock gave her admission to the cell.

"Here," she said to me, "you will see a contumacious sister. Beware lest the same fate should happen to yourself."

"May the remark not be ominous!" I thought to myself, for I had the strongest disinclination to solitary confinement and the spare diet of bread and water.

The pale rays of the light streamed into the cell, illumining its dimensions and exhibiting it in all its naked hideousness, revealing the attenuated form of a fair girl, who was reclining upon a truss of straw. If the passage outside was chill and cold, the cell itself was much more so. The girl shaded her eyes with her hand, to keep the light from them; but presently becoming accustomed to it, she looked up in a shrinking way. I had never seen Evelyn St. Vincent; but Alfred Wriniker had so faithfully described her to me, that I saw at a glance that the hardly-treated captive before me, suffering from infamous oppression, was the heiress for whose wealth the designing abbess was scheming. A strong and healthy girl such as Evelyn might have become under good treatment and kind, considerate behaviour, would have probably outlived the abbess; what good, then, would her money have been to the present administratress of the affairs of the convent? Literally none at all. As it was at present, Evelyn was not entitled to the possession of her property for the space of three years - that is, until she was of age. But I soon discovered that the cause of Evelyn's disgrace was her refusal of a request made her by the abbess. The latter was acquainted with certain means of borrowing money on contingent reversions, and it was the height of her ambition to purchase a large piece of ground adjoining the convent, on which she could erect a handsome building in connexion with her present establishment; but it was necessary to get Evelyn's written consent to this course, which the spirited girl refused to give. She said she had come to the convent to prepare herself for a heavenly life. She did not mind endowing the convent to a certain extent, but the bulk of her property she intended to secure to her cousin, Alfred Wriniker.

I was not acquainted with these facts until afterwards. Miss St. Vincent was lightly clad in a robe of serge, and I could see that she was gradually wasting beneath the rigour of her imprisonment, and the poignancy of her regrets at having placed herself within the power of an unscrupulous and designing woman. Setting the light down on the floor the abbess turned to me, and exclaimed -

"See nothing, hear nothing, or your turn may come next."

I inclined my head, and she addressed herself to the prisoner.

"Has the hardness departed from your heart, sister Evelyn?"

This remark told me that my suspicions were correct. It was Evelyn St. Vincent that I saw before me.

"If you mean will I consent to your request, I reply no."

"And why not?"

"You would scarcely understand me if I told you," she replied in a faint voice.

"You excite my curiosity."

"It is easy to gratify it. Before I became the bride of Heaven I loved my cousin. He must think me a treacherous ingrate. In order to dispel this idea, I wish to leave him all the landed property I am told I shall be entitled to, to show him that in my last moments I was not forgetful of him. If I give you half and him half, surely it will be an equitable distribution."

"Does he require it?"

"I have not considered that question. I want it to be a tribute of affection."

"Do you know it is sinful to talk like that."

"Is it not more so to use me as you are using me at present?" replied Evelyn, with mildly reproachful eyes.

"You must not make me such replies. I am the best judge of my own actions, and I am able to discriminate between right and wrong."

"I always looked upon you," said Evelyn, "as the one under heaven to whom my allegiance, obedience, and submission were due; but what am I to think when the first thing I hear is a grasping request for gold. Oh! I have been cruelly deceived, and I wish I were dead!"

The unhappy object of religious persecution buried her face in her hands, and wept bitterly.

"Come, come!" exclaimed the abbess, "I have no time to waste on a sentimental display; will you sign the paper I hold in my hand, or will you not?"

She had drawn a paper from her pocket, and had flourished it before the eyes of the young nun.

Evelyn rose to her feet, and replied deprecatingly, "You ought not to ask me. Let me follow the devotional life I have chosen, or leave me here to die. The gloom and solitude of those vaults will soon kill me; but do not hasten my end by your continual persecutions; you only force my thoughts to return to a world I thought they had left for ever. It is enough to madden me to reflect that I might have been so happy as the wife of another, and that I have renounced all that for an existence of the most profound misery."

'Will you sign?" demanded the abbes, savagely.

"I will not do what my conscience tells me I ought to refuse," replied Evelyn, firmly.

"You defy me - eh?" said the abbess, with a cruel look.

Evelyn was silent.

"Very well," she continued; "we will try some other means, which may prove more persuasive."

Addressing herself to me, the abbess said, "Take her by the arm, and conduct her along the passage after me."

I did as I was directed without a murmur, for I knew that to refuse any of the abbess's commands would be fatal to all my schemes, and of no use whatever to Evelyn St. Vincent. Perhaps if I were recalcitrant the act of disobedience would only consign me to a dungeon and a life-long imprisonment. So, with an affectation of roughness, I seized Evelyn by the arm, and told her to come with me. The abbess led the way; but as we were leaving the cell I contrived to whisper to Evelyn, "Alfred is well - friends are watching over you."

As I uttered these words she gave vent to a scream; it was not very loud; but the abbess confronted us in a moment, and asked why she uttered the cry.

"I pinched her arm, and I suppose her flesh is tender," I exclaimed.

"Oh!" said the abbess, apparently satisfied with my explanation of the occurrence, "she will have more cause to cry out presently."

I wondered what this remark might portend. I was afraid it boded little good to the ill-starred Evelyn St. Vincent, who with tottering steps accompanied me along the corridor, at a loss to interpret the meaning of the strange speech I had just made.

CHAPTER V

TORTURE

THE abbess led the way into a room at the end of the passage, which was lighted by gas, there being no windows to the place. It was a square apartment. Its size was about twelve feet by ten. The only article of furniture it possessed was a chair which stood in the centre. Just above the chair a rope was dangling from the ceiling. It was fastened to an iron hook. I was at a loss to imagine the use of the rope and the chair, but I was not long kept in ignorance of the purpose to which the superior of the Ursuline Convent put them. Shutting the door, the abbess advanced to Evelyn, and asked her if she had finally decided to be disobedient to the commands. Evelyn, with the firm determination of a martyr, replied that she thought herself justified in replying in the affirmative. Whereupon the abbess dragged her to the chair, and told her to mount it. She did so. The abbess then placed her hands behind her back, and fastened the rope to them. When she had accomplished this to her satisfaction, she pushed the chair away, and Evelyn was suspended in mid-air by her arms. It was a very painful position to be placed in; her feet were at least two feet from the floor, and the weight of her body wrenched her arms nearly out of their sockets. Every moment aggravated her misery, and rendered the torture more unbearable. The abbess looked on with equanimity, and seemed positively to gloat over her agony. I could have rushed forward and have done battle for Evelyn, but my sense told me that although my efforts might, and probably would, be temporarily successful, I could not hope to liberate the girl by a *coup-de-main*, in which I should have to rely entirely upon my own exertions and my own personal prowess.

Evelyn uttered a succession of tiny screams. Her fortitude was not proof against the severity of the discipline to which she was exposed.

"Will you sign?" groaned the abbess.

"Oh, yes! yes! I will sign anything if you will only take me down!" replied Evelyn, gaspingly.

At this concession to her wishes, the abbess placed the chair under her feet once more, so that the pressure under the arms was relieved.

The rope was soon untied, and Evelyn stood trembling like a leaf on the ground once more The abbess produced the document she had before exhibited for Evelyn's signature, and opening it, displayed it upon the chair. She placed a pen and a portable inkstand by its side. Evelyn's hand shook so much that she could scarcely grasp the pen; but at length she succeeded in doing so, and with difficulty affixed her name to the bottom of the deed.

A glance of triumph suffused the face of the abbess, who folded up the paper; but suddenly she seemed to remember something, for she untied it again, and exclaimed, "Put your name here, it is necessary that there should be a witness, I believe."

I did as she asked me with alacrity, because I knew it would give me a stronger hold than ever over her. If she attempted to deny the whole transaction, I could point to the deed, and show my signature attached to it. Of course, the abbess would not keep the deed in her possession. It would be transferred to the person of whom she intended to borrow money. I did not doubt that I should be able to discover him. It seemed to me to be a dubious transaction altogether; but one thing I understood clearly, that any one who assisted the abbess in her designs ran a great risk, because Evelyn when of age could, if she were a free agent, dispute the validity of any documents signed by her when under age; but the abbess relied upon her renewing the signature when she should have arrived at years of discretion - when the property she was entitled to became hers, and she had a right to dispose of it as she thought best.

Evelyn's life was necessary to the abbess; but the poor, imprisoned thing did not think of that. She only wished to escape from her present agony, which she thought might be prolonged indefinitely, till exhaustion and death resulted. So she submitted to the extortionate demands of the abbess, whose conduct did not redound to her credit, or the credit of those with whom she was associated. After this event Evelyn was allowed to rejoin her companions, and she was treated with every kindness and consideration. The best of everything was given her, that she might nerve her strength and live until she was of age; *then*, the abbess did not care what became of her. The seal of secrecy was imposed upon her as to the events which had taken place during her captivity. I found, at length, an opportunity of speaking to her when we were free from observation. She told me that she loved Alfred Wriniker passionately and dearly. She was sorry - bitterly sorry - for taking the fatal step she had taken, and she wished very much she could escape from the convent.

Up to this point of our conversation I had not told her that I had entered the convent to rescue her; but when I gave her to understand that such was the case, her joy knew no bounds. She declared that she should feel no compunction in breaking her oath since she had been so shamefully treated and so grievously deceived. I told her that it would be impolitic for us to be seen together again, because suspicion might be excited in the crafty mind of the abbess, who was never so happy as when playing the part of the spy or the eavesdropper. Before we separated I instilled all the encouragement I could into her breast, and succeeded in bringing back a hopeful smile to her lips. She was a nice amiable girl, and I took a liking to her at once.

I now had to hit upon some means of escaping from the convent, and of otherwise maturing my plans. I had discovered Evelyn St. Vincent and I had witnessed one or two transactions which so clever a woman as the abbess of the Ursulines would scarcely like to hear published to the world, and I felt certain that she would, as far as lay in her power, deprecate any delicate attentions on the part of the police when those attentions were directed specially towards herself. I thought it would strengthen my position if I could gain possession of the deed which Evelyn had signed, and take my departure with it. I had every opportunity of stealing it because I was constantly in the abbess's presence. I knew that she kept her papers in a cabinet in her bedroom. I resolved when occasion offered, to decamp with the cabinet, which was of small size, and easy to carry beneath the folds of one's robe. It was known all through the convent that I was in attendance upon the abbess, so that I came and went as I chose. I had never as yet ventured beyond the walls of the convent, but I thought that if I attempted to do so I should not meet with any opposition from those whose task it was to guard the door. The janitors were astute female griffins, and would not have neglected their duty to save their lives; but one night I succeeded in eluding their vigilance. I told them that I was going out on important business for the abbess, they believed me, and I was free. I hastened at once to the private residence of Colonel Warner. He started when he saw me in my conventual dress, but we were soon eagerly discussing the chance of rescuing Evelyn St. Vincent. Colonel Warner did not, in this instance, act in his official capacity, for it was not a case of which he could even take cognisance, but he befriended Alfred Wriniker as much as lay in his power. A messenger was despatched for the expectant lover, and we talked upon in different matters until he arrived.

Alfred Wriniker made his appearance in an anxious and expectant state. He bowed to the colonel, and grasped me nervously by the hand; his excessive agitation for a time deprived him of the power of speech. I hastened to gratify the evident curiosity depicted on his countenance.

"She is alive and well," I exclaimed.

Sinking into a chair, he said, in a husky voice, "Thank Heaven for that!"

We broke open the cabinet by our united efforts, although Colonel Warner turned his back upon us, and said that we were engaged in a burglarious operation, with which he would have nothing to do.

I discovered, amongst others, the document I was in search of. There were one or two of a similar nature, fully revealing the nefarious nature of the abbess's transactions with those whom their infatuated folly, aided by the fanaticism of youth, placed in her power. We were unanimously of opinion that with such documents in our possession we could coerce the abbess, and make her consent to the liberation of Evelyn. When I recounted the scene in the torture-room, the truss of straw, the gloomy cell, and the stern, implacable demeanour of the lady superior, I thought Mr. Wriniker would have gone out of his mind with rage and ungovernable passion. I pacified him by saying that in all likelihood he would be able to call her his own in the course of a day or two. We separated very well satisfied with the success of our intrigue. The next day, accompanied by two officers of the detective police, I paid the abbess of the Ursuline Convent a visit. She received us in her state apartment, little guessing the object of our call. She started slightly at first, as if she recognised my face, but she made no remark. I spoke to her, and in a few words explained my business.

"You have," I began, "a young lady, named Evelyn St. Vincent, under your charge. Some of her friends wish her to be liberated from your control."

"That is impossible."

"Why so?"

"Because she is the bride of Heaven. Her vows are irrevocable, and cannot be broken."

"I am of a different opinion, and I flatter myself you will agree with me when you hear what I have to say."

The abbess smiled, as if nothing could alter her ideas upon that point.

"Permit me to explain, before we go any further, who and what I am."

"Certainly," she replied, blandly.

"I am by profession a female detective."

"What!" cried the abbess, springing from her chair, her face blanched, and her confident air vanished.

"The gentlemen who accompany me are also connected with the London Detective Police."

I stopped to see what effect my words had upon her. She had recovered her serenity, and by a nod intimated that she wished to hear more.

"I am acquainted with many secrets of this prison-house: such as the gloomy cells, the torture-chamber - - "

"How - how do you know all this?" asked the abbess, interrupting me. "I fancy I know your face, and yet - - "

"Because," I replied, sternly, "I have been an inmate of the convent."

"An inmate! - you?"

"Yes, for a limited period; but during that time I kept my eyes open, as you may imagine, since I became a Roman Catholic for a purpose. But to a detective all creeds are alike."

"I see now - I remember. Oh! how egregiously I have been duped!" cried the abbess, in despairing accents.

"I was certainly obliged to use a little harmless deception."

"And the casket? It was you who robbed me?"

"I am not prepared to admit that; but I have certain papers in my possession - such as a deed of gift, signed by Evelyn St. Vincent."

"You have that?"

"Yes; would you like to have it made public? The press is always ready and willing to take up any scandal connected with monastic institutions, which you are doubtless aware are not held in very great estimation in this country."

The abbess was certainly a clever woman. She comprehended the state of affairs at once, and she exclaimed -

"You have outwitted me. I admire your talent. Are you willing to make terms?"

"Yes, provided the terms you offer are reasonable. Of course you do not want the girl so much as her money?"

She smiled grimly, and replied -

"If I consent to her liberation, will you allow her to promise me the sum of a hundred thousand pounds when she comes of age? If she made me such a promise, I would rely upon her native honesty and integrity for its fulfilment when the time arrived."

"It is a king's ransom," I remarked, elevating my eyebrows.

"Those are my terms. If you accept them, I let the girl go; if not, we will fight it out."

"Your terms are preposterously extravagant."

"Never mind."

"I have you at a disadvantage."

Again, "Never mind."

"You are in my power."

"If so, the girl is in mine, and I would ship her off to the Continent to-night, and you would not have the slightest clue to her whereabouts."

I felt the force of this remark. I knew that I was labouring under many disadvantages, and although the sum demanded was enormous, I thought it would be better to accept her terms than go to war with her. She might, for what I know, make away with the poor girl; so I said -

"I accept your terms. Will you be good enough to send for Miss St. Vincent, so that they may be ratified in her presence."

The abbess smiled triumphantly, and tinkled a small bell. An attendant here entered, and receiving his instructions left the room, shortly returning with Evelyn. I advanced towards her, and shook her warmly by the hand, saying,

"You wish to return to the world, do you not?"

She hesitated, looking askance at the abbess, of whom she was evidently afraid.

"You regret your vows - circumstances have compelled you to do so."

Still she made no reply.

"Never mind me," said the abbess. "Say what you think."

"I should like to leave the convent," she exclaimed, trembling.

"Very well. You can do so on certain conditions," said the abbess."

A flush of pleasure mantled the girl's pale cheek.

"If," resumed the abbess, "you will promise to pay me the sum of one hundred thousand pounds when you come of age, you can leave with your friend."

"Now?" asked Evelyn.

"At once."

"I promise gladly."

The abbess gave her a Bible to kiss, and having imprinted upon it a chaste salute, the abbess exclaimed, "I am perfectly satisfied; with young and innocent nature like yours a word is as good as a bond."

Evelyn could hardly believe the evidence of her senses. She thought she was the sport of some phantasmagoria - some will-o'-the-wisp - some living marsh fire. I did not doubt that I could have defeated the abbess in the long run, but she could have caused Evelyn much annoyance; her persecutions might have resulted in the poor girl's death. Abroad it would have been difficult to trace her. Her mother would, in all probability, acting upon the advice of Father Romaine, have instigated her to sanction all the acts of the abbess. I thought it better to sacrifice a trifle of money than to condemn the lover to further suspense and anxiety. I say a trifle of money, for the sum asked was not quite half of Miss St. Vincent's fortune. Mr. Wriniker did not care about her money; he loved her for herself; and after she had satisfied the rapacity of the abbess, they would still have a magnificent sum to live upon. A hundred thousand pounds in these days of Guaranteed Government Loans, which pay seven per cent, is worth more than it was in the prosaic times, when an investment in the Three Per Cent. Consols was considered the *summum bonum* of speculative life. I agreed to surrender all the papers I had found in the cabinet, except the one bearing Miss St. Vincent's signature. That I kept as a weapon to use either offensively or defensively against the abbess. Evelyn left the convent leaning on my arm. To her it was a moment of ecstatic bliss.

*   *   *   *   *

As Mrs. Wriniker, Evelyn was supremely happy. The young married couple lived abroad until Evelyn attained her majority. Then they returned to England. Evelyn paid the abbess to the uttermost farthing. Mrs. St. Vincent and Father Romaine forgave the runaways, who proved themselves better Catholics than they would have been had their union been frustrated by the living death of a convent.

WHICH IS THE HEIR?

CHAPTER I

LORD NORTHEND IS
TROUBLED IN HIS MIND

WHEN Lord Northend arrived at the age of five-and-twenty certain events happened which annoyed him excessively. His father had obligingly died a few years before, and left him the title and estates, which were of considerable value. Lady Northend had also been carried to the family vault, and the present lord was alone in his glory; but he was not destined to have quiet possession either of his title or the estates, for the most extraordinary claim was made to both. So astounding and so improbable were the whole of the circumstances attendant upon the claim, that his lordship thought the plainest and simplest course he could pursue would be to consult the Commissioners of Police, and place the case in their hands. Accordingly he did so. The main facts of the case, as his lordship related them to Colonel Warner and myself, are briefly these: -

While staying at his country-house his servant one morning apprised him of the visit of a gipsy woman, who demanded an immediate interview with him. In a good-natured way he granted her request, and she was shown into the library, where she was shortly joined by his lordship. Without the slightest preface, the woman, whose olive-tint denoted her to be a thorough-bred Gitana, declared that Lord Northend had no real title to the estates, and that he had usurped the rank his title gave him, which of right belonged to another. He indignantly asked her reason for making such an unprecedented charge, which, from its utter absence of foundation, was simply ridiculous. In grave and earnest accents the woman replied that more than three-and-twenty years ago she had been employed upon some menial work in the late Lord Northend's house; it was then that an idea struck her. If she could succeed in removing the child, of which Lord Northend was the happy father, and place another in its place, she could bring the stolen one up, and by uniformly treating it with kindness and consideration, have a claim upon its gratitude, which would be satisfied in after days, when, through her instrumentality, he came to his own, or some compromise was effected. She pondered over this idea until it took such firm root in her mind that she knew no rest until she had accomplished her design, which she did without exciting suspicion. The exchange was never detected. Years had glided by and the time had now arrived for justice to be done to the injured man.

"And you expect me to believe this infamous concoction?" exclaimed Lord Northend.

"Believe it or not, as you like," returned the gipsy; "I am not without proof to substantiate the assertion I have just made."

"It is the most impudent fabrication I ever heard of."

"Such a remark might be expected from your lordship; but a denial coming from an interested party has seldom much weight with a jury."

"A jury?" repeated Lord Northend, astonished at the woman's cool impudence and unabashed audacity.

"Certainly, my lord; it is a question of right, and we shall try it, without - - "

"Without what?"

"Without you think fit to compromise the matter. The real Lord Northend - - "

"Come, my good woman, I have had enough of this nonsense; you had better leave the house before I ring for my servants."

"You refuse to listen to me?"

"Unquestionably I do."

"Then you drive me to extremities."

"It is a matter of the most perfect indifference to me where you are driven, or what you do."

"Good morning," said the gipsy; "you shall hear from my solicitor, although I must say I should have been glad to settle the matter amicably. It is unpleasant to be turned out of what one has been taught to look upon as an ancestral home."

"Will you go?" vociferated Lord Northend, becoming seriously enraged.

The woman lingered as if she wished to be assaulted. If violent hands were laid upon her it would, she thought, strengthen the case; but Lord Northend's prudence over-ruled his passion, and she departed in peace.

Soon afterwards a letter arrived from a Mr. Jacob Jarvis, a solicitor, recapitulating the preceding facts, and adding that, if some arrangement was not speedily come to respecting this painful and unusual case, it would be his imperative duty to bring an action of ejectment against his lordship, and let it be tried on its merits by one of the judges of the law and a British jury. The glorious uncertainty of the law was well known, but that remark cut more ways than one. If it was uncertain for the plaintiff, it was equally so for the defendant. The foster-mother of his client, Mrs. Zitella Lambrook, had fully instructed him in all the particulars of the case, and although she had unquestionably been guilty of a serious offence, and exposed herself by so doing to the penalties of the law, that was no bar to his client's claims. Because she had been guilty, it was no reason why the innocent should suffer. His client had taken the name of Lambrook in ignorance of his real cognomen, and the action would be entitled Lambrook *v.* Lord Northend. If a favourable letter was not sent within twelve days, proposing the basis of a conference which might lead to a compromise, the copy of a writ in the action would be forthwith served upon his lordship. In conclusion, Mr. Jacob Jarvis said -

"A solicitor is, to a certain extent, a disinterested party, but he has his duty to his client to perform, and that is all - he must do that to the best of his ability. I trust I shall not be in any way departing from the high standard of morality I have even set up for myself, if I venture to suggest to your lordship that it would be better for all parties concerned that this melancholy case should not come into court. My client, Mr. Lambrook, will be glad to make you a specific offer if you write him word that you entertain the proposal. Again let me beg of you not to be rash and obstinate. Mr. Lambrook is of a quiet retiring disposition, and would, were the means supplied, forego long years of litigation, although in the end he must be the victor, and quitting the busy whirl of great cities, return into the arcadian simplicity of the country, where he would forget the wrong that had been done him, and endeavour to be at peace with all mankind. As a well-wisher of your lordship, I emphatically say, compromise."

This precious epistle was at once put in the hands of the police. The superscription of the letter annoyed Lord Northend very much, it was directed to "Thomas Wendell (his family name), falsely calling himself Lord Northend."

Colonel Warner handed this letter to me. After I had perused it, with a smile upon my face, he exclaimed, "Well, what do you think of that, Mrs. Paschal?"

"As clear a case of extortion as I ever met with."

"So I think. Would you like the handling of these rogues?"

"Nothing would please me better."

"Lord Northend has no doubt as to the ultimate result, even if Mr. Jacob Jarvis and his client, Lambrook, have the hardihood to bring the case into Court, but he does not like the idea of his title being called in question. There are some people who are naturally so malignant that they always shake their heads and declare that there must be something in it. It is always unpleasant to hear your name brought prominently before the public, whether you are in the right or in the wrong. His lordship's enemies might, were the story promulgated, affect to believe that he was not the lawful possessor of the estates he at present enjoys. To avoid this he told me he would gladly pay a small sum to the extortioners. I, however, forbad his doing so. 'Once give them a halfpenny,' I said, 'and you injure your position: to make such a concession is a confession of weakness; besides, they would never leave you, they would lead you a life of misery and drain you as dry as an empty well. Set them at defiance, my lord, and leave them to me.' "

"Very good advice too," I remarked.

"It's understood that you will help his lordship out of his difficulty?" queried the colonel.

I replied in the affirmative, and prepared for vigorous action.

CHAPTER II

EATING RATS

I HAD no doubt whatever that it was attempted to make Lord Northend the victim of a somewhat blundering conspiracy, of which Mr. Jacob Jarvis was the originator. The Lambrooks were simply his tools. My inquiries were first of all directed towards the man of law. I consulted the Law-list, but I could not find the name of Jacob Jarvis. Going to a law-stationer's I looked over a file of law-lists extending over a period of thirty years. When I arrived at the year '48 I found the name I was in search of. But it was in none of the subsequent lists. The presumption was then that Mr. Jarvis had been unfortunate, and had incurred the resentment of the authorities, who had ordered him to be struck off the rolls. Subsequent inquiries proved that this hypothesis was correct. This was a great step to have achieved. To find that the prime mover and instigator of the plot was an unqualified practitioner was like laying the axe to the root of the tree and toppling it over at a single blow. I next turned my attention in an affectionate manner towards the Lambrooks, whose nomadic habits were of such a nature that they would not allow them to remain long in one place. The open sky and the fluttering canvas which made their tent was their delight. They condescended occasionally to attend fairs and catch the nimble ninepence by erecting sticks upon which cocoanuts, china dogs, and sawdust-filled pin-cushions were placed, at which the juvenile mind much delights to throw the heavy stick. I tracked them to their lair by waiting outside Mr. Jacob Jarvis's office day after day for nearly a whole week. At length my exertions were rewarded by the appearance of an olive-tinted woman and a dusky-hued young man of commanding stature and handsome features. From the wonderful facial resemblance between the two I set them down at once as mother and son. The woman was past forty, but although time and exposure to hardships of every description, together with inclement weather, had made great ravages, she still preserved the vestiges of former beauty, as the faded rose-leaf retains the perfume which was diffused throughout the air.

Their interview with Mr. Jarvis was a long one, but my stock of patience was inexhaustible. I knew how to wait, and if many an applicant for office possessed half the power of long suffering that I do, he would have waited himself into place long ago. There is nothing like patient waiting. Its efficacy is grand. If you are in the Church, and you wish to bore your patron for a bishop's mitre, wait. Lay siege to him. Never take no for an answer. Sit down on his doorstep if need be. Make yourself an eyesore. Lie in wait for him in the street, in public places, in his own house. Keep him perpetually aware of your existence; and, simply to get rid of you, he will give you the diocese you ask for. If you are in Parliament, and you want a place, be always on your legs, ask impertinent and irrelevant questions; sting the Government like a precocious gadfly; keep your name before the public; take exception to items of supply; worry the Chancellor of the

Exchequer; move for returns; render the Home Secretary's life miserable, and the unanimous chorus of ministers will be, "for God's sake, get rid of him."

And so it is in every walk of life. "Wait, watch, and worry" should be the motto of those who wish to get on; but, above all things, never make the fatal mistake of relying upon innate worth or intrinsic merit. *They* will not obtain you a crust of bread and cheese - no, not if you were dying of hunger.

There happened to be a fair at Twickenham at the time of the Lambrooks' visit to the ex-attorney, and it was to this pretty suburban town that the nomads went after leaving the office of their chief. I followed them to the railway-station, got into the same third-class carriage with them, and, while pretending to be asleep, overheard little scraps of conversation between them, which served to show me how the wind blew.

"He don't bite," observed the man Lambrook.

"We can't tell yet," replied the woman.

"Jacob don't know what to make of him."

"We'll work him - don't you fear, my lord." This was said with a smile.

"My lord!" echoed the young man. "Oh! ain't that fine? I thought I should have died a-laughing when you first put me fly to it."

"Don't talk so loud."

"What are you afraid on?"

"Never mind; it's just as well to keep a quiet tongue in your head."

"You're always a-going on at me, mother."

"Oh! don't talk - I'm upset."

With a growl, the young gipsy looked out of the window. As for me, I rejoiced secretly, for I had discovered what I very much wanted to know, that they were mother and son, and that their claim was entirely spurious, and trumped up for the purposes of extortion. At Twickenham they got out, and walked moodily to a small close near the river, which was filled with tents and caravans. I noticed their entry into a caravan, and feeling sure of finding them again the next day, should I want them, I strolled through the fair; and at the invitation of a hirsute man, with a huge gong before him, entered a show. I did not know what the entertainment was to consist of. If I had been aware of its nature I should not have gone in. When the benches were well filled, a man appeared on the stage with an iron cage in which were three live rats. I looked at this carelessly, wondering what he was going to do, when I all at once recognised Lambrook the gipsy. A nice situation, certainly, I thought, for the claimant to the peerage of Northend. No doubt he did not allow - perhaps his pecuniary resources, which were, unhappily, limited, would not permit of his doing so - his ambitious designs to interfere with his professional avocations. Amidst the sounding of the resonant gong and the shrill treble of an antiquated trumpet he proceeded to business. Taking one of the rats by the nape of the neck, he withdrew it from the cage, and to my inexpressible disgust, attacked it with his teeth, breaking its neck and killing it. The unutterable horror of his next performance was so shocking even to my somewhat callous nature that I have always preserved a vivid recollection of so filthy an occurrence. He tore off the animal's legs, and made believe that he was eating them. The blood trickled down his lips, and the crunching of the bones was plainly audible. I could bear it no longer, but rushed from the place. I was told afterwards that this sort of amusement is very popular with the lower orders, who gloat over such scenes. Where are the officers of the Society for the Prevention of Cruelty to Animals? I thought large sums are given them every year. Why do they not look to these atrocities?

Certainly, the Peerage would have been honoured by the accession of Mr. Lambrook to the dignity of the Barony of Northend.

Having made all the discoveries I was desirous of making, I thought it better to put a stop at once to the nefarious practices of Mr. Jacob Jarvis. I saw him at his offices, which he had taken for one month merely for an address to impress Lord Northend. He gained his living by his connexion with the fair people. It was necessary that some one should take the land upon which the fair was held, and as there are fairs every week in different parts of the country, it became an onerous duty. Jarvis would pay so many pounds for the accommodation, and let the ground off to the different showmen at so much a yard. By this means he made a tolerable living. While in the neighbourhood of Lord Northend's estate, his fertile brain conceived the idea of extorting money from that nobleman through the ingenious mode he had already essayed. He pitched upon the Lambrooks, and, as I had surmised, made them his tools. These particulars Zitella Lambrook afterwards supplied me with. Mr. Jacobs looked at me rather timidly as he opened the door and admitted me.

"Are you an attorney, Mr. Jacobs?" I said.

"Why do you ask?" he replied, eyeing me keenly.

"Because I have a little business which I should like to confide to some trustworthy person."

"I am not an attorney," he replied; "but I dare say I could assist you by my experience and knowledge of legal matters. Pray who recommended me to you?"

"Lord Northend," I said, calmly, but distinctly. The reply took Mr. Jacob Jarvis completely by surprise.

"Who are you?" he said, "and why do you come here?"

"Merely to make a few inquiries respecting Mrs. Lambrook and her amiable son, who I am given to understand are friends of yours."

"What business is it of yours to know anything about them?"

"Perhaps," I replied, carelessly, "I take an interest in enterprising people, or I may be in some way connected with the police."

"The police!" he almost screamed. "Do they employ women?"

"Sometimes," I said; "when they think it necessary to do so."

A pause ensued, during which Mr. Jacobs walked uneasily up and down the room. At last he exclaimed - "I'm afraid I am stumped out. What do you mean to do?"

"Nothing, provided we hear no more of this imaginary peer. If we do, Mr. Jarvis, we shall indict your friends the Lambrooks and yourself for conspiracy at the Central Criminal, when Mr. Lambrook's fondness for rats will not improve his character."

"I'll drop it," he replied, eagerly. "I can see the game's up, more's the pity, as I did think I should get a cool thousand out of it. Well, I never yet cried over spilled milk, and I ain't going to begin now."

Mr. Jacob Jarvis kept his word; Lord Northend was not again molested. I kept my eye upon Mr. Jarvis, but that gentleman one fine morning took it into his head to go to America, where for his own sake it is to be hoped he conducts his plots and conspiracies in a less bungling manner.

FOUND DROWNED

THE PRETTY SHOP-GIRL

IN one of the streets at the West-end of London there was a baker's shop, which did a better trade than any of its rivals in the neighbourhood, and this fact was not owing to the intrinsic excellence of its bread, nor the virtue of its flour, nor the flavour of its biscuits - all no doubt excellent in their way; but, nevertheless, not the magnet which attracted customers in shoals. The cause of the baker's prosperity was a pretty girl, whom he employed in his shop to wait upon those who came in, and stand behind the counter. Her name was Laura Harwell; she belonged to poor parents, who, unable to keep her at home, were glad to see her earning an honest livelihood by her own exertions. Laura was unquestionably very beautiful. She was not one of those languishing fair ones, with delicate faces, white complexions, liquid blue eyes, and sandy eyebrows. Nor was she one of those queens of tragedy, those majestic creatures who glory in their length of black hair, which, when unrolled, is often to the touch as coarse as a horse's mane; with flashing eyes which throw back scorn for scorn; and when they love, conceive an undying passion, which is much too sentimental to be agreeable to the recipient of it. Laura was simply a well-made, plump, pretty little woman, going on for nineteen. Her hair was of a darkish-brown colour; but its texture was as soft as that of floss-silk. Her teeth were as white as pieces of lump-sugar. Her eyes were hazel, and what are called laughing eyes. Her nose had a narrow escape of being a snub, and she had the most charming dimple in her chin that ever one saw. An amiable expression pervaded her countenance, which had not the slightest pretension to be called angelic. It was much too good-natured, fat, and rosy for that. You could see she was a daughter of earth at the first glance, just as much as Eve or Helen. I don't know whether the beholder would have been tempted to do as much for her as was done for those two historic ladies, through one of whom man gained a heritage of toil and labour - elegantly but graphically called the sweat of his brow; and for the other a ten-years' bloody war waged.

As the shop in which she worked was situated in a leading thoroughfare, much frequented by the votaries of fashion, men noticed the pretty shop-girl through the window, and got to talk about her. The penny-bun trade increased to a wonderful extent for it used to be a favourite pastime with gentlemen who had nothing better to do with their time to stroll up from their lodgings and their clubs to buy penny buns at Wilcox's - which was the name of the baker who happened to be the fortunate possessor of the services of Laura Harwell. Laura tolerated the well-bred staring of which she was the object with becoming gravity, and if a beau more venturesome than his fellows went so far as to ask her to accompany him to the theatre or for a walk, she replied that she never went out after dark. So steadfast was her resolution in this respect that she acquired new celebrity as an impregnable rock of virtue. And those who would not come to look at Hebe, came to gaze upon a modern Claudia.

There was an apprentice at Mr. Wilcox's named Stephen Bardsley. He was a devoted admirer of Laura's, and he made no secret of his attachment to her. He was a good, honest, horny-handed fellow, and a great favourite with his master, owing to his steady habits of untiring industry, and his general good behaviour. He rather encouraged his preference for Laura, saying that the lad, who was just out of his teens, would some day make her a good husband; and when they had served a few years longer he would be the first to give them a helping hand. Laura did not snub her ingenuous lover. She did not think herself too good for him; on the contrary, she smiled upon his simple addresses, and usually went out with him on Sundays, which, amongst the poorer classes, is not, as might be expected, a sign of being engaged to one another; but that they are standing in those peculiar relations called "passive company." Stephen Bardsley looked forward to the time when he could call Laura his own with the utmost expectation, and prophesied that it would be the proudest moment of his life when he dared to speak with trembling voice upon this momentous subject. Laura smilingly checked him, telling him that there was plenty of time for the consideration of so weighty a subject. Stephen would, when his night's baking was over, write silly sonnets, and slip them under the door of Laura's bedroom, so that she might see them directly she woke up. She used to read them and put them away in the drawer of the dressing-table, amongst various superannuated articles of a woman's toilet. "An ode to Laura," written while the dough was rising, would repose side by side with an empty wooden box, which, from its aroma, once held tooth-powder; and "A few Lines, hastily scribbled while the muffins were in the oven," would clash with an old pin-paper or a piece of chalk.

The fame of Laura Harwell penetrated to the ears of Sir Castle Clewer, who was the foremost rake and libertine of the age: and he determined to pay a visit to the baker's shop and see if she merited the reputation she had attained. He saw her, took a fancy to her, and vowed that before long he would teach her to love him. His friends, on hearing his determination, told him that he was embarking on a perilous enterprise which in the end would demonstrate his tastes. He laughed at their monitions and said that he was too old a hand to be frightened off the scent by an affectation of virtue, which was a quality he did not believe any woman possessed if she was properly handled. This coarse speech denoted the utter absence of morality from the man's nature, and demonstrated the libertinism of his nature beyond the power of contradiction. Sir Castle Clewer was not one of those who go fiercely to work when they undertake an enterprise; his was the slow way and sure. As long as there was a chance of success he did not care whether the success came in six weeks or six months, but when he once embarked in a thing he considered his reputation staked upon the result, and he consequently became a most formidable antagonist to cope with. In total ignorance of the design of the serpent who was about to invade his Paradise, Stephen Bardsley worked on bravely, labouring like Jacob when he served his seven years for Rachel, and Laura served the customers with the innocence of a ringdove.

CHAPTER II

CAUGHT AT LAST

THE first intimation that I had that there ever was such a being in existence as the pretty shop-girl was through a paragraph in the newspaper, and the universal excitement which followed its appearance. It was headed with the true sensational headed type, "Found Drowned. - This morning at an early hour, as some park rangers were passing by the Serpentine, they discovered the body of a female floating upon the surface of the water. Drags were procured and the unfortunate female brought to land. She was promptly taken to the receiving-house of the Royal Humane Society, and there awaited identification by her friends. In the course of an hour or so the body was visited by numbers of people and at length recognised by Mr. Wilcox, a baker, in whose employ she had been for many months. Her name was Laura Harwell, better known as the 'Pretty Shop-girl.' There were sundry marks of violence about her person which led to the belief that she had been the victim of foul play. The case is in the hands of the police, who are actively at work. Government, it is reported, will offer a reward of 100*l.* for the apprehension of Laura Harwell's murderer, should it prove that she has been the victim of a crime."

After reading the paragraph attentively, I made up my mind to compete for the reward, and discover the circumstances attendant upon the death of the "pretty shop-girl," but which were at present shrouded in impenetrable mystery.

By dint of pushing investigation and constant inquiries, I learnt all the facts related in the preceding chapter. But my first care was to go down to the receiving-house on the banks

of the Serpentine, and form my own opinion upon the state
in which the girl was when taken out of the water. I found her
lying upon a bed, just as she was when first discovered. They
had not removed a single article of her attire. I set my face at
once against a theory of suicide, because there was not that
resolute expression upon her features, which is made up of the
resignation of despair, and a firmness superinduced by extreme
misery. Her face was convulsed as if she had perished in a state
of great terror. Her dress was torn and otherwise disarranged,
finding one ground for the supposition that prior to her
immersion in the water there had been a struggle between herself and her murderer. Her wrists were discoloured, showing
that they had been tightly grasped. There could be no doubt
whatever that the unfortunate girl had been foully murdered.
By whom? was the next question which arose. I walked slowly
back through the park, meeting crowds of people on my way
who were going towards the place where the crime had been
committed, animated by a morbid curiosity which did them
very little credit. Probably a reed shaken by the wind, if the
incident had been noticed in a newspaper, would have proved
equally attractive to them. For the mob there is no magnet so
powerful as blood. Shed blood by drops and they turn the matter over admiringly, shed it by bucketfuls and they go frantic
over it. It is much more interesting than a royal procession, or a
Drawing-room, or the opening of Parliament, or the arrival in
London of a patriotic hero. When you are hanged the women
turn out in force to see you, and there is hardly one who does
not pity you and regard you more as a martyr than a criminal.
So much for the effect of capital punishment on the people. I
pondered over the cruel fate of the pretty shop-girl without
arriving at an elucidation of the mystery. How could I? At

present I was ignorant of the main facts and leading incidents of her history. These, however, I was not long in gleaning. I must confess that my suspicions fell upon Sir Castle Clewer. It appeared from what I heard that the baronet had been indefatigable in his attentions - perhaps it would be more correct to say, his persecutions - to Laura Harwell; and that on the evening of the murder she had consented to dine with him. They had gone out together. They had dinner at a fashionable tavern at Richmond, and the baronet's coachman deposed that he put them down at the entrance to the park, which he saw them enter arm-in-arm. The girl appeared happy and joyous. Stephen Bardsley had disappeared, he was nowhere to be found. Mr. Wilcox declared that he had gone out on the evening of the murder shaking his fists and talking incoherently. He did not return that night, and he had not been seen since. It was a case full of perplexity. I was positive that one of the two men - either Sir Castle Clewer or Stephen Bardsley - must have committed the murder, but the difficulty was to say which was the actual culprit. As I have before observed, I inclined to the belief that the guilt rested upon the shoulders of Sir Castle Clewer. He was in amatory affairs quite unscrupulous, and accustomed to throw himself into sudden transports of rage which were by no means creditable to him. While in a state of mental fury it was more than likely that he had so far forgotten himself as to have perpetrated the crime of which I was prepared to accuse him. Yet it was strange that Stephen Bardsley should have disappeared as he had done. If he had not dreaded something he would have remained to face the coroner and abide the result of the inquest. In a conversation I had with Colonel Warner I strongly advised the immediate arrest of Sir Castle Clewer. "Let us arrest him on suspicion," I said.

"Does it seem to you that we have sufficient grounds to go upon?" he replied.

"Certainly it does. Is it not proved beyond the power of contradiction that they went out together? He was seen with the murdered girl."

"That is all very true, but I have seen Sir Castle Clewer and had his explanation."

"What does he say?"

"He admits that he was in the girl's society, and that they entered the park together. When half way over she entreated him to leave her. She would rather run home by herself. If any of the neighbours saw her with him they would immediately scandalize and calumniate her. 'Is that your only reason?' said Sir Castle Clewer. She looked confused. He attributed her confusion to her fear of meeting Stephen Bardsley, of whom he had heard. Yielding to her earnest solicitations he left her. She ran swiftly like a young deer through the park, and he soon lost sight of her in the haze of a summer's evening. He returned to his house, and was intensely surprised to hear of the terrible catastrophe which had evidently happened during the night."

"Do you believe his version of the affair?"

"I see no reason to disbelieve it."

"You forget he is an interested party?"

"Yes; but I can generally form a shrewd opinion from a man's manner. Sir Castle Clewer who, in spite of his faults, is in every respect a most polished gentleman, said to me in the most earnest, and apparently truthful manner, 'I give you my word, Colonel Warner, that I know no more than yourself about the means by which this poor girl came to her end. I am perfectly willing to undergo an examination.' "

"That was explicit," I said.

"I thought it so; but to-morrow, as you are aware, the inquest is held. He will be interrogated by counsel on the occasion, and the jury will give in their verdict. If they find him guilty, he will at once be taken into custody; out of consideration for him, I thought it better to leave him at large until that time, more especially as he is closely watched, and cannot by any possibility escape. I repeat that I do not think Sir Castle Clewer is the murderer of Laura Harwell."

"I disagree with you," I replied; "but I admit there is much in Stephen Bardsley's behaviour which requires clearing up."

"If you take my advice, Mrs. Paschal," exclaimed the colonel, "you will do what I am going to suggest."

I replied, "I should be glad to take into consideration any suggestion he liked to throw out."

"Very well. Here you have it, then, in these words: - Follow up Bardsley; numerous officers are already on his track, but the glory of his capture may yet be reserved for you."

I left Colonel Warner fully determined to take his advice. It was no use following Sir Castle Clewer because he had not attempted to conceal himself; he had adopted a line of defence and expressed himself perfectly willing to adhere to it. Some credit, if nothing else, was to be acquired through the capture of Stephen Bardsley. I did not believe him to be the guilty man; but his apprehension would further the ends of justice. I paid a visit to Mr. Wilcox, the baker, whose house was now more celebrated than ever, and he furnished me with full particulars respecting his missing apprentice. He told me his height, the colour of his hair, and the shape of his features. When I considered myself sufficiently well posted up in these important details, I began my operations.

For some time I could learn nothing of Stephen Bardsley. The inquest had been held, and the evidence so clear against Sir Castle Clewer, that the baronet was, by the verdict of the jury, committed to take his trial for wilful murder. Popular indignation rose high, and he was, owing to his well-known immoral character, universally looked upon as the destroyer of Laura Harwell. A fortnight had to elapse before his trial at the Old Bailey, and if condemned to death, another fortnight would pass before the law took its course. He had then, if no miracle intervened to save him, on a moderate computation, about a month and a few days to live. Much could be done in that time, and as there was a doubt as to the baronet's guilt until Bardsley was arrested, I determined to do all I could to effect the seizure of the runaway apprentice. Popular feeling took a different turn after a time, and the police were loudly blamed for their inability to lay their hands upon Bardsley; but still the baronet was in imminent peril.

One evening I happened to be passing along the Strand; it was close upon ten o'clock, and quite dark. There is a small street or place with a sloping pavement which leads down to what are called the Adelphi arches. As I went by I heard the harsh voice of a policeman, who was telling some one to expedite his movements, and go on with greater celerity. Turning round, and going a small distance down the declivity, I watched the scene which was taking place between the officer and the vagrant. I was frequently in the habit of doing this, for I never liked to hear of a policeman exceeding his duty, which some of them are very apt to do occasionally. My vigilance, and that of some others with whom I was acquainted, exercised a salutary check upon those constables who, from innate malignity or a brutal nature, were in the habit of treating coarsely all the unfortunates with whom they came in contact.

The man who was being driven along by the policeman was in the shadow caused by an angle of the wall, so that I could not see him very plainly. Posting myself near a gas-lamp, I waited until he should come within the scope of its rays. When he did so I looked at him steadily. His face was pale and attenuated; he had evidently been trying to get a night's lodging in the arches, ignorant of the police regulation, which forbids any such proceeding. A constable is always on duty to drive beggars and vagrants out of the vaults, which are cold looking and uninviting, but which nevertheless afford a tolerable shelter to the homeless wanderer when the snow is on the ground, the water congealed into ice, owing to the severity of the frost and the inclemency of the weather. So many harrowing tales were told, once upon a time, about poor creatures who obtained a night's lodging in the Adelphi arches, that the municipal authorities bestirred themselves, thinking it a scandal to the parish and humanity, and so the pariahs of civilization were driven to some other covert. The blemish was removed, but not eradicated, as I can testify.

As I continued to look on the vagrant who, from the condition of his clothing, was a perfect tatterdemalion, I thought I saw some resemblance between him and my conception of Stephen Bardsley. I was unable to speak distinctly, but if the stoop in the back had been corrected the height corresponded with the standard I had been supplied with. His hair, although unkempt and dirty, was of a light brown, and one or two other trifling peculiarities made me think that I had succeeded in finding the clue at last. I was never hasty or precipitate; had I been so I could have at once ordered him into custody on suspicion, but I thought it would be advisable to follow him and watch his movements. From the inflamed state of his eyes I could see that he had been drinking deeply.

He passed me by and staggered into the Strand. I was close upon his heels. He wandered about in a purposeless manner - going a short distance and then suddenly retracing his steps, as if he did not know what to do. Two hours ran away in this uninteresting pursuit. But still, with the pertinacity and indefatigable industry of an Indian scout, I trod in his footsteps. He left the town at last and walked in the direction of some suburb. I was completely out of my reckoning. I still followed him. In the course of time he reached a cemetery. Standing still, he scanned the lofty gates in a contemplative manner, and then clambered up them with the agility of a wild-cat, descending on the other side without in any way hurting himself. My going after him was out of the question, so I looked about for some easier mode of entrance. A bell-handle caught my eye, and it immediately occurred to me that it communicated with the lodge of some man appointed to watch the cemetery. I lost no time in ringing the bell, and was rewarded for my effort by hearing a loud jangling, which was followed by the appearance of a sleepy-looking man, whose indignant glances demonstrated pretty clearly that he had an invincible objection to being disturbed in the midst of a sound slumber. He held a lantern in his hand, and flashed its light upon me through the lens of a bull's-eye. I was nearly blinded by the vivid rays, and edged a little on one side to avoid them.

"What's your business?" exclaimed the night-porter, in a voice more distinguishable for its gruffness than its melody.

I at once replied that I was connected with the police, and was following an offender who had taken refuge in the cemetery. I ended by calling upon the porter to render me all the assistance he could, and to at once admit me to the cemetery. Rather surprised at my story, but believing the truth of it through the earnestness of my demeanour, he opened a small gate constructed in one of the larger ones, and I was quickly standing by his side on the neatly gravelled walk.

"Which way did he go?" asked the porter.

"That I can't say; it was too dark to see."

"In that case we had better go up the main road to the catacombs."

Walking at a rapid pace, we did as he had suggested. The catacombs were a long range of semicircular vaults, surmounted by a double Ionic screen, which formed a series of cloisters. The moon suddenly broke from a bank of clouds which had hitherto concealed it, and a shower of silvery light descended, illuminating the scene with a bright radiance. A dusky figure flitting between the cloisters, now concealed by a pillar, now clearly revealed as it crossed an open space, caught my attention.

"There he is," I cried.

"Where?" demanded the porter, turning on his lantern, and following its light on the spot indicated by my finger.

In a moment the figure reappeared, and the porter led the way up some steps into the cloisters; but although we threaded their mazes with great care we could discover no trace of the man we were in search of. The porter turned a shade pale. I am not prepared to say that he stood in solemn terror of ghosts, but he might have supposed we were following a vampire, which some years ago was solemnly believed in by the sextons and grave-diggers of Paris, who in their ignorance took wily doctors and skilful resurrectionists for bad spirits - who, like the Eastern ghosts, were fond of human flesh after it was dead and buried.

We reached the entrance to the catacombs. The porter threw a flash of light upon the entrance. There was no door to the entrance to the vault, because in the daytime any one was at liberty to promenade the gloomy space, and in melancholy mood to feast upon the spectacle of frail humanity gone to its long account.

The porter proposed that we should investigate the interior of the catacombs. I made no opposition to his suggestion, and we accordingly did so. Long rows of coffins piled up one on the top of the other with the regularity of bodies in an Egyptian mummy house caught my eye, but I turned away from them with an involuntary shudder. We had not proceeded far before we heard the sound of footsteps. Our own must have struck upon the ear of the person preceding us, just as his were heard by us. He stopped to listen; we did the same. Apparently dissatisfied - perhaps terrified at what he must have considered a supernatural occurrence - he took to his heels and ran with amazing velocity along the dismal passages. The rays of the moon penetrated through small slits like loopholes made in the wall to let in air and light, and guided by these he made his way out of the catacombs as he had entered them; we were not far behind him. I felt firmly persuaded that the man I had pursued to the cemetery was before us, and I redoubled my exertions. Puffing and panting, the night-porter, who was, I thought by his hard breathing, slightly given to asthma, led the way. The moonlight plainly revealed the chase who was leading across country - if the expression may be used without profanity, for he was jumping over graves in a scientific manner. All at once he disappeared - we could see nothing of him. I rubbed my eyes thinking I was the sport of some hallucination. A loud laugh from the porter made me turn towards him for an explanation.

"We've tired our 'coon at last," he said, laughing louder than ever.

"How is that?" I demanded.

"So you hear nothing?"

"I thought I heard a splash."

"That's right."

"But how does that explain the mystery?"

"Easy enough; he's fell into a new-made grave with upwards of three feet of water in it; if that don't cool him, I'm a Dutchman."

I now began to understand. The man had not looked before him - the consequence of his inattention being that he made acquaintance with a formidable pit, going down into the grave literally and not figuratively. Coming up to the pit and looking over the side, we saw him crouching down with the water up to his chin. I called to him to stand upright, and we would pull him out. He replied in faint tones that he could not move, he was afraid his leg was broken. After some search and trouble the porter found a ladder, which he let drop into the grave. Descending by this, he pulled the man up by main force, and laid him, all dripping wet, upon the green sward. He could not stand, and in his sorry plight, presented a pitiable spectacle. It was as he had surmised - his leg was broken.

"Who are you, and where are you going to take me?" he murmured.

"I am a detective," I replied, promptly.

At hearing this declaration he uttered a scream of terror.

"I arrest you on a charge of murder," I continued.

"Murder!" he shrieked; "whose murder?"

"The murder of Laura Harwell."

"It's false, I didn't do it."

"I must warn you not to say anything that may criminate yourself, because it will be used against you afterwards in evidence."

"Hang him," he cried; "let him swing for it. What matter who did it. Let him swing for it."

"Who?" I asked.

"Sir Castle Clewer; he stole her heart from me - curse him. That's what drove me to it."

"Again I must caution you," I said, temperately, feeling sure that I had limed the right bird. The last incautious admission proved to my mind incontestably that I had all along been upon a false scent. The wincing, crippled, ragged wretch before me was Stephen Bardsley, and he was the real culprit.

With some trouble we got him out of the cemetery, and with the assistance of a policeman removed him to the nearest station-house. The result of Stephen Barnsley's examination fully acquitted Sir Castle Clewer. The unhappy apprentice owned his guilt, and said that he had been driven to the commission of the crime through jealousy. He was hanged at Newgate, amidst a unanimous shout of execration, for every breast was full of pity and commiseration for the pretty shop-girl, Laura Harwell, who, amidst the astonishment of every one, had been found drowned.

FIFTY POUNDS REWARD

MRS. WILKINSON

JOHN ESKELL was as fine a fellow as ever put a quill behind his ear. Not having been born with a silver spoon in his mouth, he was obliged to work for his living, which he was not ashamed of. He had no silly pride about him, such as some people affect. He thought himself quite as good a man as my Lord Tom Noddy, and he paid his way, which is a thing my Lord T. N. has frequently a disinclination to do. He received a hundred and fifty pounds a year from Messrs. Nugget, Gold, and Co., the eminent bankers of Lombard-street, at whose place of business he punctually made his appearance every morning at ten. There was not a man more regular in his attendance than Mr. Eskell, who was generally considered a rising young man. At the age of four-and-twenty he contracted a marriage with his cousin, a pretty little woman enough, with an engaging manner, but without any mind. She was a bad manager, as John Eskell was subsequently to find, to his cost; in common language, a muddler. If it had not been for their only servant and housekeeper, Louisa would have often been in a great strait, but Mrs. Buzz was a clever woman, and although she did not think much of her mistress's administrative ability, she was wont to make allowances and palliate offences against domestic economy, by saying, "There's always a something."

John used to laugh at the persistency with which the old lady reiterated her favourite phrase, and when he reflected upon his wife's shortcomings, he got into Mrs. Buzz's way of thinking, and muttered to himself, "There's always a something."

The Eskells lived at Bow, because it was handy to the City, and John saved the expense of an omnibus by walking to and from his house and Lombard-street every morning and evening.

John's cottage, which was pleasantly situated, stood him in eighteen pounds a year; the taxes were not heavy, and he managed to get along pretty well in spite of his baby wife's unintentional extravagance. He had a small plot of garden-ground, in which he grew cabbages and potatoes, and mustard and cress, together with various herbs, which all came in handy, and served to lessen the length of the greengrocer's bill; but Louisa wanted sadly to tear up the esculents and plant flowers and shrubs, and John was so fond of her, that he would have allowed her to do it if she had bothered him into it. Louisa had her pets. One was a little dog of the terrier species; a sweet pretty little thing, with a wonderfully sleek coat and thin hair, and an excellent tan, which, for some reason or other, she called Porkins. Another was a Guineapig, which played great ravages amongst John's cabbages, and from the peculiar noise he made, he was called "Week-week." Porkins was a greater favourite than Week. He had a house all to himself and a cushion to lie upon. The third and last pet was Brunow the house-dog. He was a great, rough shaggy dog, with long curly hair, and he would lie outside upon the doorstep and bark at everybody who came near the place. Brunow was a great coward, and would bite no one, although he made a great noise. The postman and the newspaper man were always in a great state of terror when they saw Brunow, who always rushed at their legs and made them believe he was going to bite them, and they put thorough credence in his hostile demonstrations, and then Brunow would go back to his place, lick his paws, and laugh at them.

Mrs. Buzz had been John Eskell's father's housekeeper until he died. Then she had lived with his widow, but when she followed her husband to the grave, Mrs. Buzz threw in her lot with her son, whom she loved for old associations' sake. She did not much like animals.

The worthy woman was more like one of the family than a servant. She generally sat in the sitting-room in the evening with John and his wife, and was privileged to say anything that she liked. She had saved a little money during her life, and she used to buy what things she wanted, out of the interest of the small sum she had in the bank - always steadily refusing to receive one halfpenny in the shape of wages from John. Now and then she received handsome presents; that handsome Paisley shawl she wore on Sundays came from John; so did that black silk dress. Consequently if she did not get her wages in malt, she got them in meal; with regard to Mrs. Eskell and her pets, Mrs. Buzz used to say, "I can't abear the fawning things myself; but, lor'! there's always a something. Let her wait till she's been married a year or so, and then maybe she'll have something more worth her cuddling and kissing."

Louisa used to blush at this, and reply -

"Mrs. Buzz, you shouldn't."

And John would kiss his little wife tenderly, and earnestly hope Mrs. Buzz might turn out a true prophet. After which Louisa would take her pet on her lap, and toss him up and down amidst snarls and snaps, and say - "Was it 'ittle Porkin's dog, 'ittle beauty!"

"I'd beauty it," growled Mrs. Buzz, "But there, it ain't no use talking, there's always a something."

Laura was very much in the habit of talking amicably to the tradespeople, who would ask her into their parlours when she went to pay the bills. If she had been a man she would have been an excellent prey for skittle-sharpers.

One of the tradespeople Mrs. Buzz very much disapproved of, and that was Mrs. Wilkinson, whose husband kept a pork and butter shop. Wilkinson was a man who found more entertainment in betting circles than he did in attending to his business. He was accustomed with gross indelicacy to speak before his wife as he would have done before his sporting friends, and the consequence was that her mind became vitiated, and her manners contaminated. She was an adept in the slang of the prize-ring and the race-course, and she frequently uttered the most disgusting speeches in the presence of her servants and her guests. She was enormously stout, and to such a size did her corpulence extend, that at the first glance the beholder imagined he was regarding a phenomenon who by some accident had escaped from the caravan in which she was carted from fair to fair, to be shown to the curious as a monstrous mass of humanity, whose adipose tissue had grown to a size altogether beyond reasonable or decent limits. In a house in which beetles abounded she would have been invaluable, for few of the poor insects could have effected their escape from the crushing tread of those huge feet, which more resembled the hoofs of an elephant or a gouty rhinoceros than the lower extremities of a woman. The bloated and swollen lumps of flesh which in her composition represented hands, were like patches of dough formed into half-quartern loaves before they were subjected to the heat of the oven. Her face might have been made by the amalgamation of two turnips and a pumpkin, with two pig's eyes deeply sunk in the fatty mass. Nature was to blame for having created such a monstrosity, or if creation was unavoidable, for permitting it to cumber the earth, whose surface groaned beneath the imposition. Her voice was hoarse like that of a raven, and when she endeavoured to talk, her verbal efforts resulted in dismal croaks that a jackdaw with a sore throat would have indignantly disdained. The grand climacteric was attained by an unpleasant way she had of twitching her upper lip when she spoke. This action was so repulsive that you turned away with an irrepressible shudder, thinking that the palm of hideousness should be accorded to so ungainly a creature.

This woman, by some unaccountable means, obtained an extraordinary influence over Louisa Eskell. This was the more to be regretted because, until she had the misfortune to come in contact with one who in every way deserves the epithet of moral leper, there was not a purer minded, or a woman of a better disposition than Louisa. At first it must be confessed that the young wife shrank with instinctive dread from the mountainous mass; but with characteristic cunning, Mrs. Wilkinson hid her real nature under a specious mask until it should suit her purpose to drag the frail covering away, and show herself a female prophet of Khorassan. Her husband frequently made large sums of money by backing dogs, and horses, and men. He was never so happy as when watching the work of disfigurement and mutilation. Two men battering one another's faces out of the semblance of humanity; two dogs tearing, worrying, and biting the life out of their miserable carcases; a score or two of rats expiring under the practised fangs of their canine executioners, raised a half inebriated smile to his lips, and transported him into a sort of blackguard heaven, where brutal instincts revel and expand. Of such a callous nature, and so indifferent to the sufferings of others was his wife, that nothing delighted her so much as to see one animal tormented by another, and she frequently desecrated the sanctity of the Sabbath by permitting a sanguinary contest between ferocious dogs, who were hounded on to kill, and slay, and battle to the death, to gratify the cruel and morbid feelings of those who were raised but a very little above them in the scale of creation.

Mrs. Wilkinson obtained large sums from her husband, which he could never have obtained in the way of legitimate trade, and this money she spent in the adornment of her person, declaring, with an oath, that she saw no reason why she should not be as well dressed as the first woman in the land; but with all her lavish extravagance her bad taste shone out at every opening. She could never, in spite of all her efforts, be anything else but what she was - a craven and vulgar woman, one of the lowest and commonest extraction. And this was the person with whom poor, weak-minded Louisa Eskell contracted an intimacy. "Heaven help John!" exclaimed Mrs. Buzz when she remarked their growing acquaintanceship, at which she was so horrified that she was unable to say "there's always a something."

CHAPTER II

A VERY BAD WOMAN

"I WANT to talk to you, my dear," exclaimed John Eskell to his wife one morning, after breakfast, before he started for the Bank.

"I'm busy just now," replied Louisa, petulantly.

She was nursing Porkins - certainly a very important occupation.

"Just one moment," said John, putting on a stern look, altogether unusual to him.

"Oh! how you do bother," returned Louisa. "I wish I'd never married."

"Don't say that, Louey, dear."

"So I do. I ought to have married a gentleman."

"And what is your idea of a gentleman?" asked John, very quietly and composedly.

"Somebody who - who doesn't work."

"Oh! indeed; that definition would amuse the Philological Society. So, because I work for my living I am not a gentleman? How long is it, Louisa, since you imagined I was not good enough for you."

Louisa hung down her head and said nothing. Her attentions to the dog were more vehement than ever.

"Just oblige me by putting that dog down, will you, my dear, and attend to me?" said John.

Louisa complied with her husband's request, saying, as she deposited the dog on the ground, "Poor Porkins! was he driven away from his mother's arms?"

"I am going to talk to you very seriously, Louey," began John. "I have been speaking to Mrs. Buzz, and - - "

"I wish Mrs. Buzz was dead," cried Louisa, angrily.

"Why, Louisa, you surprise me. I never saw a woman so altered in my life as you have become within the last few weeks. What in the name of goodness has happened to you?"

"If you are going to scold me I shall run away."

"Excuse me, but you will not before you have heard what I am going to say to you," said John, with the light of determination in his eyes.

"Make haste, then."

"You have lately made the acquaintance of a woman of whom nobody speaks well."

"I suppose I can choose my own acquaintances?" was the reply.

"Certainly not; I am the proper person to regulate such things, and to tell you who you shall know and who you shall not."

"Indeed!" she exclaimed, slightly elevating her eyebrows; "I was not aware of that before."

"At all events you are now; and I must tell you that I strongly disapprove of your knowing Mrs. Wilkinson."

"She has always been very kind to me."

"That does not matter; I am your husband, Louey, and I consider myself a better judge of those matters than you are."

"I won't be dictated to," said Louisa, stamping her feet on the ground. "If I like to talk to Mrs. Wilkinson I shall."

"If you are disobedient to me, Louisa," replied John, sternly, "your folly will raise a gulf between us which you will never by future submission be able to bridge over."

"I don't care what you say," cried Louisa, in whom the full tide of rebellion seemed to be rapidly rising.

"I should be sorry to think so."

"Why should I? I am your wife, and you must keep me. You have nothing to live upon except what you get from the Bank, so I can always find you."

"Is that what Mrs. Wilkinson has been instilling into your mind," replied John, with a hard, bitter smile.

"Never mind who told me: a wife ought to be mistress in her own house, and a woman who submits to a man is little better than a fool. The more she does submit the more she will have to knock under."

"I am very sorry indeed to see this, Louisa," said John, gravely. "If this sort of behaviour on your part continues, I shall send you home to your mother."

"You can't, because I won't go, and you mustn't hit me, because I can give you six months for it," replied Louisa, triumphantly.

"Can it be possible?" exclaimed John, in amazement.

"And you can't keep Mrs. Wilkinson out of the house either, because you're not at home always, and she comes when you are away," continued Louisa, who proved herself an apt pupil.

"If I saw Mrs. Wilkinson I should probably tell her what I thought of her conduct. She ought to be ashamed of herself to corrupt so young and innocent a mind as yours."

A knock was heard at the door. Louisa ran to the window to look out, and exclaimed, "There is Mrs. Wilkinson. You can say what you like to her."

John turned a shade paler and walked to the door. He met Mrs. Buzz in the passage, who was going to answer the summons, but he waved her back with his hand, saying -

"It is that bad woman."

When he opened the door, Mrs. Wilkinson said -

"Is Mrs. Eskell in?"

"May I ask who I am talking to?" demanded John.

"Oh! my name's Wilkinson, if you want to know," she replied; "and I suppose you're Louisa's husband."

"I am," replied John, "and I beg to inform you that your visits at my house are not desirable."

"That don't matter," she exclaimed; "I don't come to see you."

"I am perfectly aware of that; but it is my wish and my determination that your visits to my wife shall cease."

"Oh! stand on one side; don't talk to me," said Mrs. Wilkinson. "I hate a parcel of men jawing and cackling."

"I am sorry, but I cannot allow you to enter my house," replied John, firmly, with a strange light in his eyes.

"Oh, but I must. You'll like me well enough when you know me."

"I am of a different opinion."

"Now don't you stand there and insult me," she cried, impudently. "If you do I'll get my husband to break every bone in your body."

"Will you oblige me by going away?"

"No, I wont, and that's flat."

"Mrs. Buzz," said John, "go for a policeman."

Mrs. Buzz went down the kitchen stairs, and out the area-way on a mission she found most congenial to her feelings.

"You'll send for a policeman for me, will you?" exclaimed Mrs. Wilkinson, in a towering passion. "Louisa, why don't you come out? Do you see what this low fellow's done?"

Up to the present time Louisa had listened to the altercation in silence, hardly knowing what to do; but now she came out in the passage, and said to John, "Let her in. She has come to see me; you must be a tyrant not to let me have a single acquaintance."

"I disapprove of this woman as an acquaintance for you," he rejoined.

"This woman! If you put me out," cried Mrs. Wilkinson, "you'll repent it, I can tell you. I'm not going to be insulted by any clerk in the City. It's hard enough to be cheeked by a gentleman; but from a man like you, why, I can't stand it. I'll smash all the windows in the place. My husband's always got twenty or thirty pounds put by, and he wont mind paying for any little amusement of mine."

"Let her come in," said Louisa; "she will do as she says; she's not afraid of anybody."

"I certainly shall not," replied John. "I shall oppose violence by violence, and if this woman makes a blackguard of herself she must take the consequences."

"You take that first," said Mrs. Wilkinson, striking him in the face; "that's how this woman makes a blackguard of herself."

Fortunately for John a policeman at this juncture came up with Mrs. Buzz. He witnessed the assault, and did not hesitate to take Mrs. Wilkinson into custody.

"I must trouble you to come with me," he exclaimed, as John said "I give her in charge."

"All the peelers in London shan't take me," she replied, boldly.

"You'd better come quietly."

"I shan't come at all."

"We'll see about that."

The policemen seized her by the wrist and dragged her down the steps into the street, when she fell down on her back on the pavement, and kicked and screamed, uttering the most awful curses and blasphemous exclamations all the time. It required the aid of two more constables before she was removed. Without speaking to his wife, John accompanied the *cortège* to the police-station, and preferred a charge against her; then he walked moodily to the Bank, where, for the first time in his life he arrived an hour late. He began to see that the clouds were gathering about his hitherto happy home.

CHAPTER III

THE FAGINS

Mrs. Wilkinson, with all her bombastic raving, did not care to dare the terrors of a prison. The magistrate before whom the case was brought, declared that if she were brought before him again on a similar charge he would at once commit her to prison for fourteen days, so she contented herself with carrying on a clandestine intimacy with Mrs. Eskell who, during her husband's absence, often stole down to the shop on the pretence of ordering some butter or eggs. Very frequently she told a palpable falsehood to Mrs. Buzz, whom John had entreated to look after his erratic wife during his unavoidable absence. Mrs. Wilkinson since her *fracas* with John Eskell had imbibed the most violent hatred and detestation for him, and inwardly vowed that she would in some way or other ruin him for life. The means she resorted to were worthy of her devilish ingenuity. She resolved to injure him through his wife. Louisa fell readily into the trap, and was an easy victim. She was urged to dress in a better way than she was in the habit of doing. She was told to go to theatres and places of amusement. "What!" exclaimed Mrs. Wilkinson, "are you always to be shut up in the house with that old frump, Mrs. Buzz?"

It was well that the old frump did not overhear the remark.

"Are you never to have any enjoyment? My old man gives me plenty of money, and lets me do as I like, but then he is not like your husband. He thinks a woman is somebody, and ought to have some relaxation; you must confess yours does not."

"He doesn't study me much," replied Louisa, in an inane manner.

"Of course not. He even grumbles at your having a dog."

"I don't think he likes Porkins much, and he positively hates Week-week, while I saw him kick Brunow the other day for barking, and I called him a beast for doing it."

"Just what I thought."

"I don't deserve it. I am very good to him."

"Any one can see that, my dear," replied Mrs. Wilkinson. "But why do you stand it."

"What can I do?"

"Oh, a thousand things."

"Tell me one?"

"A dozen if you like."

"I wish I knew how to alter it; but you see I am married."

"So am I; yet my husband never attempts to domineer over me. He knows better."

"I am not so strong-minded as you are," said Louisa, with a simper.

"Why should you not be? you only want a little more spirit."

"Will you give me the benefit of your experience? I want some one to advise me."

"Yes, with pleasure."

"I don't think I am treated well."

"Well? I should think not, any one can see that with half an eye."

"I have not been happy for a long time," remarked Louisa, trying to put on a look of long-suffering.

"How could you be? I'm sure my husband and I often talk about you, and he says 'Poor little thing! what a beast he is to her.'"

"Does he really?"

"Should I say so if he didn't. Why, your husband's treatment of you is the subject of conversation all round about!"

"What do they say?" asked Louisa.

"All sorts of things. People will talk, you know, especially in a quiet place like this."

"You know it is a chattering neighbourhood."

"They say amongst other things, since you will know," replied Mr. Wilkinson, "that you are entirely governed by that Mrs. Buzz and that you are no more mistress of your own house than I am."

"That is not true," replied Louisa, with warmth.

"Well, you know best, my dear. I don't want to interfere between you and Mrs. Buzz, although I know one thing."

"What is that?"

"Oh! not much; only if an old woman like that came into my house dictating this and that, she'd go out again a precious sight quicker than ever she came into it."

"I never liked her much."

"I should think not," replied Mrs. Wilkinson, with a cold, sarcastic smile. "I should think not - who could? I never came across such a woman; but you are the fool not to get rid of her. Have you no influence over your husband, or are you his slave?"

"I hope not."

"Do you mean to be his drudge for life?"

"His drudge? I am not a drudge. I don't work."

"I don't know what you call it, then; you are always at his beck and call. You never have a moment that you can call your own. Do you go anywhere?"

"No, I don't; but you must remember that he does not either?"

"What consolation is that to you? If *he* is obliged to work you might enjoy yourself, nevertheless."

"So I might."

This was said in a slightly diffident tone of voice. Louisa was feeling a few pricks of conscience. Her mind's eye pictured honest, hard-working John chained to the ledger and the desk, working to get bread for her, and keep her in indolence and idleness. She fancied him casting up figures and settling accounts with all the indefatigable industry of which she well knew him to be possessed. He never spent any money on himself. Since he had been married he had given up smoking cigars, and if he did smoke, which was seldom, he brought home a modest ounce of bird's-eye, and put it in the bowl of a cheap brier-root. If this was not abnegation of self, what was? He would go out with five shillings in his pocket on Monday morning, and on Monday night he would have half-a-crown left. Didn't that speak of cheap City dinners, and a meritorious pinching which ought to have met with its reward? But Louisa's mind was perverted by evil-counselling, and she had fallen under the influence of a designing serpent, very much as Eve did in Paradise in the days of trees of knowledge of good and evil.

"I am going to the Opera tomorrow night," remarked Mrs. Wilkinson. "Mine brought me some tickets for the stalls. He is always giving me something, and he is not so *very* well off either."

The truth was, that Mr. Wilkinson had made a bet with a theatrical gentleman, and had taken the orders in part payment of the obligation.

"Oh! I should so like to go to the Opera," sighed silly Louisa. "It is a place I have never yet been to."

"Never?" ejaculated her friend in a tone of profound disdain.

"Never."

"Why don't you go, then?"

"In the first place, I haven't the things to go in."

"Get them, then."

"How?" exclaimed Louisa, astonished, in spite of herself.

"Why, do a bill."

"I thought married women couldn't sign bills."

Mrs. Wilkinson said, "Oh," and continued, "if you don't like flying a kite, get one of your husband's cheques out of his book and bring it to me."

"What good will that be?"

"Never you mind; bring it to me, and I'll tell you what to do with it."

This proposal took Louisa by surprise, but her innate honesty and goodness of heart would not allow her to suspect any evil, and she listened greedily to the voice of the temptress. Mrs. Wilkinson depicted in flowing, gushing, and grandiloquent language the glories and beauties of the Opera House. According to her description it was a scene of enchantment. Such melody was not to be heard by mortal ears in any other place. Louisa, full of her anxiety to go to the Opera, went home to commit the deed that was to ruin her peace of mind for ever, and involve herself and her husband in difficulties innumerable. John had so much confidence in his wife, that he seldom if ever took the trouble to lock anything up; consequently she went to his desk, and, after a search amongst his papers, found his cheque-book. This, together with a letter in his handwriting, with his signature attached, she took to Mrs. Wilkinson.

"Have you brought the letter, my dear, and the book? Yes; that is all right. Can you imitate John's hand-writing, eh?"

"I don't think I can," replied Louisa, timidly; "wouldn't he be angry if I did!"

"Possibly he might; but you are his wife, and he could do nothing to you; he would look upon it as a joke most likely."

"Do you really think so?"

"Of course he would. He loves you; and if it were your whim or your caprice to imitate his signature, for the fun of the thing, only just to get a little money to go to the Opera with, he would laugh at it, and love you more than ever."

"You forget he is not rich."

"Oh! never mind - fifteen or twenty pounds wont hurt him. It wont make any difference one way or the other."

"I should not mind doing it if I thought so," said Louisa, hesitatingly.

"Don't think one way or the other; take this pen and practice his handwriting on this sheet of paper," replied Mrs. Wilkinson, decisively.

Louisa, ever ready to be led, took up the pen, and placing the letter before her, began to scribble. She was one of

"Those who are born to be controlled;
Who yield to the foremost and the bold."

After about half an hour's practice she succeeded to Mrs. Wilkinson's satisfaction, and produced a very decent forgery. Her friend now tore a cheque out of the book and gave it her to fill up. Never stopping to reflect upon the crime of which she was guilty - for which in days not very remote many a poor fellow has swung upon a gibbet - she imitated her husband's writing to the best of her ability.

"Give me the draft," cried Mrs. Wilkinson, triumphantly. "It will be better for me to get it cashed than that you should try to convert it into money; because in the latter case suspicion would at once fall upon you. I shall take care that it shall be directed into other channels."

Louisa felt sorry after the deed was done, and with tears in her eyes, exclaimed, "I - I don't think I care about going to the Opera, Mrs. Wilkinson; give me back the cheque?"

"What for?" said her friend, elevating her eyebrows in profound amazement.

"To tear it up! I really don't care about the Opera."

"That is a pity."

"Will you give it me?"

"Certainly not; I wont listen to such nonsense," replied Mrs. Wilkinson.

"Oh, do!" pleaded Louisa. "Please do!"

Mrs. Wilkinson went to a drawer in a bureau and took out a handful of gold and some notes, amounting in all to twenty pounds, which she handed over to Louisa, saying, "Take that, my dear; you see I have so much confidence in your husband that I don't at all mind discounting the cheque for you."

"I don't want the money now," sobbed Louisa.

"Why not? A moment ago you were mad after it. Take it and go home. Buy what you want for the Opera to-morrow night, and mind you are ready at six o'clock when I call for you."

"But he will ask where I am going, and where I got the things from," said Louisa, as fresh difficulties rose up before her.

"Then I should let him ask," was the reply, in a tone of frigid indifference.

At last Louisa was persuaded, as she always was, and she walked home in a melancholy mood, in time to replace the letter and the cheque-book before her husband's return. As she left the house, Mrs. Wilkinson took the cheque up in her hand and soliloquized, "Nugget, Gold, and Co." - that's in Lombard-street. It is not a bad forgery. I wonder if he has a balance of twenty pounds there; if not, they will think he is anticipating his salary. I should think he had, though. He is the sort of man who would make a purse on the sly. Won't he be put about when he finds it all out. I'll try it myself the first thing to-morrow morning. If anything happens I shall swear that she gave it me for money lent. Anyhow, I'm all right, if it isn't square with her! Shan't I laugh if it smashes them both up and ends in a separation."

Mrs. Wilkinson forgot one essential particular, which constitutes an important item of our criminal law. She was *de facto* an accomplice both before and after the fact.

The cheque was duly cashed by the cashier at the Bank on presentation, and it was not until the afternoon that the forgery was discovered. Mr. Nugget, who was a great friend of John's, insisted upon offering fifty pounds reward for the detection of the forger, and a notification to that effect was sent to the principal police-offices in London. The case being one of some importance was placed in my hands, and my first care was to call upon Mr. Eskell at his house. He received me with every courtesy, and took me into his private sitting-room, expressing himself not only prepared, but anxious to answer any questions I liked to put to him. My first interrogation was as to the state of his cheque-book, he had looked at that, he said, and he could not see, that a cheque had been removed from it.

"How many cheques ought there to be?" I said.

He told me the number. I counted the existing drafts, and the remains of those which had been torn off, and there was one short.

"I miss one," I exclaimed. "Is it possible that the binder could have made a mistake?"

"We never heard of such an instance."

On receiving this answer I turned to the place in the book where the last cheque had been drawn, and by looking minutely at the binding, I came to the conclusion that a draft had been torn out very neatly and very cleverly.

"A cheque has been removed without your knowledge," I exclaimed.

"Are you sure of that?"

"I have very little doubt upon the subject. Who has access to your desk?"

"Only those I can trust - my wife and my housekeeper."

"Is your housekeeper trustworthy?"

"Thoroughly so, I have every reason to believe. She lived with my father for thirty years."

"And - excuse the question; I know it is a delicate one - your wife?"

"I would trust *her* with my life," he replied with warmth.

"Has she any bad acquaintances - people you disapprove of?" I demanded.

"If the truth must be told, she has one very bad acquaintance."

"Who, and what is she?"

"A Mrs. Wilkinson, the wife of a butterman. I have often had occasion to complain of her, but I am grieved to say that I believe my wife still continues on friendly terms with her."

"Have you noticed any difference in your wife's manner and behaviour lately - that is, since yesterday?"

"She has been shy."

"Where is she now?"

"She has gone out shopping."

"Have you given her any money?"

"I have not; but she has a pound or two at her disposal whenever she wants it."

"Has she been lately in Mrs. Wilkinson's society?" I asked.

"I really cannot say, for a sort of estrangement has lately sprung up between my wife and myself owing to that detestable woman. Perhaps Mrs. Buzz, my housekeeper, can inform us. I will ring the bell for her."

She made her appearance, and took a seat near me without being asked to do so. She always behaved more like the mistress of the house than the servant.

"We are talking about your mistress, Mrs. Buzz," explained John Eskell.

"She has her faults Mr. John, I wont deny that," replied Mrs. Buzz. "But law, there is always a something."

"You are quite right, but I want to know if you saw your mistress go out the day before yesterday, and if so, where did she go to?"

"She went to Mrs. Wilkinson's, sir, and was there the best part of the day, because I slipped on my bonnet and shawl when I saw her go out, and followed her. She came home once about the middle of the day and had a glass of sherry, and then went back again to the butter-shop."

"Did she go into your master's private room?" I asked, calmly.

"Now I come to think of it, she did," said Mrs. Buzz; "she was in and out again, as you may say."

I looked triumphantly at Mr. Eskell, but he averted his eyes in hard set sorrow and chagrin.

"When Mrs. Eskell came back," resumed Mrs. Buzz, "I remarked that she had been crying a little, but I have told her upon my Bible oath upwards of a score of times, that there is no good to be got out of that woman, and I repeat it, sir, although I say it before you, she is no good to anybody."

After this important evidence Mrs. Buzz was dismissed, and Mr. Eskell and myself talked matters over calmly and dispassionately. I advised him to wait until his wife came home. I wanted to see the result of her shopping expedition. When Louisa arrived she seemed tired and out of sorts, and expressed herself very much surprised at seeing her husband, whom she had imagined at the Bank. A cab brought her back - quite an unusual event in her prosaic life, for John's limited income would not permit such extravagances. The vehicle was full of packages. John Eskell regarded them with a critical eye as they were laid on the drawing-room table. Louisa, from her manner, appeared to deprecate any remarks. She would have given worlds if her husband had been out of the way. Very solemnly, and in quite a business-like manner, John cut the string of one of the bundles with his pocket-knife, and turning back the brown paper wrapping, displayed to view a handsome evening dress ready made. The ticket marked with the price was attached to the silk, and it informed us that the fabric had cost four pounds ten shillings. A bill which had been enclosed in the package fell upon the table. It was receipted, and represented a sum total of fourteen pounds. This damning evidence deprived Louisa of the hazardous refuge which she might temporarily have obtained by saying that she received credit for the things she had brought with her.

"Why do you interfere with my purchases?" she exclaimed, trying to be angry, but too sick and faint at heart to succeed in an irate demonstration.

"Because it is my duty as a husband; and I have a right to," replied John Eskell.

"I wish you had Mrs. Wilkinson for a wife, you would not dare to speak to her as you do to me," muttered Louisa.

"Mrs. Wilkinson is a very bad, wicked woman, and she has been your ruin."

"My ruin! What on earth do you mean?" cried the guilty woman, her cheeks blanching and her knees knocking together.

"I can soon tell. A cheque was surreptitiously abstracted from my book."

"What has that to do with me?" she asked, in a trembling voice.

"Stop a bit, and you shall hear. It was subsequently filled up for twenty pounds. I happened to have that sum placed to my credit, and the cheque was cashed. It was, however, a forgery, and there is very little doubt that either Mrs. Wilkinson or yourself forged my signature. The heaviest suspicion falls upon you owing to your lavish expenditure this morning."

"Why do you talk to me like this before people?" asked Louisa, making a pointed allusion to my presence in the room.

"Because this lady is a female detective; and it is mainly owing to her practised wit that you are found out at the commencement of your criminal career."

Finding herself checked at all points, Louisa hid her face in her hands and burst into a violent flood of tears. When the paroxysm had somewhat subsided, she beckoned her husband to her in a penitent way, and made a full confession - stating how Mrs. Wilkinson had instigated her to the commission of the act, from the commencement. How she had represented the glories of the Opera in glowing colours, and told her that she was a weak and silly fool to pine in obscurity when she might go out and enjoy herself.

After all, Mrs. Wilkinson's cleverness was of a vulgar order. She might have obtained a tremendous hold over Louisa if she had kept the forged cheque in her possession, and threatened to make use of it in a way detrimental to her interest whenever the young wife refused to do as she directed her. But like a bull at a gate she went to work in a blundering way, wishing to destroy her enemy at one blow. To discover that your wife has forged your name in order to rob you of your hard-earned money, is calculated to destroy all faith and confidence in the offending person; and Mrs. Wilkinson imagined that she should, by her evil machinations, succeed in throwing a blight upon the family of the Eskells, bring about a separation and drive John out of the country to begin life anew in a foreign land, where no painful reminiscences would haunt him, no harrowing recollections dog his reluctant footsteps.

When I heard Mrs. Eskell's confession, I conceived a furious detestation for Mrs. Wilkinson, who had played a part in this domestic drama more worthy of a fiend than of an educated woman in a civilized portion of the globe. I resolved if I could to frighten her a little. Five minutes' conversation with Mr. Eskell told me that he did not intend to prosecute his wife, although he regretted his feelings would not allow him to do so, owing to his hatred for Mrs. Wilkinson, which was quite as profound as mine, if not more so, because it was of longer standing and had grown by accretion. With his consent I went to Mrs. Wilkinson's shop, and inquired for her. She came out of her parlour in a swaggering manner which suggested a mixture of the bully and the cut-throat. In an insolent tone she asked me what my business was. The shop was full of people, whose attention was riveted upon us. I was the cynosure of all eyes. I replied that I was connected with the London Detective Police, and that I had come to arrest her for being an accomplice with one Louisa Eskell, now in custody for committing a forgery.

At this announcement the customers stared and opened their mouths with astonishment. Mrs. Wilkinson's puffed and bloated cheeks turned the colour of fine lard. She grasped the back of the chair for support; but the frail structure gave way beneath the mighty load imposed upon it and collapsed with a sudden crash, the result of which was that she came to the ground heavily. The most fitting epitaph for the occasion was, "Procumbit humi bos."

I told her in inexorable tones that it was imperative she should go with me.

At this she kicked and struggled and roared. When her passion was a little spent, her husband came in. He had been drinking at a neighbouring public-house, and his shopman had been to fetch him, considering the position of affairs critical.

I explained the state of the case, and Mrs. Wilkinson did not attempt to deny the truth of my statement. Her husband was much more lucid in his ideas than herself, and he at once recommended that a cab should be sent for, and that we should all adjourn to Mr. Eskell's, and see if that gentleman could not be induced to extend his clemency to the parties concerned in the transaction. After some demur, I agreed to the proposal. Mrs. Wilkinson caught rapturously at the idea, as a drowning man, spent with exertion, would at a hencoop or a plank.

I knew that Mr. Eskell would be satisfied at the humiliation of the woman who had been base enough to work him this great wrong. He could not put the law in motion against her without punishing his wife at the same time. I had done her as much harm as lay in my feeble power. Every one in the shop at the time of my arrival had heard what I said, and I had no doubt whatever that in a short time the story of the forgery would be all over the neighbourhood, and very much damage her credit and fair fame.

During our short journey in the cab Mrs. Wilkinson had an attack of violent hysterics, but was eventually soothed by a draught of brandy from a flask handed to her by her kind and considerate husband.

On our arrival, I left the Wilkinsons standing in the passage, while I prepared Mr. Eskell for the interview. It was arranged that Louisa should lie upon the sofa and simulate the most profound grief, keeping a pocket-handkerchief to her eyes, and sobbing occasionally. John was at first to be obstinate, but to yield at last to the entreaties of the Wilkinsons. Having settled the preliminaries in a satisfactory manner, I brought in my party. There was no doubt about Mrs. Wilkinson's contrition being genuine, for she howled out her penitent prayers for forgiveness with a submission that was as servile as it was disgusting. Mr. Eskell consented to compromise the matter, provided her husband would pay the amount of the forged cheque. Notes were at once produced, and handed over. The Wilkinsons took their leave much dejected, to have a conjugal dispute over their cups. Mr. Eskell forgave his wife after a time, and so the matter ended, as far as they were concerned; but the Wilkinsons were so much annoyed by their neighbours, that they were obliged to sell their business and buy a public-house, which they drank themselves out of in less than twelve months, and are now in a state of abject poverty. Mrs. Buzz took the part of the young wife, and in talking the matter over confidentially remarked sententiously to Mr. Eskell, "Ah well, there's always a something."

MISTAKEN IDENTITY

CHAPTER I

DEAD AGAINST HIM

"SEND for his friends?" I repeated, in reply to a question put to me by the inspector of a police station at which I happened to be; "Oh, yes. I see no reason to refuse his request, but I think you are fully justified in not admitting him to bail."

The prisoner in question was a tall, fair man, of gentlemanly appearance, who seemed to feel his position acutely. He had lately been brought in on a singular charge of skittle-sharping.

The prosecutor, a simple-looking countryman, deposed that he had met the prisoner three days before in Westminster, with two other men, and was by them solicited to have something to drink. After his compliance a game of skittles was proposed. Bets were made and he was ingeniously robbed of eighty pounds in gold and notes. The whole of the gang on that occasion made their escape; but the prosecutor met the prisoner while walking in the Strand, and recognising him at once gave him into the custody of the first police officer he saw. The prisoner vehemently protested his innocence, and in no measured terms declared that he was the victim of a mistake. He gave the name of Joseph Halliday and a respectable address which we afterwards found was a correct one, described himself as a civil engineer, and said that he was the scapegoat of the prosecutor's stupidity.

It was the early part of the afternoon, but the business of the court that day not being heavy, the magistrate had finished his work and gone home; so that Mr. Halliday would have to remain a prisoner until the next day, even if he were able to prove his innocence in an incontestable manner. We were accustomed to see respectable men - that is, externally respectable - brought into the station on charges of skittle-sharping; and so Mr. Halliday's decent exterior did not impress me in his favour in the least. He appeared greatly distressed, and said repeatedly, as the charge was being taken, that he was innocent. His manner had the appearance of being genuine; but I never allowed appearances to have any weight with me. Some of the rascals who infest the streets and plunder the simple are such clever actors that if they were not incorrigibly idle they would make a decent living upon the stage.

I suggested to the inspector that it might be a case of mistaken identity; and, in order to set the question at rest, it would be better to send for the landlord and the barman of the "Duke's Head," which was the name of the public-house in which the swindle had been perpetrated. The prisoner evinced the utmost signs of joy and exultation when he heard this proposal; and the prosecutor made no objection, saying that he was sure their testimony would bear out the charge he had just made against Joseph Halliday. Accordingly, messengers were despatched to the "Duke's Head," requesting the immediate attendance of the landlord and his barman. In the meantime the prisoner was conveyed into the yard of the station-house and placed in a row with nine other men. It was intended that the witnesses we had sent for should identify the prisoner from amongst a number of others. When they arrived, the landlord of the "Duke's Head" requested to be told why he had been summoned. "A case of skittle-sharping," replied the inspector, "took place in your house three days ago. Would you remember the three men who hired your skittle-ground for the best part of the afternoon?"

"Perfectly," replied the landlord; "there were four altogether, and this gentleman" (turning to prosecutor) "was one of them."

"You are quite right; but he is the victim of the three rogues. We imagine that we have one of them in custody. He is amongst some others in the back-yard. If your memory serves you, you will have no difficulty in selecting him from his companions."

"I don't think I shall have the least trouble. I have a distinct recollection of the whole party," replied the landlord, following the inspector and myself to the yard. The barman we left behind; his turn was to come next.

It must have been a moment of intense anxiety to Mr. Halliday. I was a little curious as to the result, and looked on with expectation.

The courtyard was a narrow piece of ground in which the men were drilled occasionally. It was covered with gravel and surrounded by a high wall, which, however, in no way obstructed the light, which fell in a bright stream upon the men, who were marshalled in single file, awaiting the scrutiny of the landlord, who took a critical survey of them, and, without a moment's hesitation, went up to Mr. Joseph Halliday, and, touching him on the shoulder, exclaimed, "This is the man."

A shudder of repulsion ran through the prisoner's frame, and he turned ghastly pale. I thought he would have fallen. The inspector smiled, and said, "An old hand evidently."

"Oh! I knew him again in an instant," exclaimed the landlord, who went back again with the inspector to allow the barman to commence his investigation.

A tin cup stood under a tap, and seeing that the prisoner looked faint and ill I filled it with water and presented it to him. He drank off the contents at a draught and regarded me gratefully.

"You are very kind," he murmured in a low tone.

There was something in his voice that interested me, something quiet and gentle; but the evidence against him was so strong and damning, that I could not bring myself to regard him favourably or look upon him as the victim of a mistake.

Presently the barman made his appearance; he seemed an intelligent fellow possessed of powers of discrimination. He walked along the yard and looked steadily at the men who were grouped together for his inspection, and stopped abruptly when he came to Mr. Halliday.

"This is the one;" he said triumphantly; "I could tell him amongst a thousand."

The slender hope which had hitherto animated the prisoner now deserted him, and he fell on the ground in a heap insensible. It was a terrible ordeal for him to have gone through, if innocent. Stepping up to the inspector, I said, "This is a remarkable case; but although the evidence seems to be against him, it is odd, isn't it, that he should take on so."

"I don't know. These fellows are up to as many dodges as there are days in the year. He must take his chance. He'll have a fair trial to-morrow. Perhaps he can prove an *alibi*. If you take an interest in him you can talk to him. I won't lock him up again till you've done your little bit of palaver."

Thanking the inspector, I returned to Mr. Halliday, and was glad to see that he had shown signs of returning animation. Some good Samaritan had sprinkled his face with water, and he had opened his eyes. By my order he was accommodated with a chair, and when he was sufficiently recovered I began a conversation with him.

"Do you still persist in saying that you are the victim of a mistake, Mr. Halliday?" I exclaimed.

"Most certainly I do," he replied earnestly. "Some one must have a strong and fatal resemblance to me."

"Will you tell me how you spent your time yesterday during the alleged robbery?"

"With pleasure," he answered; "but, I presume - excuse my asking the question - that I am talking to some one connected with the police."

"I am a female detective, and in my professional capacity may be of service to you."

"You are very good, and I esteem myself fortunate in having met with you. In the first place, I must tell you that I am a civil engineer by profession, and tolerably well known to people who move in scientific circles. On the day in question, when the man who gave me in charge was robbed and plundered, I was attending a meeting at Muswell Hill and giving evidence as to the advisability of extended sewerage in the vicinity before the Muswell Hill Board of Works. The solicitors to the Board will prove it. The members of the Board will prove it."

"Very good, so far," I replied. "Leave your case in my hands and make yourself easy as to the result. I shall, with your permission, instruct Mr. Sea, one of the cleverest practising barristers we have in cases of this kind, to defend you when brought before the court to-morrow morning, and to ask for a remand. You must put up with the worry and annoyance of imprisonment for a few days, bring all your philosophy to your aid, and I will see if I cannot unravel this tangled skein. By the way, I should like to ask you one thing?"

"As many as you like," he replied readily.

"Do any of your family resemble you in any way? Have you ever been taken for any one else on a previous occasion?"

"Some years ago," he replied thoughtfully, "my twin-brother was alive, and you would not have known us from one another, we were veritable Dromios."

"Is he dead now?"

"I am sorry to say he is. We were much attached to each other, but he was of a roving disposition and would never stick to anything. I started him in several professions, but he always repaid my kindness by ingratitude, which is hard to bear from a relation. At length, on my refusing to assist him any longer he ran away to sea, and the ship in which he sailed was subsequently wrecked on a voyage to Malaga."

"Oh!" I said, with a prolonged exclamation; I began to see my way a little clearer.

Wishing Mr. Halliday good-bye, I left the station-house to commence operations. If what the prisoner said about his being in attendance upon the Muswell Hill Board of Works at the very time at which he was accused of being at an obscure pothouse in Westminster, in company with two other men not in custody, to defraud a simple-minded countryman of his money, the case was at an end. I at once sent a retainer for Mr. Sea and engaged his services for Mr. Joseph

Halliday on the morrow. I had a shrewd suspicion that I was about to embark in the investigation of one of the strangest cases of mistaken identity that had ever been heard of; nor was I "mistaken," as after events tended to prove.

CHAPTER II

PEGON

I WAS acquainted with a man of the name of Pegon - a Frenchman - who had, it was popularly supposed, been a thief in his own country, although he might have left France through political motives. On arriving in England he had taken service in the police-force, and evinced such wonderful dexterity in tracking criminals that he speedily became one of our most valued detectives. The old saying - set a thief to catch a thief, was, admitting the reports about Pegon to be true, never better exemplified than in the person of the dapper little Gaul. He was not a proficient in the English language; he talked in a half-broken sort of way, rather amusing than otherwise. It was to Pegon that I betook myself after leaving Mr. Sea's offices. I found him at his favourite public-house - the "Three Spies." He was seldom at home, and when not on business he could always be discovered either at the before-mentioned tavern or else at the Welsh ambassadors - the "Goat in Boots." Pegon had probably a greater acquaintance with the skittle-sharping fraternity than any other man in London. He knew them all, and when they occasionally took a trip into the country, Pegon would miss the familiar face, find out where he was gone, and telegraph to the police of Birmingham, Manchester, or Liverpool, and they would exercise such a strict look-out that their vigilance would soon drive the sharper back to his old haunts and associates. When Pegon met him on his return, he would smile sardonically, and say -

"Back again, eh? change of air is goot for your 'elth," and his mouth would distend itself into a broad grin. It was rumoured that Pegon was occasionally heavily bribed by the thieves to allow them to remain unmolested, but his superiors took no notice of this scandal, as they always found him an active and intelligent officer; and if a man was wanted particularly, and Pegon was applied to for his apprehension, he was almost always forthcoming at a specified time. Pegon was sitting in the parlour of the "Three Spies," smoking contentedly, and drinking out of a pewter pot which contained nothing stronger than the best old and mild ale. He rose when he saw me, and exclaimed, in a genial tone -

"Ah, madam, it ees you! How you carry yourself? Sit down - 'ere is a chair."

Taking out his handkerchief, with true politeness, he dusted the bottom of it and handed it to me.

"Good morning, Pegon," I said; "I have come to consult you on a matter of some importance."

"Yaes - yaes."

"Three days ago a countryman was robbed by a skittle-sharper at the Duke's Head, in Westminster."

"Yaes," said Pegon, concentrating his attention on what I was saying.

"To-day a gentleman was arrested on suspicion of being concerned in the robbery. The barman and the landlord swore that he was one of the men."

"Ah," said Pegon, "this is strange - ver strange."

"Have you heard of the robbery?"

"No, but I have my suspicions; my good friend Toko and my dear friend Donnymore have been ver flush of their monny, and I suspect - - "

"Who is Donnymore?" I ventured to ask.

"Donnymore! oh, he ver goot fellow, Donnymore, but he go leetle too far."

"In what way?"

"I shall tell you," replied Pegon.

"Donnymore he come to my 'ouse, and he drinking my wine, but that is noting - oh, no, noting. You must know I cannot pay Donnymore; when I first com to England to show me thing or two I not know much, and Donnymore he show me the places where thieves go, and give me hint now and then, but Donnymore he ver goot fellow, only he go leetle too far - just leetle bit too far. One day he com to my 'ouse, and he drinking my wine and smoking my tabac, but that is noting - oh, noting - but he go to drawer, and he steal my stocking - oh, Donnymore he ver goot fellow, but he go leetle, leetle too far."

"Your stocking!" I said. "That was not very valuable, I should think."

"Oh, by Gar! it was. I keep all my monny in my stocking. Thirty, forty, fifty, hundred pound! Oh! Donnymore, he ver goot fellow; but, by Gar! he go leetle too far."

"So you think Donnymore had a hand in this robbery?" I said, laughing at the Frenchman's story.

"I be dam well sure," replied Pegon, slapping his fist on the table. "I say to myself, Aha! Donnymore, my boy, you been at your old games again! More stockings, eh? Donnymore, take care, sare, you do not go leetle too far."

"Who is Toko?" I asked.

"Toko! he Donnymore's pal. They stand in always."

"And the third, do you know him? I believe these fellows always walk in gangs."

"Oh! *certainement*. It most be! Let me see. It most be Fon Beest, the German. I know him. Oh! he is crafty, like one English fox - yaes, I say so!"

Von Beest I had heard of as a clever German thief, who had once been imprisoned for two years for a daring burglary in Oxford Street.

"What do you know about Toko?"

"Toko! he is what you say new mans almost; he has not been here 'bove year and half. He is sailor or something; he look like gentleman, and know how to talk, and Donnymore he make him decoy. Oh, leave Donnymore alone. I have met him before to-day. Yaes, I know Donnymore; he ver goot fellow, but he go leetle too far - just leetle bit too far."

And as the little Frenchman recalled his grievances, he pulled away somewhat vigorously at his pipe, and looked at the sanded floor as if the reminiscence of the gold-laden stocking was painful to talk about.

After a pause of a minute, he said, "Oh, yaes! I know Donnymore!" and then he chuckled as if he contemplated revenge.

"Where could you find Donnymore and his associates?" I asked.

"I say," asked the astute little Frenchman, "is there reward offered?"

"No," I replied. "But Mr. Halliday, the gentleman I was speaking of, who is in custody, is well off, and will, I have no doubt, make a couple of days' work worth our while."

"*Bien!* that is goot. I like to be on ze square, you know. You vast humbug! I vast humbug; we all vast humbug. *Tiens!* you shall hear. Donnymore, Toko, Fon Beest, all stay now at the 'Pig and Whistle,' in King Street, Seven Dials. I have my eye on one of them *toujours*. I am father, they are my children."

"Let us go, then, and reconnoitre; I want to see if this man Toko resembles Mr. Halliday in any way; if so, the mystery is cleared up at once."

"Of course it is. Well, we will go. I can spot them. I shall not touch Donnymore, I think, for Donnymore he ver goot fellow; but he go leetle too far - just leetle bit too far. Donnymore and I were pals once, *confrères*. You shall have Toko and Fon Beest, but Donnymore he shall shake loose leg a little longer. Vat you say to that, madame?"

"I have no objection," I replied. "I only want Toko."

"*Bon*! You shall have Toko, and I will be liberal - I will throw Fon Beest into the bargain."

We shook hands in order to cement the bargain; and leaving the "Three Spies," wended our way to the Seven Dials, and entered the "Pig and Whistle." It was filled with thieves and loose women, their companions. Pegon perceived no trace of the trio we were in search of. Coming near, he said. "*Attendez!* they are *en haut*."

CHAPTER III

ON ascending the stairs, we found ourselves in a spacious room, in which singing was going on. It was long and narrow, with a stage at one end, and a succession of tables on each side, with a passage up the middle for ingress and egress, very much after the manner of the cafés chantants in the Palais Royal. The room was tolerably well filled. A man who threw himself into the most awful contortions and impossible attitudes, attired in a suit of dittos of a check pattern

- something like Mr. Leech's caricature of Mr. Briggs when his mind is on hunting intent - was lilting a ditty respecting "Sairy's young man," which seemed to take the audience by storm. The success of this song was only equalled by another, beginning -

> "A cove he would a macing go,
> Whether the blueskins would or no."

An evident allusion to accomplished thieves and baffled policemen. We took up a position from which we commanded an excellent view of the room. I began to look about me, and perceived a couple of bottles of champagne standing on a particular table in one corner. At this table three men were seated. I started. Pegon asked me what was the matter. I smiled at my stupidity; I thought I saw Mr. Halliday. My explanation of the singular coincidence was, that the brother whom Mr. Halliday had thought dead had escaped the shipwreck which had induced the belief of his decease, and that on returning to England his innate vagabondism had broken out afresh, and he had allied himself with Donnymore and Von Beest.

"Who is that?" I asked Pegon, pointing out the man who bore such a marvellous resemblance to Mr. Halliday.

"That is Toko, and that is my dear friend Donnymore, while the other is that *sacré* German Fon Beest. Oh! I will make it hot for Toko and Fon Beest."

"Cannot you go up to them, and get into conversation?" I asked.

Pégon looked at me steadily for a moment, and replied, "You will have to be *ma chère amie*. I shall say you are the idol of my heart, and *mort de ma vie*, we are going to make our lives happy for ever. Donnymore, he vill jump to see me; but I shall give him the office, and say, It is no business; he is not wanted; and we shall be ver merry. When he is in luck he will spend money like a king; so vill Toko; but Fon Beest he is a screw - no good, no, not to anyone. Come 'long, *ma chère. Baisez moi*? *Non*? It is droll; is it not? Come 'long; let us go to these ruffyans."

We walked across the room; I was hanging on Pegon's arm, as if I was his wife. When we reached the table at which the thieves were seated, Von Beest looked up, and touched Donnymore on the arm. The latter jumped up as if he had been shot. The trio were struck with the utmost consternation at the sight of the clever and well-known little Frenchman, who, holding out his hand to Donnymore, exclaimed -

"Ah, how is Donnymore, my ole friend Donnymore? I always say he ver goot fellow, but he once go leetle too far - just leetle bit too far. But we will not talk 'bout that now. I have come out for what you say spree, one lark, and I am rejoice to see you here; and my friend Fon Beest too, and that dear Toko. Toko, how you do? You not shake hands with your own Pegon? That is right. Fon Beest your hand. That is right also. Now, Donnymore, you make room there for *ma chère amie et moi-même*."

Donnymore, slightly reassured, made room for us, and we sat down.

"Ah," continued the indefatigable Pegon, "you have been in luck lately. Champagne, *vin de ciel*. Give me some, Donnymore; I feel ver dry."

Donnymore called for some more glasses, and poured out some wine for both of us.

The more I looked at Toko the more surprised was I at the wonderful likeness between him and Mr. Halliday. No wonder, I thought, that the innkeeper and his barman as well as the prosecutor were deceived. The circumstance was something marvellous. I remarked the same mild-looking blue eyes, the same rather broad mouth and thick lips, the same straight nose a little dilated at the nostrils; but there was one thing about Toko which was not observable in Mr. Halliday. His face wore a restless expression, as if he had been haunted by the apprehension of arrest. You would have put him down at first sight as a man who had something upon his mind which was eternally weighing upon his spirits and depressing them. He drank heavily. His somewhat bloodshot eyes, together with their swollen lids, and the dry, parched, burnt-up, cracking skin upon his lips sufficiently proclaimed the fact of his having addicted himself to spirituous compounds in a wholesale manner.

Pegon was in his element. He carried on the part he had undertaken with admirable cleverness, and I brought all my histrionic talent into requisition. He was my lover, and I pretended to be by no means shy. Every now and then he pressed my hand before Toko and the others in an amorous manner, much to their amusement. I immediately resented a liberty of this sort by snatching the insulted member away and putting on an air of injured innocence.

"Pegon's got hold of a widow," remarked Donnymore.

"No, no, not a widow; no, thank you," cried Pegon; "I never buy ze goods in ze matrimonial market which are of ze segond-hand."

"Ha, ha!" laughed the sharpers.

"Pegon's a good judge," said Toko.

"Yes, leave him alone," replied Donnymore.

"More wine, Donnymore!" exclaimed Pegon. "Once you drinking my wine; to-day I drinking yours."

Donnymore complaisantly filled his friend's glass, paying mine the same compliment. After Pegon had to his satisfaction quaffed the foaming vintage, he exclaimed, "Donnymore, you telling me one thing."

"Fire away, old fellow."

"You will tell me true this one thing."

"Half-a-dozen, if you like."

"What you going to do now?"

"Do?" repeated Donnymore, with the light of consternation in his eyes, for Pegon's words seemed to have a strange significance for him.

"Say what you going to do."

"Oh, I don't know."

The man looked nervously around him, and eyed the door suspiciously, as if he fully expected to see a body of police standing in its immediate vicinity.

"Why not you try change of air?"

"I'm well enough."

This was said rather surlily.

"Birmingham is nice place."

"I - Brummagem," muttered Donnymore.

"Ah! you not like to leave your friends?"

"No, I don't."

"That is good, shows you have good heart. It is but natural, you are so well known, have so many *friends*."

He laid a stress upon the last word, and looked steadily at Donnymore, who said angrily -

"Look here, Pegon - what the blazes are you driving at?"

"Me! nothing, my friend - it is only anxiety for the state of your health."

"My health be blowed; what's your little game?"

"How you talk; as if I ever had little games; but he is so funny, that Pegon."

There was an awkward pause, during which the sharpers looked at one another uneasily.

"There is that dear Fon Beest," resumed Pegon. "His friends could not part with him; he is too precious to them."

"Drink your wine, and hold your row," growled the German.

"Ha! ha!" laughed Pegon.

"That dear Fon Beest is like one bear with a sore head. He is complimentary too. But I shall have the pleasure of returning his compliment some day. I never forget my debts."

"Devil doubt you," said Donnymore.

"I wish I was like you, Donnymore," exclaimed Pegon.

"What for?"

"Shall I tell you?"

"Go ahead."

"I would take a Schwostle."[3]

"What's the pull in that?"

"Oh, you'd soon learn the squeak."

It was clear now that Donnymore began to see some hidden meaning in Pegon's apparently objectless remarks. He became more and more uneasy, and it was evident that he came to the conclusion that Pegon was giving him the office in a friendly way. He did not care much for Toko or Von Beest. Self-preservation was the first law with him, and he

---

3. Punch and Judy show.

apprehended they were both wanted, whilst he was through the Frenchman's kindness allowed to escape. Rising from his chair in a careless way he put on his hat.

"You are not going yet?" asked Pegon, pretending to be surprised.

"Going! no, not till midnight. I'm game for a spree."

"Where you off to, then?"

"Back in a minute."

When his associates heard this they disposed themselves entirely to await his return.

Pegon muttered to himself, "Oh, he's fly bird, ver fly bird."

After the lapse of five minutes the sharpers began to grow fidgety, and Toko rose to take his leave. Pegon got up at the same time and exclaimed -

"Have you minute to spare?"

"What for?"

"Just one word - private conversation. You stop here, my dear."

This was to me.

Toko and Pegon walked up the room together. Suddenly there was a cry of rage and alarm. I looked up. Two men in the body of the hall were fiercely struggling together. The fight was of short duration. In less than a minute Toko was lying on his back on the floor handcuffed.

When Von Beest perceived this he turned deadly pale. I heard him utter an imprecation upon Donnymore and his treachery, and then he made a rush towards the door, but Pegon had by this time drawn his policeman's staff, which he carried concealed under his cloak, and as the German attempted to pass him, he struck him on the forehead, and he rolled heavily over upon the floor.

Toko and Von Beest were both manacled, and helpless. A smile of triumph flitted over Pegon's face; he beckoned to me. I came up and stood by the side of Toko, who was sitting disconsolately upon a bench.

The musical performance was arrested, and the people who were in the Hall manifested the most lively interest in the proceedings of Pegon and myself.

I was especially an object of remark and scrutiny.

"Mr. Halliday," I said, in a low voice to Toko.

He started; my words roused him from his listless, apathetic mood, and he asked in a hurried voice if I spoke to him.

"Certainly," I replied, "that is your name."

"How do you know?"

"That does not matter, you cannot deny it."

"I can, I do," he vociferated.

"Your violent asseverations - - " I began, when he interrupted me saying, -

"Whoever says so is guilty of an infamous falsehood."

"Possibly," I replied. "By the way, have you seen your brother lately?"

"My - my brother?" he stammered.

"Yes, the engineer."

"Who are you?" he cried, "and why do you ask me these questions?"

"I am a female detective, and I ask you these questions in order that Justice may vindicate her character and reputation for impartiality."

"A - female - detective," he repeated slowly.

"I think I said so."

"Why, I should as soon have thought of seeing a flying fish or a sea-serpent with a ring through its nose."

"You have not answered my question respecting your brother yet?"

"I have not seen him, nor do I wish to."

"What harm has he done you?"

"Only driven me to - - ; but never mind."

"He thinks you're drowned at sea."

"A good job too; let him think so."

"Do you know where he is now?"

"No," he replied, laconically.

"He is where you will soon be."

"In gaol?"

"Yes; in a prison."

"What!" he cried, with a bitter laugh, "does it run in the family?"

"Not that either."

"Explain yourself?"

"You are the cause of his arrest."

"I!" he ejaculated in astonishment.

"Yes; he is accused."

"Of what?"

"Of committing an offence, the responsibility of which rests entirely with you. He has been taken up as a skittle-sharper."

"No; you are joking?"

"I assure you that I am speaking the truth."

There seemed something so exquisitely ludicrous in the idea of his sober, steady-going, respectable brother being brought before a magistrate for a disgraceful misdemeanor, that the dissipated scamp laughed immoderately. The painful position in which he was did not affect his hilarity or his flow of animal spirits.

"That is capital," he said at last. "I am only sorry he was not committed for trial."

"There is no chance of that now."

"I suppose not, as I have fallen into your clutches through the infernal treachery of that fellow, Donnymore. But I'll be one with him some day."

"He had nothing to do with it; you must lay your misfortune to the astuteness of Mr. Pegon."

"I wish you and Pegon, and the whole kit of you, were at the bottom of the sea!" he growled.

Presently Von Beest returned to consciousness, and glanced fiercely around him.

"Ah!" said Pegon, with cruel levity, "that dear Fon Beest is himself once more. Do I not pay my debts well; have I not returned your compliment, my amiable Fon Beest. Come along, you shall go to the Government Hotel to-night; and if the beds should turn out hard, come and complain to me, and I will get you a new chamber-maid. Come here, my dear Fon Beest. Come along, my good Toko."

*   *   *   *

When the magistrate saw Toko he was not less astonished than the prosecutor, who at once admitted that he had fallen into an error which, he trusted, was excusable, owing to the wonderful likeness existing between the brothers. Mr. Halliday, the engineer, and Mr. Halliday, the skittlesharper, must have been cast in the same mould. The prisoner was at once discharged, and his brother placed in the dock. Mr. Halliday's joy at seeing his brother once more was considerably damped by the reflection that he had provoked the doom of a felon; and taking me on one side, he asked me to add to the favour I had already done him, and try to make terms with the prosecutor.

I found this worthy rather obdurate at first, but when I told him that Mr. Halliday would refund all the money he had lost, and make him a handsome present besides, his resentment gave way and he consented to withdraw from the prosecution. Toko was so much affected by this proof of his brother's good-nature that he gave up his evil way of living, and addicted himself to honest pursuits. He thought it unadvisable to stay in England, so he went out to Australia (not at the expense of the Government as he was once ambitious of doing - but by his brother's assistance), and set up in New South Wales as a sheep-farmer; and the last time his friends heard of him he was doing remarkably well and turning out better than the most sanguine of his acquaintances had ever anticipated; and so ended this marvellous case of mistaken identity.

INCOGNITA

I HAPPENED one morning to be at Colonel Warner's office when a messenger came up and said that a lady wished to see him on particular and private business.

"Who is she?" asked the colonel.

"I don't know, sir; didn't say," replied the messenger.

"Did she give you no card?"

"No, sir."

"No name?"

"No, sir."

"Then go down stairs and ask for either one or the other."

The man made an inclination of the head, which was intended as an affirmative bow, and so interpreted, and then left the room.

During his absence we continued our conversation, which related to some clever and impudent frauds of a pawnbroker's, and arranged our plan of action as to the steps to be taken to discover the thieves.

When the messenger returned he held a card between his fingers, and presented it to Colonel Warner, who looked at the name and address, and said, "Show her up."

"You must excuse me," he added, addressing myself. "I shall not keep you long. Probably this lady may require your services, and it may be worth your while to pay her a little attention."

I replied that I was in no particular hurry, and left the room to take up a position in one below, which was known as the waiting-room.

On my way downstairs I passed a lady, whom I at once took to be the one who had demanded an interview with Colonel Warner. She was between forty and fifty, apparently, and extremely ladylike. I was unable to scrutinize her face well and thoroughly, owing to the fact of her wearing a thick Maltese lace veil. The rest of her attire consisted of a black silk dress and a black embroidered shawl of a very rich texture. Her bonnet was chiefly remarkable for its exquisite shape and the grace with which she wore it.

She gave me a sidelong look through the meshes of her veil, and walked on preceded by the messenger.

The waiting-room at the office in Whitehall is not an agreeable place to pass an hour or two in. It is well carpeted as far as substantial matting goes, and it is well supplied with severe-looking tables and chairs, the latter being rather hard and unyielding when you venture to sit down upon them, highly suggestive of cramp and rheumatism in an aggravated degree. The window is a strange mixture of glass, wood, putty, and iron bars; and in winter the polished grate contains a fire sufficiently large to roast half-a-dozen oxen, let alone the same number of inoffensive human beings. I had to wait about five-and-thirty minutes - if I could place any reliance upon my "Benson," which was generally addicted to accuracy, and seldom took erratic fits into its mechanical head except on Sundays, when its Sabbatic proclivities became apparent, as it gained sometimes as much as three quarters of a minute, a fact, in all probability, not without a parallel in the history of watches.

The messenger came downstairs at the expiration of the time I have stated, and asked me to come to Colonel Warner, who was waiting to see me. On the staircase, I again passed the sombre-looking lady, still discreetly veiled.

"I am glad you waited," said the colonel, "because I can give you a little work."

"Of what description?"

"Not altogether novel, but rather out of your usual line."

"Indeed! You excite my curiosity."

Colonel Warner handed me a card, saying, "That is the name of the lady who was with me just now."

I took the piece of pasteboard, and read, "Mrs. Foster Wareham, Shanklin-street, Belgrave-square."

"Has she been robbed?" I inquired.

"No. Guess again."

"Has she lost anything?"

"Not a halfpenny that I am aware of."

"What on earth, then, brought her to you?"

"I thought I should make you curious."

"Pray enlighten me."

"I had better tell you the story as briefly as I can. I assure you Mrs. Wareham interlarded it with sighs and tears in quite a dramatic manner. It appears that her son has just come into a very large property, worth I don't know how much, which he inherited under his father's will. No one can deprive him of this, and he is, in plain language, making ducks and drakes of it, and an egregious ass of himself."

"I begin to see," I exclaimed.

"Wait a bit. About a month ago, some woman got hold of him, and is easing him of his superfluous cash in a most dexterous manner."

"What has that to do with us?" I asked, in some surprise.

"Nothing whatever," he replied, calmly.

"Why, then, should she have come here?"

"Because she wanted some clever person, man or woman, who would in some way help her to reclaim her son. She knows very well that the law cannot assist her. The woman, who goes by the name of 'Incognita,' certainly fleeces him in a way that would make the hair of a professed skittle-sharper stand on end, but she is not guilty of an indictable offence. If 'Incognita' and her associates retain their hold over him for six months, young Wareham will not have a penny."

"It ought to be prevented."

"So I think; and I told the lady that I would send her some one perfectly competent to undertake so arduous and delicate a case. You must have recourse to stratagem."

"Of course."

"Perhaps she has more than one lover. Most women - I may say all in her position, and who pursue the calling she does - are deceitful, and I will wager a new hat that she is no exception to the rule."

"I quite agree with you."

"Very well, then; all you have to do is to prove her infidelity beyond a doubt, and the young simpleton will open his eyes, and confess that he has been made a fool and a tool of."

"Did you tell her I would call upon her?"

"I did; and she said she should be at home the whole of to-morrow, and should expect to see you. Keep her card, and do not fail to go. She will be pleased beyond measure if you succeed. She told me she was rich and would reward you liberally. You are like a gold-digger at Ballarat who is in luck; you have an auriferous claim, and it only requires work and perseverance to bring out the nuggets."

I thanked Colonel Warner for his kindness, and said that I would do all I could for the unfortunate mother, who saw her only son doing what was extremely distasteful to her maternal feelings.

At no time is it agreeable to a mother to see her son led away by unworthy persons, whether they are men or women. A fine fortune and a noble estate can be soon wasted and squandered at the gaming-table; but a designing and unprincipled woman, if she is an expert at the business, can do the work of destruction sooner than half-a-dozen others put together. It was nothing very unusual for us to have an application of this nature made to us; people always think that the "police" can help them out of every difficulty. If a man loses his umbrella at his club, or a lady leaves an opera-glass in a cab, the police are applied to, as though they were omniscient and infallible. I rather liked a case of the kind in which I was about to embark. There was more money to be made out of it than there was in the legitimate way, and generally less danger and fewer risks.

I lost no time in paying Mrs. Foster Wareham a visit at her residence in Shanklin-street. The house was a large one, and, as far as I could judge by the aspect of the drawing-room, not only magnificently but luxuriously furnished.

Mrs. Wareham, with well-bred courtesy, did not keep me waiting long. She knew by my card who I was, and she held out her hand in a kind manner, as if she looked upon me more as a friend and ally than a Jonathan Wild in petticoats. I have met people who have turned up their noses at me for being a female detective or thief-taker, as they have thought fit to term me, but I never forgot the insult, and have had my eye upon them, and have caught more than one tripping, which perhaps, the reader will observe, is not saying much for my acquaintances.

"Pray sit down, Mrs. Paschal."

I resumed my seat.

"In a case of the sort we are going to discuss, it is as well to commence at the beginning."

"Quite so," I replied.

"My son, Walford Wareham, has not left Harrow more than a year. He is now twenty. He will not enter any profession: he says there is plenty of time, and when he feels inclined he will go into the army for a year or two, just to say he has been something. He says he has plenty of money, - and so he has - and that there is no necessity for him having a profession. It is all very well - I use his own words - for poor fellows to become professional men; but when a man is born with a silver spoon in his mouth the case is altered."

She paused, presently resuming.

"I was foolish enough to let him have his own way when I might have controlled him. Now he is out of my hands, and has taken the bit between his teeth. I have no jurisdiction over him, and he thinks no more of me than he does of that table by your side. He has unfortunately contracted an intimacy - why mince matters? - he is living with a woman of disreputable character. These women, I have been told on good authority, always begin by trying to warp and prejudice the minds of their victims against everything good and holy. They especially try and turn the poor simple boy's family into ridicule. If he talks of his mother, they laugh at him; if he makes an attempt to say his prayers, as he has been accustomed to, they call him a weak-minded idiot - physic him with Champagne, and tell him he had much better smoke a cigar. They dread home influence more than anything else, and therefore they fight against it in a most determined manner.

Since the boy has been under the spell of this woman he has treated me, his mother, with contumely and contempt. I am not angry with him for it - I am only sorry and regretful. I *know* he will see his folly some day, and then I shall forgive him all his unkindness, all his insolence, and all his ungentlemanly conduct, without one word of reproach, because I know *he* is not to blame. He is instigated by the bad and vicious woman who holds him in thrall. There is one thing, though, which is becoming very serious. She has designs upon his property. She is not satisfied, like most of her class, with a liberal allowance. She has proved herself to be a rapacious harpy. Probably there are men in the background, accomplices of hers, who tell her what to do. I do not want Walford's property - I have sufficient of my own; still, I do not want to see him fall into the hands of thieves, robbers, Jews, and sharpers, because, when all was spent and gone, he would be thrown upon my hands a ruined, drunken spendthrift, and it would be extremely mortifying to me to see the splendid estates which have been in the family for centuries pass into other hands. So you perceive I have many reasons for interfering."

"You have the best of all possible reasons," I replied. "I can, I assure you, sympathize deeply with your maternal solicitude. Anything I can do in my poor way shall be done freely, and with every wish to render you material assistance."

"I may rely upon your good offices?" she inquired.

"Certainly."

"Have you any hope of being able to induce him to abandon his vicious course of living? You must bear in mind that I have tried on more than one occasion, and have failed signally."

"I should not think of making a direct appeal to him," I replied, with a slight laugh; "that would be the height of folly. In cases of this sort we are compelled to have recourse to duplicity."

"I think I catch your meaning," answered Mrs. Foster Wareham, - "you would play the spy upon the woman?"

"Precisely so."

"And exhibit her to my misguided boy in her true light, so that the scales will fall from his eyes? Is it not so?"

"You have interpreted my meaning exactly - that is precisely the course I am about to take."

"May I inquire what steps you will take to effect your purpose?"

"My line of conduct is very often dictated by chance or accident, as often as not; but I shall endeavour in this instance to attach myself to her person in some way, and be able to insinuate myself into her confidence."

"Of course you are the best judge," she replied. "I wish you every success. May Heaven bless and smile upon your efforts, as I trust it will!"

"I have conducted more difficult affairs than this to a successful issue," I replied, with a sanguine smile, meant to reassure her and set her fears at rest.

Before I left the house, Mrs. Foster Wareham made me a handsome present in the shape of a gold ring richly studded with emeralds and diamonds. I could see at a glance that it was of great price. She also give me a large sum of money to defray my expenses, and stimulate me, I suppose, to exertion.

On making inquiries, I discovered that the lady who had incurred the hostilities of Mrs. Foster Wareham, had been a third-rate actor at a minor theatre in her early days. Now she was spoken of amongst her friends as Incognita; her real name was Fanny Williams. Walford Wareham had taken a great fancy to her, and was her devoted admirer on all occasions. She lived expensively, and drew heavily upon her lover's purse, which, although of considerable extent, was unable to withstand her repeated attacks for a very great length of time. Having found out where she lived I called upon her one morning after breakfast; the landlady opened the door and asked me what my business was. I replied, that I wanted to see Mrs. Williams. Before she could make any reply, I heard a voice, issuing apparently from the drawing-room, shout out "How much longer am I to be kept waiting for that soda-water?"

"Oh! dear me," cried the landlady. "Do you mind waiting in the passage, while I take her up the soda?"

"Not at all," I replied, smiling inwardly at the state of affairs, which this early demand for an effervescing draught revealed.

In the course of a few minutes the landlady returned, saying, "I told her you were here, and she wants to know who you are, and where you come from?"

"Just be good enough to say that I would rather tell her when I see her; it will save a good deal of time and trouble," I replied.

"Very well."

The landlady went upstairs again, and delivered her message, to which Mrs. Williams responded in a tone evidently meant for my ears,

"If she's come for any money she can't have it; you tell her so. It's no good her coming dunning for money at this time of the morning."

"It isn't money, ma'am," I exclaimed, as loudly as I could.

"Oh! then you may come up. Parsons" - this to the landlady - "show her up."

Parsons did as she was ordered, and I was ushered into the presence of Mrs. Williams, who was seated at breakfast, attired in a handsome dressing-gown of light blue flannel trimmed with cashmere. Her hair was of a golden colour, and carelessly brushed off her forehead, being tied in a knot behind. She was eating some anchovy paste as I entered.

"Sit down," she exclaimed, "and just get your business over as quick as you can; I hate being worried when I'm at breakfast. Parsons should have told you I was out; but she is such a stupid creature."

"You seem to be badly waited upon, ma'am," I replied, wishing to lead her to the discussion of what she evidently considered a grievance.

"Oh, yes! Parsons leads me a life. I never have a moment's peace. There never was any one so hunted and worried as I am. But what do you want? Pitch me your tale at once, and don't be a month over it."

"Certainly not," I rejoined. "I heard in the neighbourhood that you were in want of a maid, and I thought I would apply for the place."

I could see from Mrs. Williams's manner that a lady's-maid was a luxury she had not hitherto indulged in, but the idea evidently pleased her; she said -

"They informed you correctly; I am at present without a maid. What wages do you expect?"

"Twelve pounds a year and 'found' in everything."

"I'll take you for a month on trial," she exclaimed, "provided your references are satisfactory. You are prepared to give references, I suppose?"

"Quite," I said, and I proceeded to give her the address of two friends of mine in a respectable position, who were in the habit of recommending me whenever the necessity for doing so arose, which it often did, as gaining access to people's houses in the capacity of a domestic servant was a favourite plan of mine, and one I very frequently had recourse to.

"Call again in three days, Mrs. - - What's your name?"

"Paschal."

"Mrs. Paschal, I shall call on your referees tomorrow, or whenever I have time to spare; and when I see you again I will give you an answer."

I was much amused at her way of living, her conversation, and the ludicrous contrast presented between it and the excessive precaution she was taking before admitting me into her service.

"Do you know how to open a bottle of soda?" she asked, handing one to me.

"I'll try, ma'am," I replied.

It was not a thing I often did, but I had had some experience of the art in my younger days when employed as a barmaid at a large refreshment saloon at one of the railway stations. I carefully, but with expedition removed the wire, then I cut the string that held the cork to the bottle, afterwards bending the cork gently upwards with my thumb and finger, holding the bottle mean while in a perpendicular position, which prevents the soda-water from flying about; the gas quietly escapes, and there is no cascade of fiercely-leaping globules. If, on the other hand, you hold the bottle horizontally, the cork goes through the window or into somebody's eye, and every one in the room is more or less deluged.

"Capital!" she cried, as I gave her a foaming glassful of the refreshing beverage; "couldn't have done it better myself. Come again in three days."

I heard from my friends that Mrs. Williams had called upon them the next day in a neat little brougham; asked them a few questions; was very particular about honesty and sobriety; said she did not much care about anything else, and expressed herself much satisfied with the replies they gave.

The next time I saw Mrs. Williams, she appeared glad to see me, and exclaimed, "When can you come? I engage you at once."

"To-morrow, ma'am; I should like to say goodbye to my friends, and I shall require a day to put my things in order."

"Oh! never mind about patching your dresses up; if you want anything of that sort I can give it you, ever so much better, too, than you have been in the habit of wearing."

The only reply I made to this ostentatious speech was a sudden murmur of gratitude.

"I've got just one thing to say to you," she exclaimed.

"What is that, ma'am?"

"Only this. If you have your wits about you, and don't make a fool of yourself, you shall never regret entering my service. But you should have eyes and not use them; ears, and keep them shut; and above all, never listen to anything that old fool Parsons may tell you. She's a gossiping old story-teller, and would say anything. I shall treat you like a friend, and you'll be as happy as a grig with me if you choose to be so."

I could, in a moment, see the drift of these remarks. Mrs. Williams looked upon me as a virtuous and respectable woman, who would in all probability be shocked when I discovered who and what she was, and she was warning me not to be prejudiced against her. I replied in a manner which set her apprehensions at rest, and the next day entered upon my new place.

One of the first discoveries I made was that her beautiful golden hair was in reality of a dark brown colour. She had some expensive wash in her dressing-case, some of which she poured into a saucer every other day and put on her hair with a small sponge. This changed the colour without in the least injuring the hair; and from a semi-brunette she became a blonde of the loveliest description.

The metamorphosis astonished me not a little. She laughed when she saw my amazement, and wanted me to allow her to make my hair golden as her own; but thinking that pliability and good nature might be carried to too great an extent, I steadily refused, and after a few trials she gave up the attempt.

Mr. Walford Wareham used to call upon Fanny Williams every day about twelve o'clock. They were not living in the same house as Mrs. Wareham had apprehended and stated to me. Fanny's room was *en suite*, that is to say, all on the same floor. I was generally either in one room or the other, so that as often as not I overheard their conversation. The first time I saw Walford Wareham was the day after my arrival. He was a fine handsome young man, as dark as the night; a great smoker, hardly ever without a cigar in his mouth, and very much addicted to champagne, which wine he drank morning, noon, and night. He drank it to an injurious extent; and he persisted in doing so in spite of Fanny's remonstrances. He was on this occasion rather low-spirited; his manner was listless and his air gloomy.

"What is the matter, old fellow?" cried Fanny, gaily.

"Nothing that I'm aware of."

"Oh, yes, there is; you want waking up a little."

"Got a new slavey?" he asked, catching sight of me.

"Yes; what do you think of her?"

"Oh, she'll do; what do you call her?"

"Paschal. You see I was obliged to have some one, because old Parsons worried the life out of me."

"Paschal!" he cried, "bring me some champagne. Let's see what sort of a Phyllis you will make."

"You have not told me what makes you so out of sorts this morning," persisted Fanny, while I gave my master the wine he asked for.

He made no answer.

"The fact is, I suppose, you have seen your mother."

"If I have, what does it matter? Can't I see who I like without asking your permission?"

"No, you can't," she replied, imperiously.

"You know I hate to be dictated to, Fanny."

"Never mind, your mother's no friend of mine, and I don't thank you for calling upon or talking to my enemies. I think of it all. I suppose she has been setting you against me."

"No, she has not," he replied hesitatingly, as if deprecating the storm he had sense enough to see was lowering overhead.

"If I thought so, I'd pay her a visit and tell her what I thought of her. She wouldn't wish to see me twice, I'll lay something."

"Don't talk nonsense, Fanny."

"It is not nonsense, I mean what I say. You go talking to your mother about me again and see what I'll do."

"If you are going to talk in this violent way, Fanny, I shall leave you," he said, rising from his chair and throwing the stump of a cigar into the fireplace.

"You will do nothing of the sort," she replied, firmly; "sit where you are."

Without saying a word, he took up his hat and walked out of the room. Fanny made a movement as if to go after him and arrest his egress, but on second thoughts she considered it better not to do so. With a small smile of conscious power, she sat down in a chair and beat a devil's tattoo with her pretty little foot upon the hearthrug. She remained in this position until she heard the street door slam, and then she exclaimed - "Paschal!"

I obeyed her summons instantly.

"Give me some wine and a cigarette."

I poured her out some champagne from the bottle I had just opened, but she handed it back to me with a petulant exclamation, saying - "That is flat by this time, open another bottle. I do declare I think you are as big a fool as Parsons."

I pretended to fire up at this, and replied - "If you don't like me, ma'am, I can soon suit myself."

"I didn't mean anything," she answered, changing her tone directly. "You mustn't be huffy. Don't you see I'm put out?"

She smoked viciously at a small cigarette, and seemed to derive considerable enjoyment from the very mild tobacco of which it was composed. After this, she went to a small cabinet which was lying upon a side-table, and opening it with a silver key, took out a bundle of notes. She carefully counted them. Their collective value, so far as I could ascertain, was five hundred pounds. Rolling them up again, she hid them in the bosom of her dress, pinning them to her stays.

"Paschal!" she cried.

I presented myself like a dutiful slave of the lamp.

"Do you know what a note on the Bank of Elegance is?"

"Yes, ma'am; I have seen such things."

"How much are they at the toy-shops, or where-ever you get them?"

"A penny or twopence a-piece, ma'am, I think."

"Very well. Here's half-a-sovereign; go and get me three dozen of them."

Taking the money, I did as I was told. I had no difficulty in getting as many as I wanted at a shop where they sold valentines, and having procured them, I hastened home. Fanny Williams took them from me, glanced hastily at them, and placed them in the cabinet from which she had taken the genuine notes. I was altogether at a loss to imagine what her reason for this strange proceeding was; but I was not long kept in a state of suspense. A knock was heard at the door.

"Run to the window, Paschal; quick!" cried my mistress.

I did so.

"Who is it?" she asked.

"The gentleman, ma'am."

"Mr. Wareham?"

"Yes."

"I thought so," she muttered, while a look of pleasure irradiated her pretty countenance.

Heavy footsteps were heard approaching, and in a short while Mr. Walford Wareham stalked into the apartment with a stately step. I retired into the bedroom, but I took care to keep the door open so that I could overhear the conversation of my master and mistress, and this, too, for the matter of that, in more senses than one.

"So you've got over your ill-temper at last?" she asked.

"I'm very jolly if you'll let me alone," he replied.

"I let you alone! I won't speak to you. Will that please you?"

He lighted another cigar, carelessly allowing the fusee to fall on the floor.

"Oh, what a careless man you are!" she said, petulantly; "you will burn a great hole in the carpet. You are always doing something."

"I can pay for it if I do, I suppose!" he grumbled.

"Pay for it! you are always talking about your money," she replied, with ineffable disdain. "One would think you were a City cad instead of being a gentleman. Money isn't everything, my dear fellow."

"Isn't it?"

"No, not by a great deal."

"You seem to have some affection for it, though."

"How do you mean?"

"Oh, nothing much; only when you get it you don't throw it out of the window into the street for the little boys to scramble after."

"Oh, you *are* a beast to me," she replied, affecting to cry. "I can see what you mean. You are thinking of the notes you gave me yesterday."

She got up and ran towards the cabinet. Opening it with rapidity, she snatched up the false notes, and hastened with them to the grate in which a bright fire was burning. She flourished the notes before him for an instant, making the crisp paper crackle; but so swift were her motions, that he was unable to detect the imposition which had been practised upon him. Thinking that she was really going to burn the Bank of England notes, he rushed up to her to prevent her carrying her purpose into execution; but before he could reach her she had cast them into the fire, and while waving him off with one hand she seized the poker with the other, and held the flash notes in the blaze until they were reduced to a mass of tinder.

"That is how much I care for your money!" she cried, in a seeming transport of rage.

"If you are angry," he replied, "that is no reason, my darling, why you should destroy valuable property."

"It is every reason. You shall not accuse me of caring more for your money than I do for yourself. If I have been foolish enough to love you, I have done so because you ran after me and made me do it. One cannot control one's affections. Oh! I wish I could - I wish, I wish I could."

Having worked herself up into a very comfortable state of excitement, Mrs. Williams threw herself on a sofa and sobbed hysterically.

Mr. Wareham regarded her critically for a moment, and then walked over to the sofa upon which she was reclining, and endeavoured to comfort her to the best of his ability.

"Don't cry, my darling!" I heard him say; "don't cry."

"Your d - darling?" she sobbed. "I wi - wish I were your dar - darling."

"So you are; you know it as well as I do."

"I don't want to - to be."

"Why not?"

"Be - because you tr - treat me too cruel - cruelly."

"I may have been a little harsh and unkind; but believe me, it was not intentional."

"Oh! ye - yes, it w - was."

"I will never accuse you of selfishness again, my own!" he murmured, fondly.

"Y - yes, you w - will," sobbed the beauty.

"No, indeed, I will not, after the strong proof of disinterested affection I have just received from you."

"I do – don't want the m - money; I ha - hate it," she replied.

"But one can't get on without it," he said, reasoning practically.

She recovered herself now, and drank a glass of wine he gave her, afterwards allowing him to wipe the tears away from her eyes with his pocket-handkerchief.

"Why are you so unkind to me?" she asked.

"I don't mean to be so," he replied.

"I wish, dear Walford, you would not go near your mother; she always tries to upset you, and make you quarrel with your little wife. You must confess there is always a quarrel after you have been with her."

He made no answer.

"Isn't it so?" she persisted.

"The old woman," he said, "means well enough. She has no particular objection to you personally, more than she would have to any other woman. It is only natural she should set her back up and throw out her bristles like a fretful porcupine."

"Well, we won't talk about her," said Fanny, skilfully turning the conversation into another channel. She had gained her point, and was satisfied. "Let us talk about something else."

"By all means," he answered, helping himself to some more wine, and lighting another cigar.

"You look upon me as your little wife, don't you, dear?" she asked, taking his hand in hers, and pressing it tenderly.

He replied in the affirmative.

"Then why don't you make me your wife legally?"

"There is such a thing as moral obligation, and that is quite enough for me," he answered thoughtfully.

Before she could continue the attack the postman knocked at the door and brought a letter, which Mrs. Parsons gave to me. I carried it upstairs, knocked at the door, and gave it to my mistress, to whom it was directed. She opened it, read it, and sighed deeply. Then she threw it carelessly upon the table.

"Excuse me," asked Wareham, "but is that a private communication?"

"Oh, no!"

"May I look at it?"

"Certainly."

He stretched out his hand and took up the letter. It was not of great length; but the contents seemed to startle him considerably. It was purely on business. It ran -

"Dear Miss Williams, after many inquiries I have succeeded in discovering your address in London. If I had known where you were living, I should have written to you before. There is at present a dearth of theatrical talent in Liverpool, and I should esteem it a great favour if you would once more grace the boards with your presence. I am prepared to give you a liberal salary, and shall like to enter into a long engagement with you at once. The favour of an early reply will oblige, yours very truly, F. W., Manager and Lessee of the Liverpool Theatre."

Mr. Wareham looked annoyed; he evidently believed the letter to be authentic; but I had my doubts about its authenticity. I had been through the world and seen much more than he had. This drawing-room burlesque was becoming very interesting to me.

"Did I ever tell you I was on the stage when a girl?" asked Fanny.

"Yes, I think you told me something about it."

"You see I am not without the means of gaining an honest living if you were to desert me tomorrow," she added.

"No, you are not," he answered, in an unmeaning tone, as if he were ill at his ease and did not know what to say.

"Since I have known you, dear Walford," she resumed, "I have had better thoughts and ideas; I was always religious in my heart, and I want to lead a good life. If you do not make me your wife, I think I shall accept the offer contained in this letter, and go down to Liverpool. There I may meet with some one who will take a fancy to me, and make an honest woman of me, as they say. Of course I could never love again - *that* is out of the question. My poor little heart, which at present beats for you alone, would be crushed and broken, and would be at the mercy of every thought and every cutting recollection which chose to sweep across its snapped and broken chords. This is generally the fate of women who may be classed amongst the number of the foolish virgins. Seriously, dearest, the time has come when I must do something for myself. You have often told me that I am beautiful - that I am very lovely, and fit to be the bride of an emperor; but how long will this last? Certainly not for ever. When my beauty goes who will love me? - who will care for me? Once let me lose my good looks, and then, Heaven have mercy upon me! I cannot work - I shall not be attractive enough for the stage. I *would* work if I could, but living as I have been living, I have contracted habits of idleness and laziness, and I would rather tie a mill-stone round my neck and throw myself into the sea than labour at needlework for a shilling a day. I couldn't do it - it would kill me. When I am old and ugly you will not care for me. I am not a little fool, dearest, like some women. I have all these constantly before me. I know you are only making use of me, and although I love you very fondly and very dearly, I must look out for my own future. It will break my heart to tear myself away from you, but I *must* do something. I am too proud to wait until a man gets tired of me. If you will not marry me - if you think that you would be making a bad match - I must look out for myself. But, oh! dearest Walford, why should you think so? I would be a dear, good, kind, loving little wife to you, and you would never - never repent having married me. You say you love me. I take you at your word; I put your affection to a practical test. Marry me, Walford; make me your wife, and introduce me to the world as Mrs. Walford Wareham."

The young man listened to this impassioned appeal with evident uneasiness. Fanny Williams was undeniably lovely, and the excitement under which she laboured rendered her doubly interesting. He looked at her with admiration, but he preserved a discreet silence. Once his lips opened as if he were going to make a reply, but they closed again almost directly.

Mrs. Williams was far too skilful to jeopardize her position by any further remarks just at present. She looked at him with her full lustrous eyes, and played impatiently with a lock of her golden hair.

At last he spoke.

"I cannot answer you all at once, Fanny," he said. "You have not altogether taken me by surprise, but I am nevertheless unprepared with a reply on the spur of the moment. Give me a day or two, dearest, to think the matter over coolly, calmly, and collectedly, will you?"

"Oh yes," she murmured, with an air of resignation.

A pause ensued, during which he drank more wine.

"Why not decide at once, dearest?" she asked; "we can go to America. Let us sail for New York directly after our marriage. We can cross the Atlantic in the *Great Eastern*. Oh! it would be so nice" - she clapped her hands childishly together - "Why think of your mother? Why let her be the rock on which we are everlastingly to split? Your mother does not keep you. You have plenty of money of your own. Act independently, then; be a man for once. Marry me, and go abroad."

"Let me have time to consider, Fanny," he answered; "wait till the day after to-morrow, and then I will give you a response."

She bit her lips with vexation, but affected to acquiesce with pleasure.

"And this letter?" she said.

"Well?"

"You see the man wants an answer immediately?"

"So he does."

"Shall I deliver it?"

"Let it stand over until the day after to-morrow."

"Very well, to oblige you I will do so."

Mr. Wareham did not go away until late in the afternoon, and then my mistress accompanied him. I gathered from their conversation that they were going to dine together at some favourite place of resort, and afterwards go to the theatre or other place of amusement. I pondered over all I had heard, and thought that Fanny Williams was a clever fisherwoman, and had a net quite big enough to catch so silly a fish as Mr. Wareham. I looked upon it as certain that he would marry her, if the match were not interrupted in some way. He could not withstand her blandishments, and what I may call "the tricks of the trade." I had not witnessed the least symptom of infidelity on her part as yet, although I had made sure I should have no difficulty in discovering some mortal equally favoured as Mr. Wareham. To all appearances, Mrs. Williams conducted herself with the strictest and most irreproachable propriety. I grew rather alarmed, for the *dénouement* was approaching sooner, much sooner, than I had expected. I had pledged my cleverness, my skill, and my good faith with Mrs. Foster Wareham. I had undertaken to defeat the ambitious scheme of an unprincipled but still accomplished adventuress, and when the trial of strength between us came I found her cleverer than I had anticipated. She was a worthy antagonist. Instead of the silly, listless, pleasure-seeking woman I had expected to find "Incognita," I came in contact with a woman who not only had her wits about her, but who was fully qualified by an early theatrical education to break a lance with any one in fair and open verbal warfare. The little episode of the bank-notes opened my eyes considerably, and I saw that I had undertaken a task which would require all my generalship to bring to a successful termination. I did not believe for an instant that the letter which had arrived so opportunely really came from or was written by the lessee of the Liverpool theatre. I looked upon it as a clever device of a designing woman. My opinion was, that if she had not indited the epistle herself, she had obtained the services of some one to write it for her. She was completely mistress of Walford Wareham's affections, and in time she would make herself his wife. I had insinuated myself into her service in order to prevent such a disastrous consummation. How was I to do so? Accident supplied me with a most powerful weapon. The day after the scene which had taken place between Fanny Williams and Wareham,

I happened to be in the kitchen when some one descended the area steps and knocked timidly at the door. Looking out of the window, I saw a man, dressed in ragged attire, who had a jaunty air, although he was decidedly poverty-stricken. His hat was crushed and broken, his clothes torn, and his face wore a drunken expression, as if he were under the influence of drink the best part of his time. Mrs. Parsons was upstairs, so I opened the door and said, thinking he was a beggar - "Go away, we've nothing for you."

"Oh yes, you have, my dear," he replied, with all the confidence in the world.

"Who do you want?" I exclaimed.

"What! why, don't you know who I want? Oh, I see you are a new hand. I want Mrs. Williams, as she calls herself."

"I'm sure Mrs. Williams won't see you," I returned, with some asperity.

"It'll be all the wuss for her if she don't," he answered; "for tell her that Charley Blake's downstairs, and you see how precious quick she'll fork out the shiners."

I stood still, listening to his conversation with the utmost curiosity. I began to smell a rat. I immediately began to suspect that I should be able to extract something from the man which would prove of the utmost value and importance to Mrs. Foster Wareham and myself. A ragged, shoeless tatterdemalion like the one before me could not possibly have any influence over Mrs. Fanny Williams unless he was acquainted with some secret which gave him tremendous influence over her. If she were in his power owing to the existence of some mystery she would also be in mine, could I succeed in unraveling it.

"Who shall I tell Mrs. Williams wishes to see her?" I inquired, with an air of careless indifference.

"Say Jack's come," he replied.

"Jack!" I repeated; "anything else."

"You may stick Williams on to the end of it if you like," he answered. "May as well have it in full."

"Just come in and sit down," I exclaimed, with as much civility as I could command.

I gave him a chair in the kitchen, and went upstairs three steps at a time, so anxious was I to see what effect my communication would have upon my mistress. I found her writing a letter.

"Oh, is that you, Paschal?" she exclaimed. "I was in want of you. I have a letter to go to the post. Light a taper and bring me the sealing-wax."

"If you please, ma'am," I said, "Jack's come."

"What do you mean?" she said, turning deadly pale and letting the pen fall from her hand upon the paper.

"A man who is downstairs told me to give you that message," I replied.

"What man?"

"A ragged, dirty-looking man."

"Don't let him come up here. - Don't let him see me!" she exclaimed, in terror-stricken accents, while her face turned from red to white, and from white to red again.

"Shall I send him away?" I asked. "I am afraid it will be a difficult task; he does not appear inclined to take his departure just yet."

"Did he say he wanted money?"

"He dropped a hint to that effect."

"Then, give him some. In Heaven's name let him have what he wants. It will all go in drink, I suppose; but perhaps he will kill himself some day; and oh, what a happy relief it will be!"

She felt in her bosom for the packet of notes she had hidden there the day before, and having unpinned it, took out five amounting to the aggregate value of fifty pounds.

"Give him these," she said to me, "and send him away. Say it is all I have in the house. Go; be as quick as you can, and don't ask any questions or make any remarks, and I will give you some when you come back."

I took up the notes, and went down to the poverty-stricken individual who had such a hold upon Fanny Williams' fears as to be able to obtain fifty pounds at one time from her. I was burning with curiosity to know all about this singular man, and I resolved to cultivate his acquaintance. Giving him the money, I said, "The lady has sent you this. It is all she has in the house; but if you will leave your address with me, she will send you some more this evening or to-morrow morning."

"If I was to give you my right address, I should say, Wukus, St. Martin's," he replied, with a ludicrous grin; "but now I'm flush you'll hear of me at Tony's Hotel."

"And where is that?"

"Vinegar Yard, St. Giles's.

He stuck the notes between his fingers like an experienced cashier, regarded them affectionately, and folding them up in his waistcoat pocket, prepared to leave the house.

"So she wont see me," he grinned. "She is particularly engaged. Oh!" he cried significantly, "Nod's as good's a wink to me. I won't spoil sport. Lucky for her she had the 'ready,' or it would have been the worst for her!" When he got into the area, he added, "If your mistress sends you, my dear, with the rest of the cash, you ask anybody for Jack Williams, and they'll show you where Tony's Hotel is, and you'll find me there."

I replied in the affirmative, and he took his departure with alacrity.

When I entered the drawing-room again I found my mistress lying on the floor in a fainting state. She was suffering from severe palpitation of the heart. I attended to her as well as I could, and calmed her. When her excitement subsided, and she was a little less nervous, she murmured feebly, "Is he gone - the dreadful man?"

"Yes," I replied.

"Was he satisfied?"

"He appeared perfectly so."

"He will be the death of me some day, I know he will. Just feel how my poor heart's beating now. Give me your hand. Put it there. That's it. Do you feel it?"

I put my hand against her side, and felt her heart pulsate very quickly.

Presently she felt better, and with my assistance laid down upon the sofa. A glass of wine so far recovered her that she was able to talk in her usual animated strain, yet there was a tinge of sadness about everything she said which affected me strangely. I cannot tell how it was, but there was something about Fanny Williams which made me take an interest in her. I felt sorry for her. I was sure that there was some secret grief gnawing at her heart; and although she was what she was, I had a presentiment that she was more sinned against than sinning. However that might be, I had my duty to perform, and driving all my sentimentality back into my breast, I was once more the cool and crafty female detective.

"You are my friend, Paschal," she said; "at least I think so. Can I trust you?"

What could I do, while playing the part of Tartuffe, but be an unconscionable hypocrite? So I replied that I hoped in all sincerity she could.

"Do you know that I have pined for years for some one to whom I could confide my griefs, but I have never yet met with one?"

"Is it possible that you have griefs? It is more fitting for old people like myself to talk about sorrow," I answered.

My endeavour to rally her was unsuccessful.

"Yes," she said, "I have for years been the prey of a great and overwhelming grief."

I begged to know of what nature it was. She looked at me for a moment or so steadily, and then she replied in a low tone, as if speaking to herself, "No, no, better not; trust no one, and you will never be deceived."

She was at all times a light-hearted, merry creature; and after having been in the depths of despair, the very nadir or lowest point of misery, the reaction set in, and she became jovial and gay once more. With a sparkling, bell-like laugh, she jumped up from the sofa, and exclaimed, "Dress yourself, Paschal, and I will take you out with me. Put on the brown moiré I gave you, and the quilted bonnet. It will be such fun. People will take you for my pious maternity. What sized gloves do you wear - six and a half? Do you really? Go along with you. I don't believe sevens would fit you. Never mind, you shall try."

Falling in with her humour, I dressed myself, and having ordered her brougham, we took a drive in the Park. At the entrance at Hyde Park Corner, a policeman was stationed; talking to him was an inspector, who politely raised his hat to me.

Mrs. Williams' suspicion was aroused at once.

"Who is that man?" she asked, staring at me with tiger-like ferocity.

"Only my brother, ma'am," I replied as calmly as I could. "Did I never tell you I had a brother in the force?"

"No, I don't remember your having done so. I think we'll go home. I don't like driving about with people who know policemen. Tell the coachman 'Home.' "

I pulled the check-string, and gave him his instructions. The journey was performed in silence.

I asked permission to go out that evening. It was sullenly accorded to me. I had not intended calling upon the man who called himself "Jack" until the next day; but I felt as if a walk would do me good. I had tried to read, and I had tried to write, but I could do neither to my satisfaction. In fact,

> "Sweet inspiration, softly wooed,
> Replied in tones so very rude,
> I broke in twain the fragile quill,
> And forced in vain the stubborn will."

I knew my way about St. Giles's pretty well, and experienced no difficulty in finding the delectable and highly insalubrious locality known as Vinegar-yard. Since the time I speak of, the relieving officers have made attacks upon its inhabitants, and the sanitary inspectors have levelled its walls, and opened up its rookeries. Now they do not have all the seven plagues of Egypt there at once. Their first-born don't die, nor are they afflicted with a murrain. There are some model lodging-houses there under the control of a Government inspector, and Vinegar-yard bows its head before the genii of modern civilization and improvement. Tony's Hotel was a public-house of the worst and lowest description. It was the haunt of the most desperate characters in London. It was here that thieves sought a lodging and a place to carouse in - paying dearly for the accommodation - after a successful day. The burglar, with the jemmy and the centre-bit in his pocket, would at Tony's Hotel fortify himself for the business of the night. It was a place that ought never to have been licensed - more, it should not have been allowed to exist. I remember perfectly well having an altercation respecting Tony's Hotel with several clever thief-takers, sergeants, and inspectors. They all combated my opinions, and held out for preserving Tony's Hotel in all its integrity; and their reason for this excessive leniency was, that if they suppressed this rendezvous, the thieves and their associates would go elsewhere. As it was, the police knew where to put their hands on a man when he was wanted, and that fact was amply sufficient in their minds to justify the existence of Tony's Hotel. I asked for Mr. Jack Williams as I entered the bar, and was directed to a club-room upstairs. There were several low-looking men loafing about in the bar and on the stairs, but I took no notice of them, I stopped in the doorway of the club-room, for a strange sight presented itself to my view. Jack Williams was on his feet, with a pipe in one hand and a pot of beer in the other. Around him were grouped from twenty to five-and-twenty men. They were all thieves. Some of them I knew by sight. They were looking intently at Jack Williams, who was apparently about to sing them a song. I had not to wait a minute before he sang the following rude verses, called "Tony's Hotel," to a light, lilting tune, at once pleasant and inspiriting:

> "The beer's of the best that landlord can sell,
> Like everything else at Tony's Hotel.

The Romany sleeps in some shady dell:
He's a flat not to come to Tony's Hotel.
His pals all admire him, he treats them so well,
And spend all their dibs at Tony's Hotel.
There's not a cove but as is able to tell
Of rigs on the cross at Tony's Hotel.
When lagged - in the jug - shut up in a cell,
Oh! don't we all sigh for Tony's Hotel,
And curse the bad luck that to us befel,
Since we're far away from Tony's Hotel.
Now sing out, pals all, as clear as a bell,
Here's luck to the crib called Tony's Hotel.
Once more - "Called To-ny's Ho-tel."

The applause that followed this song was as tremendous as it is indescribable. An irresistible enthusiasm seized every listener; and Jack Williams's song was unanimously encored. He very good-humouredly obliged his friends, who positively revelled in the chorus of "Tony's Hotel," and repeated it with a vigour that did their lungs infinite credit. When the song was a second time brought to a close, an old man of venerable appearance rose to his feet and said -

"Pals all." There was a dead silence. "The Captain's done the trick, and I'm his humble servant. Pals all, here's to you."

This was Tony, and in this characteristic way did he return thanks for the song which had been sung in praise of his establishment.

Pulling a ten-pound note out of his pocket, Jack Williams handed it over to Tony, saying -

"Glasses round, guv'nor."

This liberality did not pass unnoticed by his associates.

"He's flush to-day," said one.

"Been in luck," said another.

"Ain't he flash with the tissue?" said a third.

"Look at the flimsy," said a fourth.

Just at this moment Jack Williams caught sight of me. He begged the company to excuse him for five minutes; and, getting up, came over to me.

"So you've come, my dear?" he said.

"I told you I should," I replied.

My idea was that Jack Williams was Fanny's husband; and I determined to risk the assertion upon the slender chance of his confirming it. I had some money of my own, for I had had no opportunity of spending what Mrs. Foster Wareham had given me. So I offered Jack fifteen pounds.

"Will that do?" I asked. "It was all your *wife* could send you."

"Did she tell you she was my wife?" he inquired.

"Well, I suppose so; or else how should I know it?"

"I'm a good husband, ain't I?" he said, with a grin. "But she's too flash for me now. I ain't good enough for her. Here, give us hold of the posh; I'm on the spree to-night. You're a good sort. Tell Fanny I ain't forgot her. No, nor don't mean to," he added, with a laugh full of meaning, as he turned on his heel and walked back to the room where his friends were anxiously expecting him.

I wended my way back again to Fanny's apartments in the best spirits, because I had, as I imagined, found a clue to the disentanglement of the skein which, from its complication, was beginning to give me some uneasiness. I anxiously awaited the answer Mr. Wareham was to give Fanny. I surmised that it would be fully in accordance with her wishes. I hoped it might be, because my information would come upon him like a thunderclap, and, very likely, disgusted at her duplicity, he would conceive a dislike for her quite as intense as his present love. I had often heard of such things, and I knew that love of the purest kind frequently turned to the profoundest hatred. I could not understand Fanny's tears and her allusions to a secret grief. She was thinking of her husband, whom perhaps she had married in her youthful days, before she knew her own mind, little dreaming of the future misery in store for her. Very likely in the early days of their intercourse they were both steady-going, hard-working young people. What a change! The one a blot upon her sex, the other a drunkard, perhaps a thief; at all events, the recognised companion and associate of ruffians of every grade. Mr. Walford Wareham looked rather more mildly seraphic than usual when he called to give Fanny what she termed his "answer." She had spoken to me about it when the episode of the policeman was forgotten and placed in the limbo of forgotten animosities.

"I am so anxious about my 'answer,' you know, Paschal," she said, as she was sponging her hair with the golden dye. "I wonder what it will be. Do you think he will say yes or no?"

"Decidedly yes, ma'am."

"So I think sometimes; and then again, I think he won't."

"It's hard to tell, ma'am."

"So it is. It's very difficult to say; but certainly the odds are in my favour - eh?"

"Very much, ma'am," I replied.

I always made a point of acquiescing with everything she advanced.

When Wareham entered the drawing-room, she was reclining with a languid air upon the sofa. She held out her hand in a listless way.

"Are you not well?" he asked, anxiously.

"Oh yes!" she replied.

"What is it, then?"

"Can you not guess?"

"No, indeed I cannot."

"Then I suppose I must tell you. You have something to say to me, have you not?"

"Yes."

"Do you wonder at my evincing some anxiety? I have thought of nothing else. If you do as I asked you, I shall be the happiest woman in the world. If not you consign me to despair."

He took her hand in his and sat down by her side. There was a smile on his lips; he bent down and whispered in her ear.

She started up with a tiny shriek of joy.

"Really!" she cried.

"Yes; my own."

"You will indeed make me your wife?"

"When you like."

"Oh, you are too good for me! I do not deserve it," she said, almost beside herself with joy, covering him with kisses as she spoke.

I was not at all surprised at this declaration; I had antici-pated it from what I had seen of the man's character.

"What fun a wedding will be!" she continued. "Old Paschal shall be my bridesmaid; and who will be your best-man?"

"Oh! I dare say I shall find some one."

"I declare I'm delighted. I vote we are married just before the vessel sails from Liverpool to New York."

Some hours were passed in sweet converse by the lovers, and I did not get an opportunity of speaking to Wareham till late in the afternoon. Fanny Williams had gone out for half an hour to buy something. Going up to Mr. Wareham, who was lying on the sofa, smoking as usual, I exclaimed, "Can I speak a word or two to you, sir?"

The infatuated young man turned a sleepy look upon me, and replied -

"As many as you like."

"I shouldn't like you to be deceived."

"In what way?" he asked, evincing some animation.

"In the lady you are going to make your wife."

"Your mistress?"

"Yes, sir."

"Oh!" he replied carelessly, "I know what you mean; but I don't care what she's been."

"It isn't that."

"What then?"

"Something totally different."

"Let's have it, then."

"She's married already."

"What!" he cried, pale as a ghost, "got a husband, did you say?"

"Yes; he was here last night."

"God bless me! is this true?"

He shook all over like a man in an ague.

"I can prove it," I said, emphatically.

"Curse him!" he exclaimed. "Let me hear all you have to say, and then I can draw my own conclusions."

I recounted all I had seen and heard, telling him where he could find Jack Williams, and I so impressed him with the truth of my story, that he pressed his hand against his forehead, and murmured in a wild tone of voice: "If this is true, I have no wish to live."

I saw an agonized expression steal over his countenance, and he said faintly, "Leave me."

I did so, and went about what little work I had to do. While I was engaged in this manner, he gave me the slip and left the house. What happened to him subsequently, although of a tragic nature, was supremely ludicrous. I did not, of course, hear of it till afterwards, but, for the sake of connecting the narrative, I will relate it here. Mr. Wareham went straight to the address I had given him, and found Jack Williams at "Tony's Hotel." Jack was in a happy state of inebriety, and answered to the questions of his interrogator with such drunken truthfulness as left no room for doubt in his questioner's mind. Frantic with jealousy, disgust and disappointment, Wareham rushed he hardly knew whither. Suicide was the idea which guided him like a flaming beacon. He thought he would deprive himself of an existence which was a burden to him. In order to do so, without the fear of interruption, he got into a cab and drove to a distant part of the river above Chelsea. There he dismissed his vehicle, and prepared for death with the calmness of a stoic. Unfortunately for the immediate fruition of his intentions, the tide was at a lamentably low ebb. Vast banks of mud arose on every side, whose odour was anything but refreshing. It was fast growing dark, but there was still light enough to enable him to see what he was doing. The river, such as it was, glided calmly towards the ocean at a distance of about a hundred yards from the shore. In order to commit suicide it was necessary to reach the flowing tide. But to achieve this the mud-banks must be attacked and passed through successfully. Wareham was firmly determined to kill himself by drowning. Fanny, his dearly-loved Fanny, had deceived him; his very existence was blighted, and he had nothing left to live for. Lighting a cigar, without which he never could do anything, he stepped lightly over the bank, and at once sank over his ankles in mud, of a glutinous, viscous, and adhesive kind. It was certainly suicide under difficulties: he began to wish that he had waited until high-water, but, with despair in his heart, and the light of determination in his eye, he pressed on bravely, like the one who bore a banner with a strange device. He was soon up to his knees in mud. Locomotion was difficult, and yet the tempting water was a long way off. The mud-bank seemed to be interminable. Being a man of nervous temperament, he grew horribly afraid of eels, and dreaded lest they should attack him in the region of the calf of the leg, out of which fleshy and muscular part they might derive some sustenance. At length he sank into a sort of quick-sand, which let him in up to the armpits, and out of this he was unable to extricate himself. His struggles were useless. He was mud-bound. The most terrible ideas took possession of his mind. He was the prey of gloomy terrors, and it is not too much to say that he regretted his precipitancy, and wished himself once more safely at home. As well as he could calculate, he would have to wait some hours before the tide rose up to the spot in which he was fixed. Then his fate would be too awful in the extreme. Instead of drowning himself in a romantic manner, the waters, fetid and discoloured, would overwhelm him by degrees. To add to his miseries his cigar went out, and he could not get at his fusees. At last, overcome by his fears, he shouted aloud for assistance. For some time his cries were unanswered, but he persisted until a response was heard on the bank. Finally, some good Samaritans, in the shape of bargees, with the help of ropes, got him out of the mud-hole, and landed him on the bank, half dead with cold and fatigue, added to the effects of nervous terror.

He never saw Fanny again. He roused himself from the lethargy in which a silly juvenile passion had plunged him, and putting his affairs in order, set off for the Continent, where he travelled for some time, until the memory of his meretricious love was effaced. I was always of opinion that when once the spell was broken, he would see his folly, and bring his common sense to the rescue. By his especial wish his brother joined him at Ancona, but before he left England, Mrs. Foster Wareham gave me a substantial proof of her regard. For her son - who had been dead and lost to her - was, through my instrumentality, restored to her arms, and she felt once more that she was not alone in the world.

Fanny Williams, the "Incognita" of the story, continued a syren, and speedily found a fresh victim, whom she turned to good account with her usual tact and artistic skill.

"Jack" remained a roysterer, at "Tony's Hotel," and frequently sang his famous song with much applause.

Other fiction titles available from British Library Publishing

THE NOTTING HILL MYSTERY

Charles Warren Adams

'The book is both utterly of its time and utterly ahead of it.'
Paul Collins, *New York Times Book Review*

The Notting Hill Mystery is widely considered to be the first ever detective novel. Published in 1864, the dramatic story is told by insurance investigator Ralph Henderson, who is building a case against the sinister Baron 'R___', suspected of murdering his wife. Presented in the form of diary entries, family letters, chemical analysis reports and interviews with witnesses, the novel displays innovative techniques that would not become common features of detective fiction until the 1920s. This new edition of *The Notting Hill Mystery* will be welcomed by all fans of detective fiction.

ISBN 978 0 7123 5859 0
312 pages, 8 black-and-white illustrations

Other fiction titles available from British Library Publishing

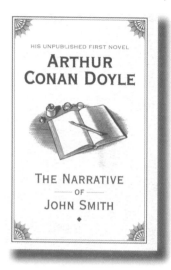

THE NARRATIVE OF JOHN SMITH

Arthur Conan Doyle

'this early piece crackles with the burning curiosity that Doyle brought to all his activities ... sheds fascinating light on the mind of its creator' David Grylls, *Sunday Times*

In 1883, when he was just 23, Arthur Conan Doyle wrote his first novel *The Narrative of John Smith* while he was living in Portsmouth and struggling to establish himself as both a doctor and a writer. The manuscript remained among his papers and this is its first publication. Many of the themes and stylistic tropes of his later writing, including his first Sherlock Holmes story, *A Study in Scarlet* (1887), can clearly be seen in this book. Though unfinished, *The Narrative of John Smith* stands as a fascinating record of the early work of a man on his way to becoming one of the best-known authors in the world.

ISBN 978 0 7123 5841 5
144 pages, Also available as an ebook (978 0 7123 6301 3)

Other fiction titles available from British Library Publishing

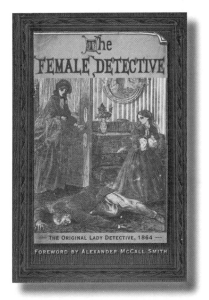

THE FEMALE DETECTIVE

Andrew Forrester

With a Foreword by Alexander McCall Smith

'Miss Gladden' is the first ever professional female detective to
feature in a crime novel. She is a determined and resourceful
figure who pursues mysterious cases with ingenuity and skills of
logic and deduction. *The Female Detective* was first published
in 1864, and it was one of only two novels featuring a female
detective to be published at this time – further stories featuring
women detectives would not be widely published until later in
the century. The reappearance of the original female detective
will be welcomed by all fans of detective fiction.

ISBN 978 0 7123 5878 1
328 pages
Also available as an ebook (978 0 7123 6304 4)